THE
LUCIDITY
PROGRAMME

J. M. BAYLISS

The Lucidity Programme

Copyright © 2020 J. M. Bayliss

This book is a work of fiction. Unless otherwise stated names, characters and incidents are the product of the authors imagination and any resemblance to actual people living or dead or any historical event is entirely by coincidence.

ISBN 978-1-5272-7590-4

"*Earth is a realm; it is not a planet. It is not an object; therefore, it has no edge. Earth would be more easily defined as a system environment. Earth is also a machine; it is a Tesla coil. The sun and moon are powered wirelessly with the electromagnetic field (the Aether). This field also suspends the celestial spheres with electromagnetic levitation. Electromagnetic levitation disproves gravity because the only force you need to counter is the electromagnetic force, not gravity. The stars are attached to the firmament.*"

NIKOLA TESLA

To Anne, Lauren and Luke

CONTENTS

CHAPTER 1
CHANGE THE DYNAMIC

Cheltenham, England - May 2019

In a second-floor meeting room overlooking a manicured inner courtyard garden, sat five women and three men. It was difficult to find a face amongst them that wasn't either deep in thought or struggling to present a positive facade. Most of them were doing some last-minute checking on their laptops and tablets of inadequate facts, and figures that didn't add up. It was an emotive meeting agenda - they were discussing a threat to British national security, and global peace.

On the south-west edge of Cheltenham in Gloucestershire sits an eye-catching, ring-shaped building. At 600 feet in diameter, 70 feet high, set on 176 acres, surrounded by dedicated car parks and the highest security imaginable. This modern, spectacular piece of architecture is GCHQ – the UK government's General Communications Headquarters, or 'Eavesdropping Central' to the locals.

The building's affectionate nickname is 'The Doughnut'. Often working in collaboration with other organisations such as the military, security services, police forces and friendly foreign governments, GCHQ keeps the UK safe from all kinds of problems from within our own country or from overseas.

Employed inside are an eclectic mix of over 4,000 well-organised, highly-focused academics – linguists, mathematicians, cryptologists, analysts, and researchers. GCHQ also advertises to recruit hackers and 'mavericks', to address the growth industry of cybercrime.

GCHQ was hosting some regular visitors from DSTL - Defence Science and Technology Laboratory - the government's famous scientific department based in Porton Down near Salisbury.

Both organisations had been working hard together for weeks. DSTL had been passed what appeared to be astonishing, technological information and needed GCHQ assistance to help fathom out its authenticity and solve a puzzle. Something, if proved to be genuine, would be a serious and dangerous threat to our armed forces and defence systems.

The collective team of people had reached an impasse and were getting nowhere. They suspected other interested parties around the world had become aware of the information and were trying to solve the same conundrum. Were those competitors progressing faster, and did they have better intelligence than DSTL?

DSTL were confident they would find the answers and a solution – at some point - *when* was the problem. The risk associated with losing the race to a hostile or unstable foreign government would be unthinkable.

They were running out of ideas. All their usual impeccable standards and successful investigation methods were not resolving the situation confronting them. They needed a fresh approach, something special to happen to change the dynamic.

CHAPTER 2

BREEZE ON THE FACE

Wales - April 2018

Wil Richardson had a year-round wind and weather-beaten complexion. He would argue the sweet 'perfumed' aroma of fresh alfalfa hay on a man was as good as any aftershave. That, combined with his dusty pick-up truck, often loaded with bales of silage, couldn't disguise his primary occupation.

A former rugby player, the size of his hands was one of the reasons it was rare for him to drop the ball back in his playing days. Working manually outdoors proved a far better regime than most gyms for Wil. His stature meant he would often have to duck to walk through some of the centuries-old Welsh pub doorways near to where he lived in Abergavenny.

He was not the kind of man to believe in fairies, ghosts, or superstitious old wives' tales. Little did he know then he was about to find himself embarking on the most emotional and mystifying episode of his entire life. Something that would change his life forever.

Wil and his wife Emma had paid off their mortgage a few years ago, well ahead of time. Bi-folding patio doors to the rear of their cottage opened onto a spacious south-facing decking. It offered stunning views of the Welsh Black Mountains with a stream running past the end of their garden. Over the years, Wil and his wife Emma had worked damned hard – now they were enjoying their idyllic rural farm.

It was a Sunday spring morning and the re-cycling boxes outside their side door were over-flowing with discarded empty cava bottles, countless beer cans and one empty pale blue gin bottle. The last of their friends hadn't left until the early hours, so the couple decided to leave the rest of the clearing up until morning. The dishwasher needed filling and the remnants of some party poppers needed sweeping up, along with a couple of 'bespoke' anniversary banners that had fallen to the kitchen floor tiles.

"Wil, where on Earth did they get the old pool pic's of us from for the banners?"

"Brilliant, I don't think I'd get into those tight blue Speedo's these days, though would I?" Wil was laughing as he said it.

"Oh, I don't know, you still scrub up, and I always liked you in those 'budgie smugglers'." Emma winked at Wil, she was still her mischievous self, even though she'd had a late night and had been the life and soul of the party – as always.

Their two sons, Haydn, and George, both in their early twenties had popped in for half an hour or so to say hello, then headed back out. The boys left claiming they didn't want to send the average age at the party crashing down.

Wil and Emma had made a successful transition from farming to glamping and outdoor pursuits. Increased bookings thanks to Emma's shrewd marketing talent meant a new 'shepherds hut' would appear almost every other week at the base of the sweeping mountains.

Haydn and George mainly ran the farm, but Wil still kept an active role in helping his sons. Emma had set up the simple but enticing website and bookings portal for the glamping business and could run the various social media accounts in her sleep. Forty-nine-year-old Emma had a long and successful background in marketing and PR, often taking on some profitable ad hoc marketing projects combined with running the business. A smart move – she had the best of both worlds. Things had worked out well for them.

However, the couple were about to experience an unexpected and radical change to their lifestyle. Three days after the party Emma was driving home late one evening from their campsite business near Crickhowell. For weeks the rain had been incessant. The water table was high, and fresh rainfall was taking a while to drain away in the vale where they lived, near to the River Usk.

It was a typical evening in Wales in the middle of April – the weather was unpredictable and unpleasant. Torrential rain on the roof of Emma's van made trying to listen to the radio almost pointless. The windscreen wipers were making a racket on their maximum speed setting. On-coming headlights were dazzling, creating reflective blurs off the wet road surface.

There was no reaction time. The steering-wheel whipped through Emma's fingers, as her little van had got caught in a huge roadside pool of standing water and was dragged side-ways.

A split second later the 'white box' she was driving found itself caught in an uncontrollable slide, nosediving down a muddy 30-degree bank. The loud noises of scrapes and bumps from boulders, bushes and saplings drowned out the screams inside the van. It was careering downwards towards the river, before ploughing head-on into an oak tree and flipping onto its side. The crumple zones and airbags did what they were meant to do, absorbing most of the obvious impacts, sending the chalky airbag dust all around the inside of the van.

A thick heavy oak bough was occupying most of the passenger side and part of the driver side of the van. The laminated glass windscreen had been pierced, pushed into the van, and wrapping the glass around the intruding piece of the tree. Curiously framing the wood like a piece of trendy installation art. Ed Sheeran had stopped abruptly long before the end of his track. Emma lay in silence, other than for the hiss of the leaking radiator, the wipers had also come to a stop. They had been ripped off and crushed like matchsticks. The seatbelt, soaked red with blood, was doing its best to suspend her as she slumped sideways – motionless.

Two young lads were taking shelter from the downpour at a nearby bus stop. Their playful banter stopped and facial expressions changed and they gave out a collective 'whoa' as they witnessed the shocking accident. They sprinted over the road, slid, and scrambled down to the van and could see Emma trapped inside the steaming overturned wreckage. As one lad called for the rescue services the other was doing his best to check on Emma. It was pointless him trying to get her out, the van was flipped onto its driver side. She was stuck, they needed help.

Two sets of blue flashing lights arrived almost simultaneously within about ten minutes of the crash. The firemen cut her out before paramedics strapped her neck-braced slender frame to a stretcher. Taking great care, they dragged her back up the rain-soaked muddy bank and through the open doors of the waiting ambulance vehicle to rush Emma to the nearest hospital. The gurney wheeled her into A&E – alive but unconscious.

~

Wil had been at Emma's bedside at the hospital in Abergavenny twice a day, every day for the past three weeks. She was in a coma and he was trying his best to keep a lid on his inability to contribute anything to her progress. All he could do was be there.

He had gotten to know most of the medical staff by their first names, and they knew all about him and the woman he'd spent most of his life with. When Wil wasn't around, he and Emma – 'that lovely farming couple' – would sometimes come up in sober conversation between some of the hospital staff members. Livestock on farms can't take holidays or sick days. Animals need to be fed, mucked out and cared for every day. But both Wil's sons, Haydn, and George had been at his side whenever they could, all sharing the anguish. Most of the time they sat in silence, looking up every time a doctor walked past – just in case, there was news.

Doctors had told Wil they were cautious but optimistic that Emma would pull through from the coma, but it might take weeks – or maybe months. The MRI scan had shown that the initial medical treatment to reduce the swelling pressure on her brain, caused by a blood clot, had been a success. Now it was a question of time.

Friends and family all agreed if anyone were capable of pulling through – it would be Emma. She was a petite, fit, and healthy woman, a regular jogger, who had been in training for her first-ever half marathon. Combined with her gritty determination, everyone had a great belief that she would be fine – sooner rather than later. She was bubbly, chatty, Emma, 'Mrs Organised' – of course, she would be fine.

~

Going about his business every day as normal and keeping himself busy was the best way for Wil to help him take his mind off things. He threw himself into the farm work - repairing fences, improving the potholed access roads that had borne the brunt of the recent rainfall. A bucket of asphalt in a pothole compared to a new front suspension strut was a no brainer for most thrifty farmers. The rangy energetic man thrived on being active and getting stuck in.

Barely a minute went by before he was again thinking of Emma or hoping to get a phone call from the hospital with some positive news. The family WhatsApp group was pinging with a constant stream of positive thoughts and updates to keep each another sane.

Wil was as concerned for his two sons' wellbeing as he was for most other things - they doted on their mother. It was exhausting, his appetite had vanished and every night he fell into a deep sleep. Then for two consecutive nights, there was an unexpected disruption to his sleep pattern.

For as long as he could remember, Wil experienced what he described as 'pretty crazy dreams', maybe once every couple of months. Typically, he would be half awake, half asleep, almost controlling the dream. Murmuring aloud was commonly caused by the dream, sometimes followed by screaming. Both were a signal that inside Wil's head he was experiencing the threat of violence.

Emma would always try to nudge him awake before the murmuring escalated into anything more disturbing or could reach any dreadful conclusion that the dream may have led to. They would often joke about it the next day and think nothing of it. Wil had looked into it once, mentioning it to his doctor, and discovered that the medical description for his night-time episodes was 'lucid dreaming'.

"You've been eating too much cheese again love," was Emma's standard response.

Wil found out his lucid dreams were a common occurrence for some people and could be disconcerting – for both dreamers and their partners.

Without Emma to rouse him from his sleep for the past two nights, Wil had found himself having some unusual lucid dreams. Again, he felt alert and engaged in these current dreams, but these were not scary and violent that was the norm. These took on a new dimension, and he found that they were becoming much harder to comprehend and were more compelling.

~

Emma's mother Maud had died several years earlier, and her dad had died when she was a little girl. Like most children with one parent, Emma had a close relationship with her mum and was devastated when she died after a short unexpected illness. Wil was like a son to Maud, he thought the world of her, she was a lovely person and they had grown to be fond of each other. At half-term and summer holidays, Emma and Wil would often take the children to the whitewashed cosy family cottage in Pembrokeshire, stay with Maud and meet with the rest of the family. They were good times.

Over the years, Emma told Wil countless stories about growing up in Pembrokeshire and the times she'd had with her older siblings and friends, roaming around the stunning coastal paths and coves. Most days, Emma said she would come home with a salty sheen on her arms and legs from the sea breeze.

~

Hospital visits with Emma often consisted of playing her favourite music, reading her favourite books and magazines aloud, narrating through sets of old photographs and talking about his work that day around the farm and the campsite.

"Hey 'Em' I've come to the conclusion I hate doing finance and marketing. I'm going to pay you double the going rate when you get back."

Wil had never underestimated Emma's influence on the business.

Family life was important to them both. Wil did his best to keep Emma up to date with their son's exploits, "The boys both scored one try each in the match last weekend. I know they've already told you, but to be fair they were excellent. George ran his try in from near the half-way line. You always said he was faster than I was, didn't you?"

Wil found himself having constant thoughts about the times they had enjoyed together and the special places and milestones in their lives. As the kids were older there was much less dependency expected of them on the family farm. They had been able to travel extensively off-season and loved every minute of it. It was rare for them to have disagreements and unheard to ever sleep on an argument. Tough times and difficult situations were few and far between, until now.

He also recalled an occasion when Emma became upset as she told him about the time she had lost her mother's beautiful solitaire diamond engagement ring. It had been a cherished family heirloom. She explained that her mother had owned a fish and chip shop in Fishguard and would always leave her engagement ring on the dressing table to go to work and wear nothing other than her wedding ring. When Emma was a little girl she loved to dress up in her mother's clothes, shoes and costume jewellery that was kept in a jewellery box. She loved to gaze at herself in the mirror pretending to be a grown-up. On that particular summer's day when Emma was about ten years old, her mother had gone to work, leaving her at home with her grandmother. Emma's siblings were much older and always out. She had been upstairs playing in her mum's bedroom, dressing up again. There was a knock at the front door and her grandmother had called upstairs to tell Emma her friends had come for her. They wanted to know if she would join them to play on the nearby beach, as they were planning to go looking for crabs in the rockpools.

An excited Emma got changed out of her mother's clothes back into her clothes and ran downstairs. She was rushing and quickly grabbed her things and a little fishing net. When they got to the beach, Emma's best friend commented on the ring that Emma had on her finger. Only then did Emma realise that in her haste to join her friends she had forgotten to take off the engagement ring.

There were no more than a couple of small fluffy clouds in the sky, the girls were laughing and having a lovely time. After a couple of hours having fun with a bucketload of crabs, the tide was in and it was time to go home.

When Emma put her sandals back on and was ready to leave the beach, to her horror she realised she was no longer wearing her mother's ring. The ring was gone - lost. With tears rolling down her face and a knotted, sick, feeling in the pit of her stomach she and her friends searched for ages, turning over every pebble and looking underneath every shred of seaweed. Without success.

The time came for the long trudge home, head down swishing at flowers on the side of the lane with her bamboo fishing net along the way. A heartbroken Emma had imagined the look on her mother's face, changing, when she told her what she had done. Her mother didn't speak more than the occasional word to Emma for days and was often seen dabbing tears from her eyes. Emma would look to her mother waiting for the affectionate glances that she was accustomed to, but none were forthcoming. Her mind kept swirling back to the beach and wanting to turn the clock back.

She never forgot the look on her mother's face. As weeks went by her mother's attitude changed, the smile returned and she forgave Emma. It was one of those silly little childhood mistakes that stayed with Emma for many years afterwards. She knew the ring was so precious to her mum because her dad had died three years earlier and Maud had never got over losing him.

~

At home, the stress of Emma's accident was beginning to tell on Wil. Exhausted from pushing himself too hard with too many hours on the farm and shuttle trips to the hospital he fell into another deep sleep. He had recently begun having strange dreams, and the strangest thing all was that Maud was appearing in them. The dreams had taken on a new dimension since Emma's accident and for some inexplicable reason, Maud was beginning to have a strong influence.

After the two previous unsettled nights, Wil got into bed and fell sound asleep. But once again, for the third night in a row, after three or four hours, he found himself in his half awake and half asleep lucid state of unrest. He appeared to be revisiting the same recurring dream. And he was not in the same full control of the situation as he had been over the years with his regular lucid dreams.

On the previous two nights, he had been unable to conclude the dream - he'd been stuck. But tonight, the sensations were significant, they were much stronger. He thought he could sense and smell a sea breeze on his face and hear the waves over the side of a cliff edge coastal path he was being led along. This place was somewhere familiar to him, in Pembrokeshire. He felt so certain he was near the sea, it was palpable. His legs were striding along, his feet were slipping on the soft narrow path and his arms brushing the undergrowth as they swung at his sides. Everything felt real to him, including a woman up ahead of him, leading him along the path. He tried hard but couldn't make any ground to catch up to her. As the dream progressed, he thought he could almost reach out and touch the woman - she appeared vaguely familiar to him - yet every extra effort to get one step closer was unsuccessful. He called out to her several times and then, she turned her head, looked back, and smiled at him. It was a young *Maud* and this time Maud was controlling the dream, not Wil.

He could hear himself asking her, "Where are we going, Maud? Where are we going?"

Maud turned, and in her unmistakable soft Welsh voice replied, "This way Wil, it's this way - we're nearly there."

In the distance, he could see a tall red and white striped lighthouse. He knew this place; he had been here with Emma and the boys. Together Wil and Maud scrambled around a narrow rocky bend which dipped a fraction towards the water. They were still high up on the cliff edge and at this point Maud stopped and pointed in a precise direction down below them towards the base of the cliff where it met the sea. She was pointing to an inaccessible, small inlet, with layer upon layer of narrow rock shelves recessed into the cliff face above the high tide mark. Some resident seals were barking and bobbing in the water just in front of it.

Once again, Wil heard Maud's distinctive voice telling him, "Now, over by there - can you see?"

Wil knew exactly what he needed to do.

CHAPTER 3
A GLIMMER

Maud was long gone. Wil's eyes opened. He was staring up towards roughly where he thought the rafters could be on his bedroom ceiling. The blackout blinds made the room so dark he wasn't sure what he was looking at or what time it was. The solitary sound he could hear was his heart beating in his head as his clammy body struggled to recalibrate after what he had experienced moments earlier. Reaching one arm over to check the time, the dazzling iPhone glare in his hand told him it was four a.m. and reaffirmed he hadn't missed any messages or calls.

He was wide awake. So he jumped out of bed, skipped his usual shower and shave, got dressed back into the same clothes he had taken off the night before, and headed out through the door.

Wil drove the usual twelve minutes to his campsite business office in less than ten. There was an urgency as he rummaged through his pockets fumbling for his security keys and alarm fobs. He opened his lock-up, disarmed the alarm system and loaded onto his pick-up truck everything he needed.

Two-and-a-half hours later, as the sun was almost rising, Wil parked in the public car park near the Strumble Head lighthouse, which is set on a spectacular island outcrop on the craggy Pembrokeshire coastline in West Wales. The clear sky had a violet-blue tone to it, with a liberal sprinkling of stars, and to his relief, the Welsh coastal wind was tolerable.

He hauled his kayak off the rack on the back of his truck, pulled on his wetsuit, helmet, surf boots and buoyancy vest. He put the paddle and kayak onto its little wheelie trolley and pulled it along the cliff path for several hundred metres. Wil found one of the handful of places where he knew it was OK for him to descend in safety, almost a hundred feet to the water, and get into his kayak.

He paddled around the headland for almost half an hour into the strong offshore breeze. It felt as though everything was against him - the wind, the tide and the current - even bits of brown seaweed was impeding him. Every little wave that the tip of the kayak skimmed and bounced over and every paddle stroke sent a cold wet spray into the air then backwards onto Wil, but it felt good, he didn't care.

He closed his eyes for a moment and imagined it was the same breeze he thought he had felt hours earlier in his bedroom. Two curious young seals had popped their heads above the water nearby to find out what was happening. Wil smiled and paddled on until he came to an inlet that looked familiar. He wasn't certain but he thought he had seen this inlet from high above when he had visited here with Emma and the kids. As he got a little closer, he saw the high tide mark and realised this was the place he needed to get to.

The rising sun cast a long silhouette from behind the outcrop of cliffs onto the water's edge, and looking into the dark shadows was tricky to make out the rocks and ledges. Luck was on his side, the currents and the waves had become more favourable for him, and he was able to pull onto a ledge and hop out of the kayak. He stood up shivering with seawater and drippers running off the end of his nose, then caught his breath and looked around him, there wasn't silence, but an eerie peacefulness. It was a special moment – Wil, his kayak, and nature. For the first time in weeks, he felt invigorated.

The lighthouse was over his shoulder in the background and for now, until the sun had risen higher, its lamp would still be rotating its powerful beam of light every thirty seconds or so. Upwards, he could see the partially hedge-lined cliff edge coastal path with a perilous drop to where he was standing.

As his eyes readjusted, he looked just ahead, then shuffled sideways a half a metre more to be sure. He waited, looking ahead in anticipation of the beam of light coming around once again from behind him.

Wil stared hard at the dark rockface where he had looked moments earlier and he hadn't been mistaken – there was no doubt, he had seen a glimmer of a reflection. Something glinting and shining back at him from within the rockface in front of him. He slid his cold wrinkled index finger into a tight crack in the rocks and scooped out the glinting item. It was a solitaire diamond ring.

~

Wil's visits to Emma continued as normal throughout the rest of the week, every day he would sit by her bedside talking and reading to her. Being as gentle as possible, he would also slide the ring he had found on and off her finger. One afternoon Wil was holding Emma's hand, whilst she was wearing the ring, when he was sure he felt a slight reaction or a squeezed response from her.

"Emma? ...Emma, please do that again."

She responded to him - she gently squeezed a hand again.

He burst out of the door and ran the short distance to the near-by nurse's station. He was frantic as he explained to one of the senior nurses what had just happened. On taking a closer look at Emma's monitors and data history, the nurse could see there had been some slight changes to the electrical activity they had been monitoring.

It felt like an eternity, but when the clinicians had finished their work, Wil moved closer to the bedside to look at Emma. He was expecting to say his usual 'see you tomorrow' to her as she lay there passively when there was an unexpected flickering and opening of her eyelids as she said his name, "Wil."

It started with his legs, then his arms and hands - he was trembling. His words were trapped - he couldn't believe what he had witnessed. Was that the turning point? She was awake and alert.

After an emotional hour and some polite cajoling from the staff, Wil left Emma to rest. When he got to the door of his cottage, he remembered leaving the hospital and putting the key in the door – nothing else about the journey home.

The next morning Wil returned to find Emma sitting a little more upright. Before the children were born, her dark hair was long and curly. Now it was shorter and straighter, and someone had brushed it for her. She had some colour in her cheeks and looked much better. Her bright blue eyes widened, and she smiled as she saw him coming.

Wil kissed her on the cheek, and in his softest voice asked, "How are you doing?"

"I'm fine, *ish*. I feel a bit weak and tired. But something weird happened, I think I had a strange dream. Mum was in it telling me that you have something important for me - and then I woke up."

An emotional Wil held her hand and said, "Yes I do, take a look."

The little object that once held such emotional value and had been lost for decades was again, sitting on Emma's finger. Despite having lost weight during the harsh effects of the coma it was still a much better fit than when she was a little girl. She looked down, shaking her head from side to side, her eyes and mouth open wide as she recognised the beautiful ring that she had lost all those years ago.

The shocked expression on Emma's face changed to one of elation as she smiled again and started to laugh. She stared at the ring, and asked, "Where, how?"

"I'll tell you later, it's a bit of a story."

~

It had been a slow frustrating process, but Emma's strength and mobility made significant improvements. Three weeks later, they made a nostalgic drive to Strumble Head and wandered hand in hand along a short stretch of the coastal path. As they walked, Wil had a sense of *deja vu* and shuddered when Emma turned and looked back at him, she was the image of the young Maud, even her voice was similar.

After a ten-minute gentle walk, filling their lungs with fresh sea breezes, they reached the exposed cliff edge high above the inlet. The light was perfect, and both the sky and the sea looked bluer than ever. Wil had done his best to explain the whole thing to Emma as soon as she left the hospital, whilst also answering a barrage of questions. She stood on the clifftop smiling, with a strange sense of calm and relief to be healthy again and to have the ring back in the family. Emma had chosen to wear the ring that day and every couple of minutes she found herself touching her finger to check and make sure it was still there.

Emma realised she had come full circle, as she gazed way out to sea and simply mouthed the words, "Thanks Mum."

CHAPTER 4
NOT A SCREAM

Late September 2018

In the months following the dramatic events of the accident and the mystery surrounding the finding of the ring, Wil and Emma had settled back into a normal way of life. Almost as if nothing had ever happened. The accident-related pounding headaches that Emma had been getting from time to time had tailed off. Then thank goodness stopped occurring three weeks ago. A couple of young grandchildren and their glamping business had been a great distraction and had no doubt helped with her healing process.

Nevertheless, most days, at the back of their minds, they both recalled something remarkable, that neither of them could explain, had happened to them. Not exactly a miracle, but it was something inexplicable.

Now and again, when out with friends and family over a glass of wine, Emma couldn't resist regaling the story.

"...Mum, God bless her, she was standing there on the path pointing down at the cove and inspired Wil to go and get his kayak and find the ring. He's lucky he isn't still there; he could have got one of those big fingers stuck in the crack."

Emma loved teasing and embarrassing a bashful Wil, reminding him that she thought he had 'superpowers'. Perhaps he did.

One September evening, Wil and Emma were returning home together after a busy day at work. They pulled up outside their home to find another car parked near to their door. It was still light, and they could see a mousey-haired middle-aged woman acknowledge them with a gentle smile and open her car door as they got out of their pick-up truck.

The woman appeared hesitant, twice stopping and starting her ten steps in their direction.

As she got closer to them, struggling to get her words out with any conviction she said, "Hello, you must be Emma, I'm Karen Jones. I'm so sorry to catch you unawares Emma, I'm a cousin of your good friend Sue. I live a few miles up the road."

Emma was taken aback, "Oh, hi, is everything OK with Sue, I haven't heard anything was wrong...?"

"No, no, it's not Sue, it's me. I don't know what to do or who else to turn to. Sue said that maybe you could help me."

The tears were starting to roll down Karen's cheeks so Wil opened the front door and Emma ushered her inside for a cup of tea.

An hour of sympathetic conversation and two cups of tea later, an invigorated happier Karen looked at her watch.

"Sue is going to think I'm such a fool for coming to see you. But I don't care. And now I'm running late, I have to make a move."

Karen put on her coat to go home. She explained she had to go and walk her dogs, as they would be 'climbing the walls'. On the way out, she thanked Wil and Emma for their patience and understanding and said she hoped they didn't think she was crazy for coming to see them as she had.

As Karen sat in her car ready to go, she wound down her window, "What else was I to do? At least I feel better for doing something instead of doing nothing. Thank you."

She left and drove off looking as though a huge weight had been lifted off her shoulders, yet all she had done was talk.

After the door closed, Emma looked at Wil and asked, "What are we going to do?"

A bewildered and subdued Wil replied, "I don't know if there's anything I can do."

Karen was in her mid-forties, a single mum, working two jobs, with two teenage kids who were studying to get the decent grades that might set them on track for college. She had a lot on her plate. Karen explained to Wil and Emma, that her father, Philip, was in his late sixties, a lovely, kind man and had always been the most amazing dad and husband to Karen's mum.

It came as earth-shattering news when three months ago Philip was arrested and charged with the theft of a valuable piece of art, a small sketch by the Norwegian artist Edvard Munch, who famously painted the work called 'The Scream'. Karen's dad ran a well-established and highly regarded art gallery, near the centre of Bath.

The gallery would not necessarily own all the valuable pieces that were on display, but they would often exhibit and sell on behalf of owners from time to time and take an agent's fee. There were also occasions when Philip had organised and run some auctions, sometimes for charities, although that wasn't the main part of his business. It was a good solid business, and he had long-standing professional clients and third parties who would use the gallery to sell their art around the world or as a base to bring in wealthy clients for pre-arranged viewings.

This was the case when one of Philip's Norwegian clients, Jorgen Karlberg, who lived on the outskirts of Bath, decided he wanted to sell his Munch sketch. It was an authenticated sketch study version of 'The Scream', with all the official provenance associated with it. Munch had painted several versions and variations of The Scream, all worth many millions.

Original sketches and studies by most celebrated artists were common practice and were their trial runs and preparations. Those were worth hundreds of thousands of pounds or more to the right buyer. Because in official terms, the Munch was described as a sketch, it was more of an unfinished doodled drawing-come-sketch and had been done on artist's paper not stretched canvas. At least half a century ago, it had also been mounted and encapsulated within a stylish handmade wooden sealed back frame. It was about the size of a piece of printer paper.

The gallery in Bath had remarkable security - it was once a bank. It even retained a back-office walk-in steel vault, the part-glazed street front of which was ram raid-proof, sledgehammer-proof, and axe-proof. It was like Fort Knox, and insurers were more than happy with all the precautions.

Philip had known wealthy collector Jorgen for many years. He was a bit of an eccentric, with the look of a typical Norwegian man. Tall and slim, with what was once a shock of blond hair, now white grey and tied back into a neat ponytail, and a matching goatee beard. They had occasionally socialised together and on one occasion Philip had acted as his proxy at a Sotheby's auction when Jorgen had been unable to attend.

The Munch had been in Jorgen's family for many years and Philip was surprised when he was told that it was for sale. Plans were made and the little framed sketch was brought in and thoroughly scrutinised and validated by Philip, who was an authority on Munch. He and other appraisers had seen and examined the sketch for Jorgen several times in the past for insurance valuation purposes. - It was valued at £1.2m.

The first of Jorgen's anonymous clients was due to come in and view it with him not long after the sketch had been placed on display in a prominent position in the gallery. Philip also had two potential clients expressing an interest and they wanted to view later in the week.

Some valuable paintings go to auction and others get sold privately by word of mouth through a network of exclusive contacts within the art world. This also saved on some of the exorbitant fees charged by auction houses, as opposed to Philip's friendly arrangement with Jorgen. To avoid transporting back and forth from Jorgen's home, overnight the sketch was kept, along with several others, in the high-security former bank vault at the gallery.

On the third day, by which time there had already been two offers well above £1.5m for the rough draft sketch, the final viewing was due to take place at midday. Jorgen arrived, as usual, soon after ten a.m. The sketch was retrieved from the vault and placed on display in a secure, well-lit viewing section of the gallery. Philip's receptionist had made them all a jug of fresh coffee just as Philip had finished a phone call near reception. At which point, in a booming voice, Jorgen shouted for Philip to join him. It sounded urgent.

As a bemused Philip approached the sketch, Jorgen said loudly, "What the hell is going on? The Munch has been switched. This is a fake - what have you done with the original, where is it?"

There was a brief stunned silence as both men looked at each other. Philip composed himself, walked up to the sketch and said, "What are you talking about? Are you crazy? This is the picture you gave me on Monday - it's still in the same frame. Can't you see?"

The sketch was taken from its display easel and laid flat on a nearby table with a 'daylight LED' neutral table light. Philip did a close examination of it and the frame using a jeweller's 15 x eye-glass. He then made some further comparisons with images of the picture that he had kept on record. Within moments, his facial expression changed from indignant indifference to absolute shock. This was not the sketch he had signed off and accepted into his care three days earlier.

Karlberg was much taller than Philip, but he looked to have grown a couple more inches. He started pointing and wagging his finger and his voice was much louder than it was moments earlier. Philip could feel his shirt starting to cling to his back. He was scanning the room faintly hoping to find a wide crack in the floorboards or some clue as to where the original might be. He was also becoming more and more concerned and confused. Without any further dialogue, Karlberg was on the phone to the police. Philip had no alternative but to cancel the forthcoming client meeting. He locked the front door, secured the rest of the building, and waited for the police to arrive.

Over the coming weeks, senior 'plain-clothes' police officers spent many hours interviewing Philip. The part-time receptionist was interviewed but was soon eliminated from enquiries as she was not a key holder and had no knowledge of the vault's codes and key sequences. All the evidence was left pointing in the direction of gallery owner Philip Jones as the main, and only, suspect. The police concluded Jones had plenty of opportunities to have made the switch when he had been inside the gallery's vault on numerous occasions. He was also well connected in the art world, so could easily find a buyer from the long list of wealthy anonymous voyeurs. Munch Scream series paintings have a reputation for being highly sought after - one of them once sold for $125m and there have been a handful of well-documented thefts of them over the years. This little sketch was worth over a million on the black market.

Philip Jones was an honest man and, rightly or wrongly, acknowledged to the police he did have the original sketch in his vault from day one. He also told the police that to have switched the sketch from its frame, reinstall the fake sketch and reseal the backing would have taken over an hour with the right tools, materials, and expertise. To the police, those comments turned out to see Philip digging a much deeper hole, incriminating himself to a far greater extent.

After much consideration and debate with the Crown Prosecution Service, plus overwhelming circumstantial evidence, Philip Jones was charged with theft and remanded on bail. Who else had the window of opportunity required, access to the safe, and the skill and ability to switch the fake into that unique original frame?

~

Over dinner, back at their cottage near Abergavenny, Wil and Emma talked about the day's events and the long conversation they'd had with poor Karen. She had shared with them all the facts she was aware of, and how it was affecting the health of her dad. Compounded with her mother being in a hospital, it was a difficult situation for her. Wil and Emma wanted to believe Karen, but based on what evidence? Rumours had been circulating about Emma and Wil's mysterious story from Karen's cousin and was why she had turned up with no introduction.

Before she left, Karen had given Emma a small black messenger bag. Inside it, there were some wedding pictures of Karen's parents and some newspaper cuttings which referred to Philip Jones. Or as some of the clippings stated, 'local hero Philip Jones'.

When he was a younger man, Philip had graduated from University with a BA in Modern Art. But instead of continuing to work in the family antique dealing business, he chose to follow his older brother Bob into the army. That explained why Philip was dressed in his immaculate Royal Welch Fusiliers uniform for his wedding.

During the mid-nineties, Philip had served as an officer for the UN peacekeeping forces during Operation Grapple in the Bosnian Civil War and was awarded a medal for gallantry. He had rescued a Muslim family from a house that was coming under mortar fire. During the rescue, one of Philip's men had been shot by a sniper, a close-up ricochet to the man's jaw. Unpleasant, but not life-threatening. Philip carried the injured man over his shoulder to safety. Whilst doing so, Philip was shot in the leg by the same sniper as he was getting the family and his teammate into the nearby armoured vehicle. Recovering from the injury was not a great success, the sniper had ended Philip's military career and was why he resumed working in the art world. He went on to meet his wife there and they made their home together in Bath.

There was something else folded up in Karen's messenger bag - it was her father's regimental dark blue beret with its nine-inch white officer's plume attached. Inside the beret were two small boxes containing his treasured Military Cross for gallantry and his UNPROFOR service medal (United Nations Protection Force). Karen had borrowed the medals and stressed earlier that her father was an honourable and trustworthy man. All the evidence in the bag along with his remarkable back story appeared to support this view.

~

The following Monday was quiet, and with the glamping season coming to an end, Wil and Emma decided to pay a visit to the beautiful Georgian city of Bath. It wasn't far, about an hour's drive for them. It was to be a lovely day out, but the priority was to help out Karen - that was the sole reason for the trip. After a pleasant stroll around the famous Royal Crescent and The Circle to begin to get a feel for the compact Georgian styled city with its opulent beige stonework everywhere you looked, they headed for the gallery.

Not far off the top end of trendy Milsom Street was the former bank, now a swanky and inviting looking art gallery. There they were met by a man called Henry, who was a friend of Karen's dad and caretaking the gallery while Philip felt unable to work there during his time on bail. Karen had simply told him that Wil and Emma were old friends doing some background research for her dad's legal team and trying to find some new angles and some fresh ideas for his defence in readiness for when the case came to court.

Once inside, they browsed around not knowing what they were looking for - if anything at all. They were shown around the front and 'back of house' by Henry, then inside the vault and, over to the small area where the Munch had been viewed. It was just as Philip and the police had left it, the table with the lamp and the easel nearby. The entire ground floor had some decent CCTV, including a camera that looked at the table and easel as you walked in that direction from the main gallery area.

The overall impression was completed as a helpful Henry gave them some more background information and a comprehensive profile dossier on Jorgen Karlberg, whom he had met two or three times. Karlberg was said to be a wealthy, likeable man, happily married to a retired lecturer with three grown-up children. He had been outspoken on the odd occasion over the years. Usually concerning some political issues and funding going to the wrong places within the Bath arts community, because Jorgen was vice chairman at the renowned Holburne Museum in Bath. Other than that, Karlberg was an innocuous man.

As they were leaving the gallery Henry gave Wil an envelope and said, "I don't know if this is of any use to you? It's a DVD with the CCTV footage for the four days that Philip had taken responsibility for the Munch. The police have seen it and they found nothing untoward. Good luck. Oh, and one more thing - there's no way Philip stole the picture, never in a million years. I'm telling you - he didn't do it."

Having spent some time at the gallery and acknowledged the facts, together with the strong emotion from Henry, the couple's drive home from Bath back to South Wales was going to be a sobering experience. As they walked through the side streets back to the car, a dispirited Wil and Emma wondered what Karen expected them to unearth that the police hadn't already been able to investigate and strike from the list of possibilities. They considered the probability that maybe Philip did steal the sketch - he wouldn't be the first good guy to go rogue, and he wouldn't be the last. But they soon dismissed that possibility, they both had the same vibe - something or somebody was 'fishy'.

They set off in the truck and were about to head in the direction of the motorway back to South Wales. All of a sudden, Wil, who had been quieter than usual for several minutes, asked Emma to plug in a new address into the sat-nav.

He then said with some renewed vigour, "It's not too far out of our way - let's go and see where this guy Karlberg lives, shall we?"

Five minutes later, Wil and Emma were parked up outside a beautiful, ultra-modern property in Percy Place on the London Road on the outskirts of Bath. It was in a secluded location, so they got out of the pick-up to try to get a closer look. They couldn't see much past the tall electric gates. As they got a little closer, they gave each other one of those 'are you thinking what I'm thinking?' looks.

There was a for-sale sign fixed to the garden wall of the house. A quick online check showed the seven thousand square feet property with six bedrooms and an indoor pool was on the market for the best part of £3m.

Wil decided to make a cheeky phone call to the local estate agent and was put through to a bubbly young lady called Chloe. After some pertinent questions, he asked how long it had been on the market and why was it for sale. She said it had been 'on' for at least six months and added, "I know they have lowered the price once and are now looking for offers for a quick sale. It's not my place to say, but off the record, I think they are an older couple and they're getting divorced."

Some cogs were beginning to turn in Wil's head.

CHAPTER 5

SALUTE

Autumn 2018

It was getting dark by the time they made it home to Wales, and Wil and Emma hadn't eaten more than a small piece of cake each since breakfast. They had been much busier than they expected to be. All their focus had been on the events of the day, so they had kept pushing on with coffees and the cake. They decided to walk to their local pub and grab a bar snack. A few beers and a full stomach later, they got home and headed for an early night. It had been a full-on, thought-provoking day.

In bed, a tired Wil found himself once again looking through the contents of Karen's messenger bag and thinking about all the information she and Henry had shared with them. He felt a connection with Philip, though he had never once met him. As his mind wandered, he soon fell into a deep sleep.

For the first time in months, Wil found himself having an unsettled night. He tossed and turned until his restlessness evolved into another of his occasional lucid dreams. As usual, the experience was vivid, colourful and in the moment. In the dream, Wil thought he could feel prickles pressing into his back and brambles snagging around his ankles every time he tried to move his feet. He had a sense that he was hiding in some bushes from someone, then with some urgency, moving through leaves half-way up his shins to another location and looking and watching something.

As the dream progressed, he was startled as he heard an unexpected voice coming from behind him, urging him on, "C'mon Wil, you can do better than that. What are you waiting for? Get on with it."

Wil glanced back over his shoulder and he could see the image of the man who was talking to him. He was dressed in military uniform and looked familiar. It was the other man in Philip's wedding photograph. Maybe it was the best man?

Once again, the man repeated his instructions to Wil, "Get on with it, will you? You know what you need to do."

Wil could sense himself stepping out from the bushes that he was hiding in and following a tall man, at a distance, along a narrow road which led into a park and along a pedestrian path. As Wil rounded a bend on the path, he could feel his heart racing with anticipation, the man had stopped thirty yards ahead of him to take a phone call. The dream 'just wasn't ready' to release Wil from its magnetism, and he felt 'locked in', compelled to continue with its exhilarating lucid chase. The man ahead was tall and had his back to Wil, but he recognised the white hair and ponytail. It was Jorgen Karlberg, he was wearing a coat and carrying a shoulder bag. The ponytailed Karlberg had picked up some speed and was walking at a brisk, purposeful, pace.

As he did so, the soldier's voice was again chirping in Wil's ear, "Don't lose him son, stay with him."

As they walked through the park they came to a pause in front of an incredible looking Georgian public building with a tall new glass and ceramic extension grafted on to its side. Wil recognised it from Henry's dossier, it was the recently refurbished Holburne Museum.

The dream led them inside the Holburne, through the café and upstairs to a private area. Karlberg had used his trustees/staff RFID (Radio-Frequency Identification) swipe card access, gliding them through door after door.

After yet more corridors and doors, they entered a small office on the second floor. Inside the empty office, there was a bank of pigeonhole lockers built into an alcove. One of them had the nameplate: 'Vice Chairman of Trustees Jorgen Karlberg'. Karlberg swiped the secure small locker door and opened it, gave a nervous glance around, before retrieving a large padded envelope from his backpack. He opened the envelope and partially slid out its contents as if double-checking something. It was the Munch sketch, removed from its frame. He slid it back into the envelope, before placing it among some other documents inside the locker. He closed the locker door, made his way back downstairs and left the building.

The last thing the determined soldier said to Wil during the lucid dream was, "Well done son, now have a close look at the bank's window on the internal CCTV film," and then he was gone.

~

Emma came downstairs for breakfast to find Wil pondering recent events over a cup of coffee.

The first thing he said to Emma was, "You remember the wedding photos that Karen gave to you? Who was the other soldier with Karen's dad, any idea?"

Emma said she didn't know but she would text Karen to find out. Five minutes later, her phone pinged with an incoming message.

"Wil, Karen has replied to me," said Emma.

"She says the other soldier was Philip's best man. It was his brother, Bob - Captain Robert Jones - who I'm sad to say, was killed in an ambush in Northern Ireland four months after Philip's wedding. Why do you ask?"

~

It was Thursday morning before Wil was back in Bath, once again at the gallery, chatting with Henry. The visitor Wil was expecting turned up at the time they had agreed. It was Detective Inspector Vicky Strong, who was leading the Philip Jones investigation. Wil asked Henry if he would mind giving him and his visitor some privacy for an hour in the viewing area so they could sit at the table for a discussion. Wil had something to show Strong.

The meeting with Strong had been arranged over the phone after Wil had explained he had some powerful new evidence for her to consider. He also said he had been tipped off from 'a reliable source' as to the whereabouts of the stolen Munch. She couldn't refuse, why would she, Strong was keen to hear what he had to say. They both sat around the table and Wil powered up his laptop.

The previous two days, Wil and Emma had been busy calling in a favour from an old friend who worked at a local television production company.

The laptop came to life and Wil said to Strong he was about to show her the real-time footage of a two-minute section taken from the same HD quality CCTV that the police had a copy of. It was the Tuesday afternoon soon after Jorgen Karlberg had hosted one of his pre-arranged private viewings of the Munch – notably, Philip Jones had not been asked to join them.

The video showed Karlberg talking through the famous history and provenance of the sought after Munch and finishing his sales pitch. With smiles all around he had shaken hands and said goodbye to his Chinese visitor, who gave yet another courteous bow of the head, smiled again and left. Next, Karlberg simply walked out of shot. The area was in full view of the camera, floor to ceiling, from about five meters away. The easel and picture were standing, angled in a little, in the left-hand corner of the room against a solid wall. The front wall was one of the high-security tall glass windows, providing some natural light on the picture. Karlberg came back into shot, this time wearing his knee-length Barbour raincoat, almost ready to leave, and walking with no great conviction towards the picture. With his back to the camera, he appeared to place his hands either side of the easel and move it by a fraction back squarer to the wall, away from the window.

31

Karlberg stood back, gazed in admiration at the picture, and walked away. At this point, Philip came into shot, he gave a satisfying nod and a look at the picture, he removed it and took it to the vault.

Wil looked at Strong and said, "Nothing happened right? The picture hasn't moved. Karlberg touched the easel for a split second, then Philip came in looked at the picture and took it away."

They reminded themselves what Philip Jones was reported to have said, *"Removing the original sketch from its frame and replacing it with the fake sketch back into the frame would have been a long complex process."*

Wil was setting the scene with perfection, "OK, Vicky, now let's check this out. A friend of mine who specialises in TV and film production and has done some work for me enhancing the imagery."

A new file was opened on the laptop, - this time it was a zoomed-in, slowed down, professionally digitally enhanced version of what they had seen moments earlier. Wil tugged the laptop a fraction closer and asked Strong to take a closer look, about a half a metre to the right of the easel. Vicky Strong's jaw dropped as she watched a clear reflection in the security glass window. Karlberg was using one hand to pull out of a poacher's pocket in his raincoat a fake Munch sketch in a frame and switching it with the original. Shown in super slow motion, it was a smooth deft action, the picture was barely visible. He must have practised doing it dozens of times. His back, shoulder bag and loose-fitting raincoat had obscured the main sightline, and his left hand never left the side of the easel - adding to the distraction. Ten seconds later, Philip was none the wiser. Strong looked at Wil in amazement.

"And I know where the original is being hidden," said Wil.

Late the same Thursday afternoon, an hour before the Holburne Museum was due to close, DI Vicky Strong arrived at the front desk with a warrant to search the building. She was accompanied by Wil Richardson and another police officer as they were chaperoned through various doors until they reached the familiar-looking office that Wil had experienced in his dream. They walked over to the lockers, and the museum's facilities manager opened Karlberg's locker with a master swipe card. Seconds later, Strong slid what looked like a teenage doodled sketch of a screaming face from out of a large padded envelope.

At the same time as his locker was being opened, Jorgen Karlberg was being arrested and having his rights read at his luxury home about a mile down the road.

For someone who had been so meticulous in his planning, the arrogant man never anticipated being found out and having to endure a police cell and an interrogation. Karlberg caved in and confessed within minutes of being interviewed and all charges against Philip Jones were dropped. Karlberg's wife was divorcing him, forcing them to sell the family home. He needed a lot of money as fast as possible to pay her off. He never had any intention of parting with the Munch after he had stolen it - it was too precious to him, and the insurance money would be plenty. He thought he had the perfect plan. Get paid off handsomely, get rid of his wife and keep his picture.

The Munch sketch had been in his family for a couple of generations, along with another similar small painting from a much lesser-known artist, worth a fraction of the Munch. Both 'paintings' had been mounted at the same time in identical matching picture frames that had aged in the same way. Karlberg used his knowledge and contacts to produce an exclusive fake and retouch it to look like the original. The next cunning step was to mount the fake sketch into the matching 'twin' picture frame. Once Philip Jones had validated the original picture in its frame on the Monday, Karlberg carried out his viewings early in the week with the original. As soon as he was ready, he made the switch and took it to the Holburne to hide it. An oblivious Philip stored the fake in the vault. The next morning the fake was innocently retrieved from the vault and placed on the easel – ready and waiting for Karlberg to set his plan in motion and accuse Philip Jones.

In the months that followed, Karlberg was convicted and jailed for four years. The insurance company had settled on the claim not long after the theft. Although there was a fraud case, it was the insurers who owned the sketch and they decided to sell it.

It was six weeks before Christmas. The management of the insurers was keen to express their gratitude to those involved in its recovery and agreed the auctioning of the Munch could be handled by Philip Jones from his gallery in Bath. There had been a great deal of publicity surrounding the sketch and the art world was licking its lips at the rare prospect of a Munch becoming available.

Wil and Emma finally got to meet a delighted Philip Jones along with Karen on the morning of the auction. Vicky Strong was also there and was still puzzled as to how Wil knew to look as close as he did at the video footage, and how he knew where the original was hidden. She must have asked Wil four or five times, but every time he shrugged his shoulders.

The auction began with some lower value items. The gallery sat about thirty people, with several standing at the back. With the help of Wil's TV production friend, they had kitted out the room with a 55-inch television screen. An auction software package and internet connections for online bids had ensured an excellent 4G signal for the phone bids that were expected.

The headline event began with a smiling Philip Jones on the gavel. He gave his preamble about the Munch and said, "We have a reserve price of one million pounds, - who will start me at £1.2m?". Within minutes, the online bids and phone bids were pouring in, and several of the initial starters sat in the room had dropped out. The screen was trying its best keep up with the action. The bidding had eased up and was going up in £100,000 increments. Proceedings came to a close, with the hammer coming down - to huge applause in the room - on £4.1m.

A beaming Henry turned to Wil and Emma. He knew a thing or two about auctions. He explained that the seller would be paying a fee of about four per cent to Philip as a commission, leaving what's known in the trade as 'the buyer's premium' of 25%, also paid directly to the auction house.

He concluded, "Good old Philip has just made north of one million quid in five minutes."

After the auction had finished, the group of friends and acquaintances celebrated well into the evening at a famous fish restaurant up the road.

As they were leaving, Emma turned to Wil, "What's on your mind? You seemed to be a little distracted this evening, I can read you like a book."

Wil replied, "I'm not sure, but in my sleep last night I was restless again. It wasn't clear and I didn't see anything, but I thought I heard a young woman sobbing. The next thing was she called out to me, 'Only you can find me Wil, only you know where I am'..."

CHAPTER 6
ONLY YOU CAN FIND ME

November 2018

"Only you know where I am Wil, no one else can find me. Please, please help me."

These words, the desperate sound of a young woman in great distress, kept rattling around in Wil's head on and off for most of the day, and again during the evening after the auction. Had he dreamt it or was it for real? It had come and gone. It wasn't like his usual lucid dreams, not like the crazy ones with Maud and with Captain Bob Jones. Those moments last night had been disconcerting and heartrending. They were full of emotion and fear – they were real. Based on his recent experiences, Wil knew he needed to trust his instincts. He had every right to have grave concerns.

~

Emma led the celebrations at the post-auction party, after a slow start it wasn't long before she was taking charge of affairs and being asked not to stand on her chair by the management.

"Em', we're not the only ones having dinner here, there are other people as well!"

"Really? Oh yeah, there are some others!"

Wil knew it was a lost cause. Everyone was pretty hammered by ten p.m. - and some were still going strong long after that. The couple had booked a nice hotel in the centre of Bath, not far from the final busy pub stop of the evening. The walk to their hotel had done them good and they decided to chill in the lounge area with a coffee before heading up to bed. When Emma popped to the ladies, Wil decided to have a bleary-eyed scroll through his news feed. He didn't know what to expect, and by the time Emma had returned, he had found nothing of note and was scanning his chat groups and Facebook pages.

An hour later, Wil was snoring like a demon. Emma had tried everything: reading her book, nudging him, kicking him, turning him onto his side. It took a while before he fell silent, and they both went off to sleep.

Four a.m. and Emma's sleep was again disturbed. The snoring had been replaced by what appeared to be Wil practicing his gymnastics techniques in the bed. But the worst of it was his murmuring and whispering, which had gone on far longer than the usual episodes had ever done. It almost felt like he was on the phone to someone, communicating in his sleep.

~

Doctors had told Emma recovering from severe head trauma could be a long road to recovery for many people. Following her accident, she had been one of the lucky ones - there were no obvious ongoing physical or psychological issues for her to contend with. The nurses and consultants had been amazing whilst she was in the hospital. She had also attended numerous outpatient sessions until she was given an all-clear and signed off. During that time, Wil and Emma had become friendly with the specialist consultant. He was a cheerful, helpful man, and Emma had regaled the story about Wil's dreams, Maud, and the ring.

Like all senior medical professionals, the consultant would share unusual cases and information within his UK peer group and further afield in North America and Asia. One of his group members was Dr Frea

Huckle, a highly regarded sleep specialist who had papers published on the subject and had been invited to present her findings at seminars around the world. She had a particular interest in Wil and his lucid dream sleep events because his experiences opened up many new avenues for her to explore. It appeared as though he could be unlike anything she had encountered in the past.

Frea Huckle had first met Wil when she was using a consulting room next to Emma's consultant during one of her outpatient visits and was introduced to them both. Her knowledge and enthusiasm were obvious. She explained she had a personal interest in having a proper meeting with Wil some time and exploring his lucid dream experiences at length. Wil was receptive to her idea and he took her details, but days became weeks and he had never followed it up.

~

Over breakfast at their hotel in Bath, both Wil and Emma were sharing out the paracetamol. It had been a fantastic day at the auction house and a great boozy evening. They were treated as special guests, and their secret was just about kept under wraps by an exuberant Philip Jones.

Sipping a well-sugared coffee, Wil asked Emma, "Do you still have the contact details of that sleep consultant we met during your hospital outpatients visit? Frea something wasn't it?"

"Huckle, Dr Frea Huckle." Emma looked in her purse and retrieved the details with a mobile number on it.

Emma looked at Wil, who was deep in thought as usual, and asked him, "Well, are you going to tell me why? You've just woken up with a hangover and you want to call a doctor - what's happening, are you going soft or something?"

Wil raised an eyebrow and smiled, "Yes I've got a hangover but no I'm not going soft. It's driving me nuts, I've got to get to the bottom of the dream I had last night."

Wil reminded Emma it was linked to the dream he'd had the night before last, "I've had two consecutive nights of this troubling, unresolved episode. I'm worried about this woman, something's wrong."

With his head tilted forward and eyes vacant, focusing on absolutely nothing in the distance behind her, he continued to tell Emma that last night he could sense he was at one end of a long room. The room felt dank and cold and the lighting was subdued. He had not been able to visualise it clearly but had been aware of a steel tubular bed, like those you might find in youth hostels. He had looked at the bed and he could make out the figure of a young dark-haired woman, laying still. She was also handcuffed to a length of chain which was attached to the bed.

In the dream Wil appeared to move closer to the young woman She stirred, looked up and in a tired, agitated and heavily accented voice said, "Wil you're back - you can find me, you can do it."

Wil tried to speak to the woman but he was frustrated, his words didn't always come out in is his dreams. As a rule, communication was nonverbal from him, yet he could hear things that were said. On the floor near his feet, he could see a black Samsonite executive-style flight case, on wheels with an extendable drag handle. Attached to the cabin style bag was a luggage label. He had tried to see the label in the hope of reading a name, but he wasn't able to make it out.

The young woman urged him, "Please don't leave me here - please come back for me!"

The dream came to an abrupt end, maybe because Emma had nudged Wil in the ribs in an attempt to settle him back into a restful sleep.

A worried Wil told Emma he was certain someone was in trouble somewhere. He thought maybe time was running out for the young woman, and he felt he needed to find a way to help but didn't know how to resolve things. That was when he had the idea to contact Dr Frea Huckle. Perhaps she could help him.

"She sounded like a real authority on the subject, and I'm pissed off with myself for not getting in touch with her months ago like I said he would."

~

Emma was driving them home when Wil answered his phone to an enthusiastic Dr Frea Huckle, "Hello Mr Richardson, it's Frea Huckle here - you left me a voicemail. My apologies, I was with a client. How can I help you?"

"Hi Frea thanks for calling me back. Look, it's kind of difficult to explain over the phone, I'll try my best, but it's urgent and a bit of a long shot."

Frea Huckle's schedule meant she worked certain days part-time for the NHS and a couple of other days a month she worked at a private clinic in Newport. All of that was fitted in around her thriving yoga practice.

She was fascinated as she listened to Wil, who was approaching the Severn Bridge heading home, and said, "Here's an idea Wil, why don't you come to see me now? I'm here, I'm available and I am intrigued to find out more – and it sounds urgent."

Twenty minutes later after crossing back into Wales, Wil and Emma were greeted by Frea in her consulting room at the private hospital. She made them feel welcome right away, there was a definite warmth and eagerness to gain a greater understanding of Wil's 'superpowers' as Emma had once described them months ago.

Frea was open and honest as she explained that she was writing a book, the working title of which was *The Untapped Power of Lucid Dreams*. She also said her extensive yoga knowledge and Buddhism readings of tantric milam concepts - which is the practising of dream yoga - enhanced her understanding of the subject. All the more reason why she had wanted to find an opportunity to work with Wil when they had first met during Emma's hospital appointment.

The explanation of both of Wil's previous mystifying episodes concerning the engagement ring and the Munch sketch didn't faze Frea at all. There was plenty of factual evidence to support what had happened. She knew it wasn't luck or coincidence. The simple explanation was Wil Richardson's mind and brain and his ability to 'connect' extrinsically.

An open-minded and earnest Frea said, "Guys, based on Wil's previous events, I think we should all treat the content of the previous two nights' lucid dreams as a serious situation."

"You're right Frea. I don't need a second opinion on that one. It's worrying, to say the least."

Frea added, "Listen, Wil, I'm confident I can help you – to some extent. I don't know how far that goes yet. But I think we should make a start straight away, while you're here."

Emma was nodding in agreement, as Wil said, "Yes, please, let's go for it."

They talked at length, and Wil agreed to lie on the couch and relax. Emma moved and sat at the rear of the consulting room. Frea dimmed the lights and attached some non-intrusive digital monitoring devices, a set of headphones and a small microphone to Wil's collar. Frea had put on a similar set of headphones and microphone to communicate with Wil. She asked him to close his eyes and began playing him some relaxing background sounds. Softly making comments and guiding Wil, within minutes, he found himself drifting into a controlled state of hypnotic relaxation. There was an eerie silence in the room. All that a nervous Emma could make out was the gentle tone of Frea's voice in the background and her husband gently twitching on the couch. He was drifting off to sleep.

The whole process must have taken almost an hour before Wil found himself sitting up on the couch, flickering his eyelids until they were open.

Frea asked Wil how he felt, and without any hesitation, he answered, "I feel OK, but that was crazy. There are still so many questions, but the most important thing is, I have some of the answers I was hoping to find. I know what we need to do next."

It had been easy to see. Frea's on tap capability and her guided intensity had enabled Wil to resume the lucid experience within minutes - and also to reach a deeper, more pronounced sensation.

Wil hopped off the couch and the three of them stood there. With both his hands clasped around the back of his head in trepidation, he began to tell his frantic story.

His mind had been full of visions and sensations. There had to be some order to them, but if there was, he was unable to formulate it and convey what he wanted to.

There was an urgency in his voice, "The young woman, that awful room, there's no light coming in through the windows, she's on the bed, they've tied her or chained her to the bed."

Frea intervened, touching his arm and in her calm authoritative voice, telling Wil, "Slow down, take a deep breath, clear your mind, then speak when you're ready."

"Her name," Wil announced, "Her name is Alina Usmanova."

Wil told them about the name badge on the case. This time he'd seen it close up and had read her name. Half of the words on the name badge were obscured, but the last word was "Aeroflot", the Russian airline. On the wooden floor next to the unzipped Samsonite case were two cameras, some notepad size colour prints with images on them and a laptop. Perhaps she was a reporter or journalist?

He told them, "The young woman made no obvious movement on the bed - she didn't even open her eyes this time, I think she may have been drugged?"

But she must have sensed Wil's presence and stirred.

"She told me, 'Wil - look through the window'."

The window and Wil were somehow drawn together. It was blacked out with a heavy curtain, but there was chink of light to its side. He peered through the bright opening and was able to make out the views outside the building. It was immediately obvious the location was a city, a big city with tall opulent buildings. He could see cars driving on the left-hand side of the road, a park to the right of the foreground, and he could make out way over to the east a tall familiar structure.

"I saw the BT Tower – she's being held captive in London!"

Wil explained, the buildings opposite where four storeys high, many with wide imposing doors framed by pillars. Presumably, the drama that was unfolding before him was in a similarly styled building. The lucid dream had continued to enable him to scan the surroundings outside. There was a gap between the buildings opposite, and in the distance, he could just make out the symbol of an underground station and a name.

"It said, Holland Park. And the building directly opposite had the number seventy-three emblazoned on its pillars."

They all appreciated the urgency of the situation. After they had collected their thoughts, Wil and Emma hovered over Frea as she sat at her desk made a quick internet search for Alina Usmanova, which came back with hits for several women of the same name. But one of them had an image that Wil recognised as the young woman he had encountered. More details showed she came from a wealthy Russian family, studied at Oxford and was living and working in London for a PR company. Her father originated from Uzbekistan and her mother was Russian but had been living in London. Her father had been a politician and was found dead in an apparent suicide four months earlier. Her mother was blood-related to some high-ranking Russian oligarchs with oil and gas production connections.

Frea googled 'Uzbekistan, London', which produced a link to an embassy at number forty-one on the luxurious Holland Park Road. Clicking on it then spinning the Google Maps street view arrow, the impressive property opposite had the number seventy-three displayed big and bold. Dragging the mouse and spinning back to see number forty-one, Wil recognised his vantage point, high up on the fourth floor.

"Oh my God, she's on the top floor of the Uzbekistan Embassy in London."

CHAPTER 7
LONDON CALLING

November 2018

Emma reminded everyone she'd had dealings with several foreign governments via their embassies over the years when she worked on an international *roll-out* marketing project, for a big Welsh pharmaceutical company.

"Foreign Embassy properties around the world are sacrosanct. Legally, they're just like a piece of their home country built on the soil of whatever far-flung country they're based in. We can't just go wandering in - neither can the police." After some more double-checking Emma added, "It says here, *the Vienna Convention states no one can enter without being invited by the Ambassador.*"

~

Frea said they all needed to have a good think about the situation and be careful as to how they approached things. They needed to take into account the sensitivity of the situation and likely reaction from the police. If Wil rang up and claimed to know what he knew, he would be treated as just another crazy crank caller. There was nothing Emma could see on any news feed to say Alina Usmanova was missing.

Wil said he had an idea. Two minutes later, he was on the speakerphone of his mobile to someone he hoped would listen to him with enough interest to offer some help. It was DI Vicky Strong, they had shared a glass of champagne the previous evening in Bath.

You can tell when someone is smiling when they're speaking to you on the phone. Vicky was smiling - the Scream case had been a spectacular result for her and her team. While they were celebrating, she had quietly mentioned to Wil that she was being considered for promotion before the arrest of Karlberg, and this did her chances no harm at all if it came down to fine margins and track record.

Strong answered her mobile, "Hello Wil, this is an unexpected, nice surprise, from my favourite crime fighter."

"How are things going on the promotion front Vicky, any news yet?"

"It's supposed to be a secret Wil, and give me chance will you, we've only just won the case."

Wil got straight to the point and said he needed a big favour, as soon as possible. He asked Vicky if it was possible, without going into details, for her to shed some light on a young woman and her possible whereabouts, maybe in London? It was the vaguest, most ambiguous of requests, but Vicky owed Wil a huge favour. She said she would make some enquiries. Missing persons wasn't her speciality and the neither was the Metropolitan Police in London her police force, but she knew some senior people at the Met, and she would call him back.

She also said, "Wil, why do I get the feeling this isn't going to be a wild goose chase?"

Vicky called Wil back within minutes and said she had asked the right people and drawn a blank. No one had heard of this mystery woman.

"Thanks, Vicky, that's not what I was hoping you were going to say to me though. But I'm ever so grateful to you for trying and good luck with everything else."

They ended the call. Vicky Strong was none the wiser and remained mystified by the call from Wil.

The three of them sat in Frea's office, a little bit deflated, talking for another twenty minutes. As they were about to leave to go home and take stock of things, Wil's phone rang again - it was an international mobile number. He answered to find himself speaking to a man who introduced himself as Christof. He explained that Wil's recent enquiry had been brought to his attention by a colleague based at the Russian Embassy in London.

After a short pause, Christof said, "Mr Richardson, we recognise your knowledge of the situation. We are aware of your valuable contribution to the police in Bath and hope that you can assist us."

Christof explained their conversation was being treated as a private Russian Government matter and one that the UK police would not be involved in. He then asked Wil to kindly explain what information he had to share.

Wil's first reaction was of slight reticence, thinking, *"Who was this guy called Christof?"*

Yet he had full knowledge of the situation, surely, he had to be credible. Together with the gravity and probable time pressure of the situation, it persuaded Wil to open up. With a degree of caution, he explained he was with his wife and a well-respected senior medical professional, Dr Frea Huckle, who both had some knowledge and insight into what Wil was about to explain to Christof.

Diving straight in, Wil said he had some well-informed ideas as to the location of a young woman named Alina Usmanova. He added he hadn't been sure if she was missing or in peril, but now realised that she must be.

"Christof, if I'm right then she's on the fourth floor of the Uzbekistan Embassy in London, in a room overlooking the main street... I realise this all sounds a bit strange."

Wil described Alina, what she was wearing and the possessions that were scattered on the floor of the room she was in.

Christof assimilated the information and wasn't wasting any time to progress it saying, "Thank you for your help. We can't express how grateful we are for your assistance. We will be back in touch with you... and Wil, it's not strange."

Wil's large hands were shaking, and he breathed a huge sigh of relief as he looked at Emma and Frea and asked, "What the hell just happened? What's going on?"

Frea looked at Wil, "You've just done the right thing, and maybe saved someone's life, that's what happened."

They decided to decamp to a local pub. Adrenaline does strange things to some people – in this instance, it made Wil feel hungry and in need of more alcohol. While quietly waiting for the food to arrive, Emma had been doing some research on the wealthy Usmanova family. What she discovered, to begin with, were some startling facts. She acknowledged that in today's world, high profile Russian businessmen were not boy scouts, those billionaires had climbed many greasy poles to reach the top, crushing almost anything that stood in their path. After all, evidence suggested the man who raised the bar and found himself at the top of the tree as one of the richest men in the world was Vladimir Putin himself.

Without too much more effort, it soon emerged there was a connection between Alina's mother Nadia and the head of one of Russia's largest oil and gas producers. They were siblings. He and Putin also happened to be close friends.

It wasn't rocket science to work out that Nadia was seeking help to find her daughter and behind the scenes, there had been some influential people in the Russian Embassy who were monitoring everything. Hence Christof's intervention.

~

It was late evening by the time the bill was being paid in the pub in Newport. At the same moment, on a side street in Kensington, West London, a young man, and woman had left a trendy gin bar. As they held hands approaching their car, a black nine-seater people carrier slowly eased up beside them. The timing was perfect. The door opened. The seats inside had been flipped flat, seconds later, both of the pedestrians were grabbed, bundled in through the sliding side doors and driven off. It was a professionally executed capture.

~

During her internet searches, Emma had also found some controversial news reports concerning the death of Alina's father. His name was Maximilian Usmanova. He was reported by various media channels to have jumped to his death from the top floor of the Tashkent Wyndham Hotel when he was visiting his home country of Uzbekistan.

At the time, he had been acting as a government intermediary between the fast-growing Uzbekistani oil and gas sector and various international investment suitors from UK, Russia, France, and the US. Conspiracy theorists were suggesting that several local investors had been left short-changed and the deal was going to heavily favour the Russians. Before the deal was signed and agreed, Usmanova was said to have committed suicide. As it transpired, it had no impact on the outcome of the deal and the Russians got the lion's share, anyway. The whole thing reeked of corruption and there had been some extreme anger and hostility voiced by certain Uzbekistanis.

~

At midnight, the Uzbekistan Ambassador to the UK was about to go to bed when he picked up his phone to answer a call. He looked at the number and was surprised to see it was his son, who lived in London with his family. It was unusual for him to be calling at all, let alone so late - he would sometimes send a WhatsApp message. But the voice on the phone was not his son's. Like many Uzbekistanis, the ambassador also spoke

Russian, in an instant the colour drained from his face, and he understood the harsh instructions the voice on the phone was issuing.

"жизнь за жизнь, a life for a life."

Within an hour, a stupefied but safe and well Alina Usmanova was collected from a McDonald's restaurant near Hyde Park, where she had been dropped off not long before. Other diners thought she was a bit drunk and had ignored her. The exchange had been made – a life for a life, the Ambassador's son, and his wife for Alina.

Without any doubt in the following months, there would be further political repercussions and a long list of casualties involving the 'Bratva' - Russian mafia. But at least Alina was now safe.

~

Late the following morning, at a calmer and more peaceful breakfast table near Abergavenny, big decisions were being made. Porridge, cornflakes, granola, or toast?

Wil had left his phone upstairs in the bedroom, Emma had answered it and wandered down to the kitchen.

"It's Christof, he wants to speak to you?"

Handing the phone to Wil, she shrugged her shoulders, shook her head, and stood close enough to his ear to overhear the conversation.

Christof told Wil and he was calling on behalf of the Usmanova family to thank him for his help yesterday.

"Wil, Alina is well and has explained everything ...everything. Alina and her mother hope they can meet you as soon so they can to thank you personally. We will be in touch again to make arrangements if it's OK with you Wil?"

Wil left a voicemail for Frea to tell her the exciting news.

~

Wil, Emma and Frea were sitting in some comfortable seats, about to depart for London. Several weeks had passed and they had accepted an invitation from the Usmanovas to join them for lunch at their home in London. Door-to-door transport had been efficiently organised. The three of them had not stopped smiling for the past hour.

"N560HJ, you are clear for take-off," was audible from the cockpit.

The seven-seater Cessna Citation private jet thundered down the private section of a runway on the south side of Cardiff Airport before it soared into the sky *en route* to London City Airport. A burly looking Christof was waiting there at the little airport to drive the three miles across town.

They were met inside her beautiful home by Nadia Usmanova, who shook their hands and hugged all three of them. From behind her mother, a smiling Alina emerged and made a beeline for Wil, hugging him like an old friend whom she hadn't seen for years. They went into the sitting room and talked about Wales, Russia, and London.

It wasn't long before an enthusiastic Alina began to explain how for several years, she had been experiencing similar sleep episodes to Wil. In recent months they had gone to another level, where she had been steered through her dreams to uncover damning information associated with some Uzbekistani gangsters who were being controlled by high ranking government officials. The information also included evidence that her father had been murdered and identified the people involved in orchestrating it. She had then been able to uncover sensitive transcripts of emails and phone calls and had taken photographs of meetings between some of the people involved. That was the reason she had been abducted. They were planning to kill her once they were certain they had covered their tracks. But now it was over, everyone had been exposed and dealt with.

Before they left for the return trip home, Alina's mother Nadia gave each of them a small gift package and asked the group to open them later. She insisted they accept the gifts as it was a tradition under such circumstances.

After they had taken off, they removed their seat belts and the co-pilot made them all a cocktail from the plane's minibar. The sumptuous leather seats on the Cessna all slide and rotate so Emma, Wil and Frea formed a bit of circle facing each other and with great excitement decided to open the gifts that Nadia had given to them.

Frea was outvoted to go first. Her gift was in a smart little box. She opened it and wished she had left her sunglasses on. It was a stunning white gold and diamond bracelet.

An astonished and unusually quiet Emma was next. She found herself opening a box from the jeweller Tiffany containing an amazing matching gold necklace and earrings set from its 'Flying Colours' collection.

Wil was last to go. He unwrapped the gift paper. His was a box with a small card tagged to it. The card said, '*Understated, unique, very special and with perfect timing, just like you Wil – Alina*'. The box said 'Rolex - Sky-Dweller'. It was a simple, but remarkable, white gold Rolex watch worth a small fortune.

The back had an inscription. It said – 'Спасибо' - pronounced Spasibo, translated, 'Thank you.'

CHAPTER 8
FREA'S DILEMMA

Late Spring 2019

Frea had been swept along on the mystifying and exhilarating journey with Wil and Emma and in the months that followed they had all become close friends. Wil and Emma had even become dedicated yogis and were regular participants at Frea's yoga classes and her occasional rural yoga retreats. What happened in London, and leading up to it, had a big positive impact on the relationship between the three friends.

The slender, forty-something, ponytailed Frea was a highly regarded and passionate yoga teacher. Her violet coloured hair, lotus flower-inspired full sleeve tattoo and a set of chakra stone images running down her spine completed the image. She had no commitments and her newfound friendship was proving to be refreshing. Her energy and enthusiasm were infectious, and Wil and Emma enjoyed her company immensely.

As a renowned expert in her field of sleep disorders and with her book *The Untapped Power of Lucid Dreams* almost completed, the recent emotional experiences with Wil had provided Frea with far greater insight into her subject matter. It had also given her the resolve to take the science she had within her grasp to another level. Both she and Wil had been sharing relevant information and their discussions were beginning to have a recurring common denominator. They had both fended off or ignored approaches from some unusual people over recent weeks. If there was such a thing as the dark web for discreet lucid dream problem solvers and crime fighters, they had somehow managed to find their way to the top of the list. How did these people know who they were or what they had been involved in - perhaps the walls had ears?

Frea knew Wil was blessed with something special, he had a gift. She was first and foremost a doctor, and although she disliked Emma's tongue in cheek description of it as his 'superpower', it was a fair and accurate assessment. Wil was a kind-hearted, easy-going guy, maybe too laid back for his own good sometimes. Things just seemed to happen to him for no reason - he was a lightning conductor for the energies he was proving to be able to attract.

Frea realised Wil didn't appreciate the full extent of what he was capable of. In truth, she wanted Wil to be more enthusiastic about the magic he had within him. She wondered if there was there a way for them both to work together, explore new ideas and have a more positive impact for some people in society. Frea could feel a deep and meaningful conversation looming with Wil, but she was conflicted because there was something else which had been troubling her for some time. All her other professional ideas might have to be parked for a while.

~

Twenty-six years ago, with aspirations to become a doctor, Frea had not long finished her A level exams at her home in the South Wales market town of Usk. She had a close-knit circle of friends who all went to the same school nearby. Most of them belonged to the Young Farmers group and they always created a bit of a buzz and a vibrant atmosphere whenever they were around.

It felt as though the heavy summer rain, that had poured down on and off for weeks was never going to stop. A balmy July weekend seemed like it had taken forever to arrive, and one of the young men had organised a party on his parent's farm using one of the empty barns to celebrate his birthday.

A clear sky, lights, music, booze and fifty 'young farmers' going nuts, it had all the makings of a fun, memorable evening. But as it turned out things didn't go according to plan.

By ten p.m. the party was in full swing. Some of the more boisterous lads and a handful of the girls had decided to go skinny dipping in the nearby River Usk, which under normal circumstances was a placid, safe place to swim. But the recent rains had raised its levels a little and it was flowing much faster than usual. Frea wasn't a great swimmer at the time and she decided to stay with the majority of the revellers on the grass, well away from the water and the muddy banks.

"C'mon Frea, it's not that cold once you get in."

"No chance, we haven't got any towels - are you nuts?"

Frea's best friend Ruth Harris had tried several times without any success to persuade her to take a dip. Frea was staying put – dry and on the grass.

Flame-haired Ruth was a free spirit - nothing was going to hold her back. She had been involved in some drinking games with the lads - without much success. Her penalties had involved 'bolting' two pints of strong cider and several tequila shots. At the best of times, Ruth could be feisty, and Frea was aware she had also been arguing with her boyfriend earlier in the day and had told him it was over.

That evening, no doubt Ruth was proving a point to herself and her friends that she could do whatever she pleased. Her boyfriend's name was Mike Armstrong, he was four years older than Ruth and worked in a local hotel. He wasn't part of the young farmers' scene and was always jealous of Ruth mixing with the crowd and having a great time with them whenever he wasn't around. He had been seen driving past much earlier in the evening and had tried to gate crash the party. He was told he wasn't welcome and moved on. He had said he wasn't bothered, and he had work to go to later anyway.

As midnight approached, the party was still in full swing. Several more had turned up after the pubs had shut, but Frea had agreed with her parents to be home at a sensible time. She looked for Ruth to see if she would walk home with her, but there was no sign of her. The skinny dipping had finished long ago and Frea had seen Ruth a couple of times since then, chatting to a lad from their school year who they both knew. Frea assumed Ruth had wandered off with him and decided to go home instead with a lad she'd had her eye on all evening. He had offered to walk her home, so that's what she did.

At nine a.m. the next morning there was a knock on Frea's bedroom door - it was her mum, "Frea the police are here. They want to speak to you."

A startled Frea threw her clothes on and rushed downstairs, wondering, "*Oh my God, what's happened?*"

She was met by the local sergeant who explained that Ruth's parents were frantic, she hadn't arrived home last night. Ruth had never stayed out that late, she may have been a free spirit, but she loved her parents. Ruth would never put a foot wrong with them. Frea knew that.

Over the coming days, a huge police search ensued. Mike Armstrong was interviewed, but he had a reasonable alibi: later during that Saturday evening, he had been seen working near the hotel kitchen by a cleaner. All along the police suspected Ruth had slipped into the River Usk. Her bag, containing cash, was found near the water's edge, along with one of her tennis shoes. After three weeks, the search was called off and Ruth's disappearance was classified as missing presumed dead. Her body was never found.

~

It's true, time is indeed a healer. The pain and anguish of devastating events might diminish, and memories might fade, but they never completely disappear. Frea's memories of her friendship with the effervescent Ruth had always stayed with her. She never forgot that fateful evening close to the river. There were many unanswered questions in Frea's mind. What if she had joined Ruth skinny dipping? Or not spent so much time with the lad who had walked her home? Then perhaps, maybe, the whole dynamic of the rest of the evening might have changed and Ruth would not have been lost. Frea tried her best not to blame herself, but she often wished she could have had those hours over again. She wanted some kind of closure.

~

Wil and Frea had started to have some occasional experimental workshops after an evening yoga class. They would discuss more openly the subject matter of lucid dreams and Wil's long history of them. The 'savasana' yoga relaxation and meditation pose at the end of each class, was perfect preparation for her to connect with Wil and for him to connect with his mind.

Working together, trusting each other, as a tight little team was proving beneficial. They were learning from each other and finding new processes and techniques enabling Wil to instinctively recreate the intuitive nature of the dreams within a laboratory environment. With Frea's guided discovery, he was making gradual improvements and learning how to turn the lucid tap on and off.

~

One day when Wil and Emma were visiting her, Frea explained she had received another of the unsolicited approaches from someone who had somehow become aware of Wil's activities.

"He said his name was Phil Chalk. I've no idea how he knows what he does about the three of us."

"Did you say he works for the government Frea?" asked Emma.

"Yeah, that's what he said. He claims he works for the Ministry of Defence in a department called DSTL."

Emma was becoming more curious. "What does DSTL stand for Frea?"

"Defence, Science and Technology Laboratory. He said he had some important information and a commercial arrangement that he needed to discuss with all of us. And it couldn't be discussed over the phone."

"Commercial arrangement? Like a job? How do we know it's not a wind-up? I'm surprised he didn't ask you for your bank details Frea." Wil was being deliberately facetious.

Emma gave Wil a gentle kick. He was becoming irritating when they were all trying to have a serious conversation.

Frea continued, "This guy Chalk offered to come and meet the three of us down here. On the face of it, he seems legitimate. But I told him if he was for real and not from a newspaper or a scammer, he should agree for us all to meet at his offices. And pay our expenses … he said fine."

Despite being sceptical Frea had more than a grain of intrigue and wanted to find out more. She had a positive feeling about Phil Chalk's potential proposition. She chatted to Wil and Emma about it, and sold them on the idea, although they didn't need much persuading.

Asking them, "So guys, if you can get the boys to cover the glamping business for a day, would you be up for a trip to a place called Porton Down near Salisbury in Wiltshire?"

"Why not?" Emma was just as intrigued.

Wil was at an age, nearly fifty, where some men buy sports cars, hit the bottle, or might even trade their wife in for a younger model. Wil was never that way inclined and he wasn't having a mid-life crisis, but he maybe had rediscovered his taste for adventure. He also knew things were going on in his head that he hadn't resolved. He was up for it.

~

The following Wednesday, Will, Emma and Frea were sat together, three abreast, in Wil's grubby pick-up truck outside the high-security entrance to one of the world's foremost scientific organisations.

DSTL works on projects ranging from biological research investigating the threat of nerve gas to lifesaving 'invisible shield' protection against IEDs to deep space tracking. There had also been numerous conspiracy rumours an alien spacecraft had crashed in North Wales in the mid-seventies and its occupants transported to Porton Down, such is the mystique surrounding the place.

Having passed through the armed guards and customs-style security clearance, they were chaperoned to a far more relaxed breakout area. There a smiling Phil Chalk was waiting for them. He was balding, stocky man with a grey wispy beard and the hint of a cockney accent. He was also immaculately dressed.

"*How many people wear ties these days?*" Emma thought to herself, but she approved of Chalk's choice.

"Welcome to DSTL. Thanks for coming all this way."

The genial Chalk welcomed them into a cosy meeting room. He offered a selection of teas, coffees and biscuits and asked if their trip had been a pleasant one.

Frea responded, "It was fine, thanks, although Wil still thinks he's driving a tractor sometimes. I thought we'd never get here."

Frea took the opportunity to apologise for ever doubting Chalk's employers' credentials.

He laughed out loud and said, "I don't blame you. It was an unexpected and unusual request of mine. But at last, it's nice to be able to meet everyone. I've heard such a lot of intriguing information about you."

The three guests looked bemused. Then an emboldened Wil asked, "So please enlighten us, Phil, what do you know and why are we here?"

Phil Chalk smiled again saying, "Wil, what a brilliant question. Why don't I start at the beginning?"

For the next twenty minutes, Chalk explained more about the

fascinating work of DSTL. How it also worked with many private consortia and multinational FTSE defence and scientific companies. They also had a strong relationship with GCHQ (Government Communications Headquarters) in Cheltenham and, of course, MI5 and MI6. Almost with a matter of fact tone of voice, he added DSTL and GCHQ had been exploring ideas beyond the wildest imaginations of most people for many years - that was their job. You could have heard a pin drop as the three visitors listened in silence to Chalk's presentation. It didn't disappoint their expectations and soon became all the more fascinating. They were told that inexplicable lucid dreams similar to those of Wil's had a small but important segment earmarked within the huge equation of DSTL's work. They had also set up a small well-funded department to focus on it, called - *The Lucidity Programme*. It was an experimental scientific collaboration testing lucid dreamers, exploring new methods to solve crimes or serious threats.

"For years, my programme team and I have worked with other candidates similar to you Wil. The candidates were people who had the potential to take the science to new levels, but none of them made great progress for us. Until some recent events came to our attention, when we started to get what we politely describe as unexpected 'red flags' appearing. Wil, you were the red flag."

Monitoring unusual intelligence activity concerning foreign embassies or wealthy kidnapped Russians is commonplace by GCHQ.

A small GCHQ team had been working hand in hand with Chalk's team on the science of lucid dreams for the programme. The sensitive data regarding Alina's kidnapping and Christof Sorotkin's involvement in the rescue had been collected and analysed. Wil, Emma and Frea had triggered red-flag algorithms in GCHQ who then discovered the trio had solved Alina's kidnapping.

A thorough investigation of Wil, Emma and Frea's other traceable activities and scrutiny of their communication history uncovered evidence of previous 'innocent' but inexplicable events.

GCHQ simply began working backwards and gained a full picture concerning the events in Bath. It was easy to do and was almost like the light at the end of a long dark tunnel for Phil Chalk and his associates.

Continuing in a sheepish voice Chalk said, "We did some more digging. Mostly concerning Emma and some of the speculation that was meant to have been either discreet or encrypted on social media. But it never is, is it? And here we are."

He couldn't avoid a smile as he added, "Our guys are good."

To conclude, Phil Chalk explained that he had the authority to put in place a seven-year funding programme for Wil, Emma and Frea to work on an occasional basis to develop the science.

"You can simply carry on with your lives as normal, but you would be under the loose guidance of The Lucidity Programme. There would be excellent financial rewards for helping to work towards improving national security. Will you all work with us and help us with our journey?" Chalk asked.

"Do you mean as guinea pigs or kind of like scientists?" asked Wil directly.

Chalk paused, reflected and was careful how he chose his words, "To be honest Wil, you are the science to some extent. To be precise, all three of you are the science - leading us on our journey. But we have some great people here who can help you answer some of the questions that must have been churning in your head for months. Does that help?"

Wil was silently nodding in agreement. Deep inside he had lots of unanswered questions about himself - he was yearning to get stuck in.

A smiling Wil looked Chalk in the eye and responded, "It's going to be fun, what have we got to lose?"

Emma was delighted, but not surprised, by Wil's reaction. He was a closet thrill-seeker, although he was afraid of needles and heights. She had an inkling there would be some interesting times ahead. Maybe some adventures to tell the grandchildren about when they became old enough to talk. Emma was not a shrinking violet and she was as keen as Wil to step out of their comfort zones. Frea struggled to contain herself and was doing her best to stop her feet tapping repeatedly with excitement. She felt like an equal partner in all of it and knew she had an important role to play. Her role was maybe more the scientist rather than the science. It suited her well. Emma was the organiser who kept Wil on track. Frea was delighted the meeting had gone in the direction that it had and couldn't wait to get started.

~

As they drove away from the complex Wil joked, "Well Frea, he wasn't a journalist or a scammer, was he?"

There was some more light-hearted debate between them about what had they signed up for, what had they agreed to do and whether they would they have to carry guns.

"Welcome to The Lucidity Programme, guys," said a jubilant Frea.

~

Not long before midnight on a Saturday evening late July in 2004, a man in his thirties was seen climbing onto the balustrades of the old Severn Bridge. He stood there for several seconds, waiting and wobbling. Mike Armstrong's shirt was flapping in the strong breeze as he leapt off on the tenth anniversary of the disappearance of his former girlfriend, Ruth. His car was found near the bridge, it was littered with empty bottles of strong cider. His body was never found. He had decided not to leave a note and cause his family any further embarrassment.

~

The early evening yoga class had finished. In advance of them coming, Frea had asked Wil and Emma if they could both stay a little later as she had something different to show them.

62

Once the yoga studio had cleared of people, an old friend of Frea's arrived and began to set up his equipment. She explained to Wil this was going to be something new and experimental for him. It would be done in conjunction with the usual scientific techniques they used to encourage the exploration of Wil's lucid dreams. This was to be a 'gong bath'. A soothing sound vibration experience. The man hanging up his metre diameter gongs, and smaller sound bowls was the percussionist. He would create therapeutic sound waves, which would hopefully enhance Wil's usual meditative state that Frea guided and controlled with her gentle voice and yogic breathing.

Emma watched as Frea dimmed the lights and made Wil comfortable with some blankets, pillows, and a small soft bag that she specifically asked him to hold. She kneeled close to his head and led him into the meditative state as she had done several times in the past. Softly speaking to him, she allowed him to free his mind. At one point, she invited Wil to focus on the bag that he was holding. The unique sound vibrations from the gong bath were providing a different reaction within Wil. Readings transmitted from state-of-the-art discreet digital transponders confirmed it. The amazing new 'micro-tech' had been promptly provided by Phil Chalk along with many other goodies that Frea had requested. All thanks to the recent financial backing of the programme.

After the gong bath, Wil thought he was inside someone else's body. His limbs and torso were still resonating from the extraordinary effects of the sensations created by its sounds. He was assured he would feel calm, chilled, and zingy for a day or so. Reconnecting with his surroundings he sat down with Frea and Emma to talk. This was a routine they had developed within their workshops to immediately extract any relevant information that had come into his mind.

It looked as though Wil hadn't come out of his deep slumber, and with closed eyes, he quietly said, "Yes, something happened to me tonight. Something significant."

He went on to explain he had dreamt he was alone walking through a quiet country village. Walking with real purpose and energy, and breathing heavily. He wasn't being chased, as was often the case, but he sensed the need to get somewhere. The village with its huge circular green was familiar to him as he headed on, through some quiet side roads, carrying on down a secluded farm track into open countryside. He said he knew he was being drawn somewhere. His mind and body in his lucid state had allowed him to carry on getting closer - he wasn't fighting it.

His final recollection, he said, he sensed himself moving through a small farmyard, stepping over a moss-tinged stile and up ahead was an old church. It was sitting on a tiny hill in front of him. No roads led to it. Simply the old church in the middle of a field. It was beautiful. It was almost magnetic. The church had a low dry-stone wall circling it, with a wooden gate for access to the small churchyard that surrounded it. He found himself standing in the churchyard beside a single grave which appeared to be on an elaborate flat stone monument, almost like a crypt. It had the name of a child on its headstone. She was Phoebe Lees and she was fourteen years old when she died in 1919.

As Wil started to open his eyes he said, "And she began to speak to me, Phoebe, I didn't see her, although I heard her speak to me. She said, 'Ruth and I are here, together. It's OK Wil, but we have something to show you,' and that was all she said to me."

Frea was still sat crossed legged, in silence, clutching a tissue, with tears rolling down her cheeks.

Emma comforted her friend and realised that something Wil had encountered had triggered the strong emotions that they had not seen in her before. After several minutes, Frea composed herself, turned the lights up and told them the story of her friend Ruth. How her disappearance had always troubled her and that the tears were part sadness and in part because she felt a deceitful fraud. Frea said she had selfishly used Wil and his abilities in the hope of finding her lost friend Ruth. The soft bag she had given to Wil to hold earlier was the purse that was found beside the river. It contained some of Ruth's personal effects and it had been given to Frea by Ruth's mother as a memento.

"I should have shared this with you first. You are such good friends. I feel awful, but I hoped you could help me discover what happened that night."

A pragmatic Wil said, "It's fine, things happen for a reason. We all need to see this through now. Please don't fret about it Frea, we want to help you – we're a team remember."

They talked it through and agreed to speak again the next day. They all knew the challenge would be to get permission to exhume the grave of a young girl who had been buried over a hundred years ago.

By mid-morning the next day, they had a plan and it would be the first real test from them of someone's apparent wide-ranging powers of authority. Of equal importance, it would also be further evidence to the same person that The Lucidity Programme was the real deal. Frea said she would make the call to Phil Chalk, but first, they had to find the church.

Wil said he knew the village was called Devauden and he would know how to find the church nearby, although he had never been there, and it had no roads leading directly to it.

They arrived at the village, parked up and followed Wil as he led them on the twenty-minute mostly downhill walk to the remote church. His instincts had been correct.

All three of them stood there with their heads bowed in front of Phoebe Lees's grave. Not a word was spoken between any of them. They walked in silence inside the little church and Frea said a prayer.

~

When Mike Armstrong was a young man studying for his exams, to earn some extra cash he had worked as a builder for his uncle. He found the building trade hard graft and it wasn't long before Armstrong decided to quit and move into the hospitality industry where he worked long fragmented hours as a hotel junior duty manager.

Before he finished working for his uncle, one building project he was involved in was the refurbishment of a roof and landscaping of the grounds of the tiny ancient Celtic church, Kilgwrrwg, in the middle of Monmouthshire. It happens to be one of the UK's most remote churches, located in a beautiful and peaceful setting.

~

As soon as they got back to the village, Frea made the call to Chalk.

Phil Chalk had decided to come and meet with his new associates in South Wales. It had been twenty-one days since he had listened to their story about the remote church, Frea's missing friend and the request for his help to somehow organise an exhumation. Chalk had delivered. Publicly the police stated they had received an anonymous tip-off concerning a crime. In reality, someone high up at GCHQ had fixed things with a single phone call to Gwent Police. A complex night-time exhumation was not needed. The gravestone and other elements were simply slid and moved off. As expected, within the small tomb the remains of a second young woman were found. From her clothing and dental records, she was identified as Ruth Harris.

In the pocket of Ruth's denim jacket was a handwritten note. It was a confession and apology from a man called Mike Armstrong, who said it was he who had placed Ruth's body in the grave. When he was working on the church, he had seen the gravestone and understood how it had been constructed. It was easy for him to manhandle the horizontal stone to the side and place Ruth's body inside, and that he didn't know what else to do. He had felt ashamed.

His letter also explained he did not kill Ruth - he had been standing on the opposite riverbank and had seen her flirting with another lad. He stayed and watched as Ruth returned alone to the riverbank, where she must have left her small shoulder bag or purse. She was so drunk she had a job to stand up. Armstrong shouted to her. She was startled, fell into the water and in her drunken state she struggled to get out. Realising Ruth was in trouble

Armstrong said he stripped off, waded in, and began swimming across in a desperate attempt to rescue her. Ruth was thrashing and splashing, and he got closer and closer. He was almost within touching distance of her when Ruth became lifeless - the current had been strong, and it was too late. It was dark. No one had seen either him or Ruth. His mind was scrambled. He realised because he had been seen hanging around earlier - he would be in trouble and panicked.

'*Oh my God, oh my God*' - he was distraught and shaking like a leaf from his wet clothes as they clung to his body - and from his mind as it tried to rationalise the uncertainty and fear of a knock on his parent's door. He knew he would be accused of her death. After searching for almost half an hour he found her body caught in a branch downstream. It was difficult but alone he managed to pull Ruth's limp body out of the water. He carried her a short distance, placed her in his car and took her to the church four miles away. Sometimes, when they are under stress, young people make foolish decisions in their lives – it happens every day. The foolish decision was to weigh heavily on Mike Armstrong for the rest of his short life.

A few days later a sombre Chalk contacted Wil, "Not sure if you're aware, but the remains of a man have been found in the muddy banks of the Severn estuary, not long after the exhumation of Ruth. The dental records showed it to be Mike Armstrong."

~

Less than a week later, Frea attended an emotional funeral for her old friend. She was reunited with some of her old school friends and the Young Farmers to give Ruth a proper send-off. Wil and Emma discreetly attended to pay their respects and to be with Frea.

Although she lived not far from Usk where the funeral was taking place, Frea had lost touch with so many people. She had bumped into Ruth's parents maybe once or twice in decades. They were pleased to see Frea again and remembered how friendly she and Ruth had been as youngsters and had some pictures of them together.

It was a surreal experience for Frea. The reason why the funeral was taking place and that many people had now found some closure after all the years was because she and her friends had found Ruth's body. Yet no one would ever know the full truth of the discovery.

~

The one reason Chalk had come to South Wales a week before the funeral was to meet the team and to thank them all personally. They were all saddened by events but were also pleased with what they had all been able to achieve. It was remarkable, and it had been good teamwork.

But there was also another reason. Chalk's new team had demonstrated an unequivocal validation of themselves. It was time to raise the bar. Phil Chalk was now totally comfortable with them and confident in their abilities.

Before he left to go back to Porton Down he handed Wil Richardson a small package and said, "Maybe you can help us with something vitally important."

CHAPTER 9
OPEN YOUR MIND

June 2019

I t had been was almost three weeks since Phil Chalk took the call from Frea, absorbing and savouring every word she was saying as she sat in her car having earlier found the church.

Most of the time Chalk was a serious and disciplined man in his business life. It was essential in his line of work as there were occasions when people's lives were at stake. Whilst speaking with Frea that day, his instincts would have been to make copious notes. Tabulating everything meticulously into his black small Moleskine lined notebook, in his perfect handwriting. That was his way, although all his phone calls were automatically recorded anyway, the note making prevailed. It irritated the hell out of some people. If ever a man needed a mind-mapping seminar it was him.

He had not been expecting to find himself answering her call and simply listened to Frea's information about the church, what they expected to find there and what was required of him - it was as if his world stood still. He sat there motionless at the end of the phone as though all his Christmases had come at once. He hadn't made a single note.

For three years he and his team had been open-minded and positive as they worked with possible candidates like Wil Richardson. Desperately searching for something - anything - that could give them some hope they were on the right track with their plans for the Lucidity Programme. So far, every attempt to harness someone's 'lucid ability' had been a failure and a false alarm. Questions were being asked. Was there was ever going to be some tangible progress?

Chalk had seen the various reports, phone transcripts and corroborated evidence - with some of it translated from Russian - concerning Wil and the others. All of that had been compiled over several months, but he didn't doubt its validity for one second, not this time. And now, at last, he had been personally involved, hands-on and helping out. Staring success in the face, that phone call concerning the grave was the final breakthrough and affirmation he needed.

The breakthrough was needed for another reason though. Time was against them and Chalk could smell a faint whiff of competition gaining ground on him. He also knew the competition was bound to be aware of Wil and the team. Nothing to worry about for now, but Chalk intended to be careful. Soon, he would engage the services of Wil Richardson and hoped he and the others could shed some light where there was a desperate need for it.

~

Following Ruth Harris's funeral service in the small town of Usk, Wil and Emma had tried their best to sit quietly in a corner of a local hotel where the wake was being held.

It wasn't going to be a quiet affair. Although the 'young farmers' were now 'old farmers', they still knew how to party and remember Ruth and celebrated her passing with gusto, as sad as it was.

Poor Mike Armstrong's funeral had quietly taken place two days earlier.

Above the noise, Emma asked Wil, "Have you had a closer look at the package Phil Chalk gave to you?"

"No, not yet I just haven't felt able to get my head around it. Not with everything else that's been happening."

Emma placed her hand on his forearm and squeezed it. She realised he had been the central focus of a lot of crazy things of late.

"Are you still certain about us embarking on this 'journey' with Phil and this Lucidity Programme thing? I can read you like a book Wil; I know you're struggling to get your head around it all and deal with it sometimes aren't you?"

She needed to know and wanted to be helpful if she could in any way.

Wil explained, "When it all started with finding the ring, I kind of thought - pardon the pun - like I was dreaming. It had all been a bit of fun. But one thing has led to another and although most things have been private, I sometimes wonder if there's something wrong with me."

Emma's hand was enveloped inside Wil's as she held it.

"Emma, this isn't normal, is it? I'm not normal, am I? Why me, for God's sake?"

Wil was a tough character, he had physical and mental resilience. A tall wiry man, with a shock of dark curly hair. Over six feet and had been in more than enough scrapes when he was younger. On top of that, he had run the family farm for many years before converting part of it to the glamping business. Nothing ever fazed him or scared him that much - he simply got on with stuff.

He told Emma, "I suppose I'm feeling the pressure a little bit now. Everything so far has 'just happened', but now we're under a microscope and getting paid a handsome sum of money for doing next to nothing."

There were expectations and deep down, he wondered if he had enough fire in his belly. It was exciting, but he knew he needed to come to terms with it and grasp the nettle. He wasn't sure if he could perform to order.

Emma reassured him, "Wil, we aren't just a couple, we're a great team. Not only that, I like and I trust Phil Chalk, it'll all be OK – we'll be OK."

Her instinct told her that Chalk was a 'solid' guy, and they also had faith in their good friend Frea, who was in their corner.

Still holding Wil's hand, she looked him in the eye and said, "Let's not forget, any time you or any of us want to stop the bus and get off this crazy ride we can. No one is forcing us to do anything. So, for now, let's ride the wave, have this Lucidity Programme adventure and see where it takes us. It could be fun."

Wil smiled, "Sounds like a plan, I'm in - let's have another drink."

~

The day after the funeral, Wil's head was in a better place. His curiosity got the better of him and he decided to open the package that Chalk had given him. It was a shoebox encapsulated in bubble wrap which Chalk must have applied. Stuck down, and sealed with some grey gaffa tape. It had 'Wil' in blue permanent marker pen written on the front of the tape.

Wil peeled it open and took the lid off the box. Not knowing how gentle he needed to be, he took great care and began placing its contents onto the breakfast bar in his kitchen.

Emma was curious and hovering, "What is it?"

There were five items in the box. A small envelope, once again with Wil's name on it. Two round grey tins, each a fraction bigger than the size of a tin of tuna, with slim screw-on lids. A black leather-bound diary written in what appeared to be German, with its blue silk page marker protruding from the middle pages. The final item was some kind of slim well-worn black leather case about the size of a decent hardback book, with a popper holding down its side flap. He un-popped the case and slid out an old-fashioned cine camera - it had a fold-out winding handle on it with an embossed tag at the base of the camera body stating it was a Cine-Kodak Eight Model 20. He twisted open one of the tins and when opened it made sense. The Kodak paper logos on the lids must have peeled off or rubbed off decades ago, but each tin was boldly stamped top and bottom - A and the other B and contained two rolls of cine film on spools. Fascinating.

Wil opened the letter with his name on. It was a note from Phil Chalk with an SD memory card attached to the note.

The note read *"Hi Wil, isn't this a beautiful piece of old kit? No need to try and play the films, we have copied them onto the attached SD cards. One SD card for each of you, each of the two film runs for about two minutes. The diary is in German, some of the pages are gone, but we have translated the remainder and transcribed it onto another file which can also be found on the SD card. I will explain everything when you have had the chance to look through. Please call me as soon as possible, or perhaps if Frea is with you guys, maybe the four of us can have a group Skype or Zoom call? – Thanks, Phil. P.S. Wil, if the wider public knew what you had been able to do in recent times, they wouldn't believe. When we chat and I share my confidential information with you guys, best if you all keep an open mind. Remember what I once said about beyond wildest dreams and all that, eh?"*

As a recent innovation, Phil Chalk had provided Frea with the slick portable micro-tech equipment for her monitoring of Wil's sleep reactions. His I.T. guys had also furnished each of them with new encrypted laptops, VPN lines and mobile phones. They were encouraged not to use their personal phones or computers for anything concerning the Lucidity Programme. They had also been posted a platinum American Express card each.

An intrigued Wil looked at Emma, who was still shaking her head and said, "Best we have another cup of coffee, look through the information again and set up a time to call Phil a bit later today. Bloody hell!"

~

Later that afternoon the four associates were about to log into their respective Skype connections. Emma had electronically shared with Frea her copy of the SD card containing the films and the information. The three friends had been having a long chat about it well in advance of the Skype call with Phil.

The level-headed Frea had never been so animated with her friends, "Was that for real? Have you ever seen anything like that in Mid Wales Wil? You're kidding me, right?"

"No, never, I can't wait to hear what Phil has got to say! I'm so excited!" Wil was loud and full of enthusiasm.

"Frea, I've been trying to calm him down all day, but I can't wait to speak to Phil either. We've seen both films half a dozen times already."

Each film was two minutes long. They were grainy, but they could tell that Phil Chalk had must have enhanced them.

The first film appeared to be a short selection of home movies. It started with a family with four young blonde-haired children, appearing to be all below the age of twelve. Two older brothers maybe aged ten and eleven, and sisters aged five and eight. They were running around chasing a dog in the garden of a big house with some stunning snow-capped mountains behind them in the background. It may have been the Austrian or German Alps. The slim dark-haired mother, in a calf-length summer dress, was stood laughing as she watched her children trying to catch the tail of the big fluffy dog. There was a brief clip of the husband and wife with the three younger children, sat on a patterned blanket on some grass with a picnic. Perhaps the eldest son was operating the camera?

The fair-haired well-groomed man was wearing a smart grey suit and tie and had a pipe on which he was puffing, causing the odd plume of smoke to emerge. The final clip showed his family waving to him as he was about to set off down the road as a passenger in an old black car complete with running boards, from the same house. The hand holding the pipe was in shot gesticulating to his family while he filmed with the other hand.

The second film was not a 'family' movie. It appeared to be filmed adjacent to a huge concrete building built into the vertical sides of a mountain or ravine. There were some tall doors which were sliding open. Some men in uniform were surrounding a vehicle that was pulling something out from the inside of what may have been an aircraft hangar. The truck moved away, leaving the object exposed and easier to see. It was obvious, the men were soldiers, German wartime soldiers.

The sun was reflecting at all angles off the shimmering object which looked smaller than the truck, more like the size of a tall six-man camping tent. It was 'rounded', conical, and symmetrical. A man approached the gleaming tent-like object and nimbly walked up some steps and entered it. Thirty seconds later, there was some clear daylight underneath it, the truck and the hanger doors could be seen beneath it. It bobbed at head height for a moment before ascending high into the sky, skirting the granite mountainside, and vanishing out of sight in a split second. It was some kind of aircraft - with no wings, no engines, and no vapour trail.

The credibility of the whole film looked like a dodgy B movie from the twenties, but the quality of the film was good. What was portrayed was nothing like a traditional aircraft, jet, or rocket. There was no thrust, dust, or commotion as it launched. It defied gravity, hovered, and accelerated in almost a blur straight up into the sky. The camera struggled to follow it.

~

Everyone had logged into the conference call with Phil Chalk, Wil and Emma logged in from separate rooms, testing out their new equipment in different parts of the cottage. Frea was at her home, sitting and waiting in comfort.

Chalk began by welcoming everyone and started to lay out the reason for the call and what he hoped they would all agree to do as a result.

"What you have seen in the film and the documented evidence on some of the pages in the diary should be considered as genuine. The four of us need to understand we must all, including myself, be prepared to open our minds."

He asked if any of them believed one day a human would land on Mars, or Saturn or Jupiter?

"Of course, it's going to happen, one day."

Did any of them believe one day there would be an aircraft that could defy gravity without a propulsion engine or rocket motors?

"Of course, it would happen sooner or later. Maybe it's already happened?"

Chalk provided a baseline starting point, "The first manned aeroplane flight wasn't much over a hundred years ago, then about sixty years later in 1969 a man landed on the moon."

Wil, Emma and Frea were glued to their laptop screens and were all aware of the historical events. But when they were reminded of the facts, it made them realise how significant they were. Also, the speed at which and how far people, science and technology had evolved.

"Let that sink in for a moment guys - humans and aeroplanes started with the Wright brothers in 1903. Sixty-odd years later - Neil Armstrong... and Neil Armstrong was fifty years ago."

He stressed nothing was ever impossible anymore.

The Londoner's voice was resonating with them as he paused and said it one more time, "Nothing is impossible."

He continued to remind them, some of the most amazing scientific discoveries to have happened - many of them were by accident. The greatest mathematicians that ever lived were doing their thing two thousand years ago.

He added, "Within this DSTL building, I've seen some of the most incredible things that to this day remain highly classified - and no doubt there are many more amazing things way above my pay grade that I don't know about."

Emma was thinking to herself, *"I'll bet I'm probably not the only one listening here with goosebumps and hairs standing up on the back of my neck."*

She was right, she wasn't alone.

Chalk added, "Need I go on? Oh, and for the record, the aliens crash landing in the 1970s in North Wales and widely reported as being brought here, it's all bullshit!"

That lightened the tone on the Skype call and everyone was giggling.

Chalk then asked the group, "Does anyone have any initial questions before I outline my thoughts, and what I hope we can achieve with the contents of the package that I gave to Wil?"

"Thanks, Phil," said Emma, before asking, "I've read most of the German diary information. Pardon my ignorance, but what does he mean by travelling at Mach 12? What's that?"

"Now that's a great question Emma, let me put it into some context for you."

Chalk began by explaining speeds within the earth's atmosphere. Not in outer space, where far greater speeds are easily achieved.

"Mach 1 is the speed of sound at 768 mph."

"Mach 2 is Concorde at 1354 mph."

"Mach 3 is Lockheed Blackbird stealth fighter - and also a rifle bullet at 2300 mph."

Chalk had been pausing after each 'Mach definition'. He could feel the anticipation within the group building.

"Mach 5 is Theoretical Hypersonic jets. It's still years from leaving the drawing board at 3790 mph."

"Mach 12 is 9216 mph, the speed described in the diary, with no G force issues on the pilot."

"Does that make it clearer for you guys?"

There was a stunned silence for a few seconds. There were several more questions, but none were as significant as the first one for Emma.

Wil asked, "Where did the items come from Phil? And how did they get into the hands of your team?"

Chalk explained, "They once belonged to one of the senior designers on the 'anti-gravity project' - as the German diarist described it. He was the fair-haired man in the film smoking the pipe. His name was Klaus von der Heyde. Events were dated in the diary as late 1944 when the Germans were beginning to lose the war. After the films were made the airbase in the film was targeted, bombed, and destroyed. Among the survivors were some senior officers and scientists who were all beginning to make plans to escape rather than be captured. Although some would go on to work for the Americans after the war. It's unclear what happened to von der Heyde and his family. But it's thought they may have made it to South America. They had not been seen since 1944, except for one child - the most recent owner of the cine films."

After another twenty minutes, Phil Chalk became conscious of everyone's time and decided to summarise and explain what he needed from his three lucidity team members. He said he would send the team details of the German family members' names and dates of birth and any additional background history on them that was relevant and available. Also, a profile of Klaus von der Heyde was being pieced together, but it was not yet complete.

"As for the items in the parcel, we obtained them via a third party. It's a convoluted story, but von der Heyde's wife - who was the mother of the children in the film - was British. Her father was a professor at the University of Zurich in the 1920s. That was where Klaus von der Heyde studied and met his future wife. Her name was Susan. The youngest child was roughly five years old in the film, she, and her sister it seems were the only remaining family members still living. Until recently."

"Where are those surviving children now Phil? They must be in their eighties I guess?" asked Frea.

"The youngest of the two sisters is called Tilda Blake and she is alive and living in a nursing home near Oxford. It appears Tilda knew a tiny bit of the family history, but not much, and she was insistent that the items were passed to an old friend of hers to get them to us here at DSTL. We don't know why she chose to do what she did."

Everyone remained enthralled at the discussion. Secretly beginning to wonder what part they were going to be expected to play in this mystery.

Chalk's last comment was, "It goes without saying that if an unstable or unfriendly foreign government were to get their hands on the physics behind the 'aircraft', and add a twist of modern electronics and weaponry, it would be worrying for many people."

Emma gave out an audible 'wow', and was taken aback by Chalk's comments, "Is it really that serious?"

"Guys, can you imagine if China, Russia, North Korea or Iran were to have access to technology like this. No one, anywhere in the world could go to bed and sleep in safety. No missile defence system would prevent them from making demands or doing whatever they wanted. Yes, it could become a serious issue. But right now, it's a complicated fantasy - which may or may not turn out to be for real."

Wil commented, "It would be like Star Wars on steroids."

"Not funny Wil." Emma gave him 'a look' to go with her comment.

"To be fair to Wil, and not wishing to frighten anyone, it's not a bad analogy. A fleet of these 'aircraft' outrunning our missile defence systems by four times the speed - NATO would be toothless. And worried."

You could hear a 'virtual' pin drop on the Skype call.

Emma didn't speak, she had a quiet thought to herself, "*The boys, the grandchildren, our families, everyone. Bloody hell.*"

Chalk added, "It sounds embarrassing doesn't it, but the fact is, we, 'the UK Government', are in a race against time. My colleagues and I in this establishment are such open-minded people and we think you can help us. Far quicker than any other methods we have at our disposal."

Wil spotted Emma had been starting to click her pen on and off until it reached a bit of a crescendo, she stopped, "So what's expected of us, Phil?"

"Frankly, we need your help to try and find the design knowledge or the physical piece of technology or both. We hope, and this is where it begins if you are willing to continue, that perhaps you can start by uncovering more information concerning the items by meeting Tilda. Maybe Wil, with some teamwork, might be able to make a 'connection' as you have in the past. The immediate plan is to go to Oxford or wherever else in the world you need to if that's what's required. It's important and yes it's that serious."

CHAPTER 10

TILDA

Late June 2019

After their discussion with Phil Chalk, Wil and Emma played all four minutes of the two films over and over. Chalk had noted down, in some of his extra briefing information that the film reels had been tested - and they were authentic, definitely not modern fakes.

The diary was special to look at, it had seen and heard so much in its one-year life span and beyond, where it appeared to have been used simply as a notebook. Not to mention the trust it had received from all its other custodians since Klaus von der Heyde disappeared and before, finally, Tilda was old enough to own and appreciate it. They had been given a translation to accompany the diary.

The diary didn't contain regular daily entries, all it showed was occasional notable events and some meeting times. Family gatherings, birthdays, theatre visit dates, testing of equipment and the occasional technical note, but those notes were usually crossed referenced to an apparent technical journal which crucially they didn't have. There appeared to be some reference to 'Version 6', implying the anti-gravity craft on the film was not a prototype but had been well developed and was flying.

Wil scratched his head and kept asking himself, *"How on Earth could they have come up with the technology to be able to fly as well as it was claimed to do? Mach 12 - are you kidding me?"*

Many people don't appreciate that the Nazis didn't just invent the V2 Doodlebug rocket bombs. Towards the end of the war, they had the Me 262 – it was the world's first jet engine fighter. It was designed before the war even started. They were also not far off creating a nuclear bomb. Their technological capabilities were brilliant, so maybe all they had needed was a bit of luck. Perhaps von der Heyde had found his luck and had stumbled across the elephant that had been in the room for years. After all, penicillin was a mouldy mistake in a petri dish.

Wil thought maybe it was soon time to follow Chalk's plan and go and visit the beautiful 'City of Dreaming Spires' Oxford and meet Tilda for some enlightenment.

~

Three abreast in the pick-up truck was becoming a bit of habit, but it was comfortable enough.

Their request via Phil Chalk to meet Tilda had been passed on and accepted. Meanwhile, Wil and Emma's two sons were taking care of the glamping business as they often did.

The unimaginatively named nursing home The Spires wasn't in the centre of Oxford, but several miles west set in several acres of well-tended lawns and gardens. It was summer, and everything was in full bloom. The black dusty pick-up truck looked a bit incongruous parked on the crunchy loose stone driveway outside the pale-yellow Cotswold stone entrance. They were met at reception by an enthusiastic young man who introduced himself as Greg Long and said he was the shift manager. Greg didn't have a hair out of place, sparkling white teeth and wasn't a stranger to the sunbed.

Before he ushered them through, Frea asked, "How is Tilda, Greg? Is there anything we need to be aware of?"

Greg explained, "Tilda's fine, considering she's eighty-two and still recovering from a mild stroke she had over a year ago. She's got all her faculties, but her speech isn't perfect now."

Greg also said she was full of cheer and looking forward to meeting them as she didn't have many visitors.

They were shown through to the day room. It was a well-appointed sitting area with a plasma TV screen on a wall and games of draughts and crossword puzzles dotted around various tables. They sat down and waited until Tilda meandered closer and closer towards them with the use of a walking frame. Wil was convinced that she put on a hint of a spurt for the last five yards. Although she had inevitably changed from the image of a little blonde girl in the film, Tilda had aged well and had remained slender. Wil could also still see her fine features and good bone structure. He was sure she would have been an attractive woman in her prime.

The three friends stood up to meet Tilda.

Smiling and with a slight mixture of accents and a slight slur from her stroke, she said, "I've been looking forward to meeting you. I've been expecting you for some time."

The three visitors gave each other a discreet look with raised eyebrows.

Greg left them to it and promised to return with teas and cakes.

Tilda was an inquisitive old lady. She was keen to find out everything about Wil, Emma and Frea before they had a chance to get a word in edgeways. It felt more like an interview rather than the intended pleasant chat about her and her family. Wil naively assumed it was a German cultural thing, but then he remembered most of his elderly relatives in South Wales. They still did the same thing with him and they had known him all their lives. Wil thought Tilda was a fascinating character, he liked her straight away and wanted to hear her story.

Having exhausted three life stories, Emma managed to ask Tilda about her unusual accent.

Raising her voice a little louder Emma said, "I've been trying to work out your accent Tilda."

Wil was thinking to himself, "*She didn't say she was deaf Em' – just old.*"

Tilda apologised for her slight speech impediment and went on to explain that she was born in Germany. She left there when she was a young girl, many years after the film of her and her family was made by her father.

Wil said, "I thought it may have been you holding the dog's tail in the film - or was it your sister?"

"No, that was me," said a smiling Tilda.

Languages came easily to her and her siblings, explained Tilda, "We all spoke German. English was all our mother ever spoke to us, and then we grew up in Spanish-speaking Uruguay."

Her tone and happy demeanour changed as she recalled her earliest memories of being with her father, she could also remember having the dog.

She soon pointed out her father wasn't a high-ranking Nazi, "He was a weapons scientist working for his country, although he didn't have much choice in the matter at that time."

She said Klaus was worried the war was coming to an unsuccessful conclusion and there were perhaps incorrect rumours the Russians might be the first people to overrun the part of Germany where he and his family were living. They had moved from Berlin in the east to the countryside in the far south of Germany.

To avoid the allied bombing raids, they had evacuated with the children three years earlier from their home in Berlin to a summer residence south of Munich, which they sometimes shared with wider family members at that time.

The secret air base where her father worked was not far from them, near Garmisch, which was close to the Austrian border in the Alps. When they first arrived, the summer residence had been mothballed for the winter, but it soon became home for a few years. That was where they were when the day came to flee, and they were told to head for an airfield. Tilda remembered she and her sister cried for days because they had to leave their beloved dog behind.

The Russians had a terrible reputation for retribution and looting, so nothing and no one would have been safe.

"Our entire family would have been at risk and, rightly or wrongly, my father made a big decision to leave and get us as far away as possible. To South America, to avoid any other unwelcome repercussions in the aftermath of the war."

Many Germans who were well connected and could afford it were doing the same thing. Several thousand went to Argentina, thousands more to Brazil and others went to Uruguay and similar regions.

The Red Cross administration at that time was overwhelmed with requests from refugees, and documents and passports were issued to many people who may not have deserved them. A close friend of the von der Heyde's helped them out by getting all six of them aboard an aircraft that took them to north-west Spain. Tilda had some scant memories of the long perilous journey, before ending up safe and sound in Montevideo. As she got older and was more able to understand, her mother Susan recounted to the children what had happened.

Her faded memories recalled the journey, "It began at short notice. I have this vivid memory of my mother, Susan, filling several suitcases. She later told me she had collected together some valuables, including gold and jewellery, and we all fled in a hurry."

After waiting for hours in a cold and blacked out workshop building with nothing but a small lantern to keep them warm, the time came for them to board an aircraft that had Spanish insignia markings on it. There were two other men on the plane who, it later transpired, were senior Nazis making a run for it.

Tilda reflected, "Looking back, it wasn't an honourable thing my father did. It was shameful, but he did it for our family."

The flight took them ten hours to fly to a Spanish town on the Atlantic coast called Vigo, having first stopped inside the Spanish border from France to refuel.

"My mother told me many times, that for the first time in weeks she had felt safe when we got to Vigo."

The Franco regime in Spain at that time had an affinity with the Nazis and did everything they could to help their fascist counterparts. They were simply returning the favour for the military support and German bombing raids on Spanish soil during the civil war, orchestrated by General Franco. The Nazi bombing raids were simply a rehearsal for themselves in the years to come.

Klaus left Susan and the children in Vigo and went on ahead to Uruguay alone to establish a safe location for them all to re-join him. Then almost two months later after a long and difficult journey across the Atlantic, the family were reunited. They later discovered two weeks after they had flown to Spain, Klaus's secret airbase had been bombed and flattened. He thought to himself that he had been lucky.

Tilda also recalled Susan had sometimes told her that Klaus was originally meant to meet a German colleague, a pilot, who was involved in his plans in Montevideo. She said the man had ended up in a local hospital, and all the plans had to change. They all thought they were going to make a great deal of money, but something went wrong. She said the pilot's name was often mentioned in the diary, it was Lothar Muller.

Tilda said one of her older brothers returned to Germany in the late 1950s, the other remained in South America but they both had been dead for several years. Her father was killed in a tragic sailing accident in late November 1945 - he was lost overboard, and his body was never recovered. Her mother remarried, then divorced after several years. She and her mother, Susan, returned to Oxford when Tilda was in her late teens to live

86

with Susan's parents who had moved back to England. But Tilda's older sister Clara had married and remained near Montevideo.

"My mother and I brought home some of my father's personal effects, she always said they were special things, and to look after them. Clara kept some of the other items."

Tilda paused for a few moments. Her smile was gone. She poignantly explained how Clara had come to Oxford last year after Tilda had had her stroke. Clara hadn't long ago been diagnosed with a terminal illness. She told Tilda her several days visiting England would be the last time they would see each other face to face. There was some sadness, but they spent their time in Oxford reminiscing about their lives and their children. They laughed and had some fun before it was time for Clara to go back to her family in Uruguay. Clara died three months after she had come to see Tilda.

"It was Clara who convinced me I needed to do something with my father's possessions. She told me 'it was time' and she also told me to pass them to the people in Porton Down. I'm not entirely sure why, but as you can see, it wasn't long ago that I remembered and got around to doing what she asked," said Tilda, recalling Clara had been insistent at the time. "Although I do recall Clara telling me she thought some people had been nosing around back home in Montevideo. Whatever that meant."

Frea commented, "Tilda, that was very touching to hear you explain everything to us, thank you,"

"It's nice to talk about my past, it's enjoyable, although I'm still annoyed at myself for not passing the things to you sooner than I did. My son had them tucked away in his attic and I kept forgetting to ask him to get them for me."

Frea reminded Tilda, "What were the other things Clara had from your dad as keepsakes, can you remember?"

"Oh, yes," said Tilda, "She kept his pocket watch and some of the books he would forever be writing in, I think he called them his journals. I would think they are still in Montevideo with Clara's family."

When Greg had escorted Tilda in to meet them earlier, he had carried her knitting bag in for her. Tilda explained she used to knit every day but found it challenging since her stroke, although her occupational therapist had encouraged her to take up crochet, which she had tried and found was a tiny bit easier.

Tilda said she had put some things in with her wool to show them all that somehow came back to England when she had returned many years ago. She rummaged inside and produced, first of all, a couple of pictures of her and Clara when they were younger, and some were taken of them together last year. They looked so alike in all of them. She reached in a little deeper, some balls of wool rolled out, but in her hand, Tilda had some embroidery.

"These are some things we used to make when we were little girls growing up during the war."

The first thing they were shown was a what Tilda described as a 'sampler', explaining it was one Clara had made when they were young. Tilda's daughter had the one she made. The sampler was a piece of embroidery about twelve inches square. Created in wool on canvas to practise Clara's embroidery skills. Stitched across it were the alphabet and numbers, a border all around, along with the names of her siblings and 'Familie', "Mutter und Vater". It was beautifully made with not a stitch out of place. Next out of the knitting bag came another piece of embroidery in the shape of a long slim bag with an open end. Tilda slid a recorder out of the bag. Tilda explained she could never play it and it had belonged to Clara; she had been the musical one.

Tilda carefully placed the recorder back in its bag and handed it to Wil along with the sampler and photographs of the sisters.

"These are for you Wil, somehow I know Clara would have wanted me to give them to you."

Wil, Emma and Frea thanked Tilda and promised to come back and see her again. They asked Tilda not to get up but to stay seated as they said their goodbyes and left to go.

~

Phil Chalk never failed to answer a call from any of his Lucidity team members, day, or night. It wasn't late but he could have been in one of his many important meetings or doing something else.

Two rings and he answered, "Hi Emma how are you all doing, how did your discussion with Tilda go?"

Calling on years of experience, he had forced himself not to contact his team before they contacted him first. A nonchalant sounding Chalk ensured he conveyed an air of calm and collective leadership, but inside he was bursting to know what Tilda had told them.

"Hi Phil, we're on the road and we're on the hands-free. Tilda was a goldmine of useful information and we're buzzing; everything is so much clearer. We're sure we can move things forward. But we've got something important to ask you," Emma sounded excited.

There was a distinct silence at both ends of the call.

Frea intervened by saying, "Phil, Tilda was a fascinating lady to speak to. We've chatted it through, and we have come up with a plan - but we need your approval and sign off. Longer-term I'll be reducing my hours at work and right now I'm going to take some leave. Wil and Emma have lined up the family to keep an eye on their business and if you're OK with it we intend to fly to Montevideo next week."

"So much for me trying to keep you under control. It's like herding cats," said Chalk, who was quietly delighted they had taken the initiative and were undaunted.

Emma chipped in with, "Phil, we aren't ready to get off this 'Lucidity Programme bus', not yet."

"Yes, I can sense you're all full-on invested in this now," replied a smiling Chalk.

Driving and debriefing over a handsfree wasn't the best combination, but they did it for the next half hour as they headed towards Cheltenham *en route* to Wales. Chalk agreed to their plan and told them he would organise for the flights to be booked on their behalf.

What Chalk didn't tell them was he was going to discretely notify the security service at the British Embassy in Montevideo. Telling them three of his Lucidity Programme colleagues would be arriving 'in-country' and provided a full profile of each of them. He included contact details and the tracking systems which were built into each of their phones. Chalk's absolute thoroughness was always evident and first and foremost he wanted to ensure their safety at all times. He knew that fundamentally they were mere amateurs, 'pseudo-scientists', finding their way in a new field and were novices concerning any 'complications' that might emerge.

There was a lot of exciting chat in Wil's pickup truck on the way home. After it quietened down Emma began to think a little more deeply, *"What the hell are we about to get ourselves into."*

CHAPTER 11

REWIND

Early July 2019

Although he didn't recognise the number, Wil answered his vibrating phone call. The voice on the other end was Greg Long, it was almost a week since they had met him, but Wil remembered him from Tilda's nursing home.

Greg explained he had some information he thought he should share with Wil. He said that three days after Tilda met Wil, Frea and Emma, she had an unannounced visitor.

"Tilda was a bit put out, as she wasn't expecting anyone, and she was not in the slightest bit enamoured by the man who left straight away after he met her. She mentioned to me there was some relevance to her meeting with you, Wil, the previous week. It was all a bit confusing, to be honest."

Greg Long told Wil that they get the occasional chancers coming and going and he didn't always get the police involved, which is why he was calling Wil and letting him know in the first instance.

Wil decided he didn't want to go through everything over the phone with Tilda but instead arranged to drive up to see her and have another chat to Greg, who said he had a bit more detail. Having mentioned the latest development to Phil Chalk, the pair of them chatted it through and both agreed to meet at The Spires the following day. They were greeted once again by a helpful Greg Long, who took them through to Tilda, she was resting in the conservatory. She was in terrific good spirits and had got over her recent irritation about the random visitor.

Phil had been looking forward to meeting Tilda and after introductions and an obligatory cup of tea, Tilda continued to explain to Phil and Wil what had happened to her, "He turned up out of the blue and said he was an old friend of the family from Germany. I knew his accent wasn't German, so I sent him packing. We get a few cheeky rascals coming in here nosing around."

Wil and Phil Chalk took a stroll around the gardens with Tilda who still hadn't lost her ability to talk and ask questions. Chalk was absorbing everything and cross-referencing it with what he already knew should he want clarification. He was sincere and friendly, but he had a job to do. She had thoroughly enjoyed them popping in to see her, and knew they were good genuine people. But they were seeking information and were not there for a social visit, she understood and was fine with it.

They met Greg in reception as they were heading out. Wil asked him about Tilda's recent visitor. Greg said it was all a bit strange, explaining the visitor was a tall middle-aged man who arrived in a big impressive car and was smartly dressed. He had said his name was Dieter.

"I was suspicious because he was in and out in two minutes, so I made a note of his registration number."

Greg described the black car and found the registration number which he gave to Wil.

"And I've also got the CCTV if you'd like to see it?" added Greg.

Tucked behind the taller end of the reception counter was a flat-screen monitor. After several efficient keystrokes, Greg had found the date and time and played the high-quality colour footage to the two men who were observing from over his shoulder.

The shiny black Mercedes AMG 63 G Wagon looked remarkably familiar to Wil. So did the driver when he stepped out and walked towards the front entrance of The Spires. It was the same car that collected them from London city airport to take them to meet Alina Usmanova and her mother. It was also the same driver, but his name wasn't Dieter. To Wil's astonishment, it was Christof.

CHAPTER 12

COMPETITION

Early July 2019

halk asked Greg Long if there was somewhere more private where he and Wil could sit in comfort and make some phone calls. A door up the corridor was unlocked for them and they were shown into a cosy staff meeting room area, declining the offer of yet another cup of tea. Phil Chalk fleetingly smiled to himself thinking somewhere as smart and well managed as the Spires would do him just right one day when his time came.

The speakerphone call rang outbound to Emma, she answered and was with Frea who had called in to see Emma after a morning of appointments at the hospital.

Never wishing to leave any doubt in the minds of his colleagues, Chalk was keen to give everyone a full update as often as possible on any new developments. That way everyone would feel engaged and well-motivated to want to continue to work together as a team. He set the professional standards that he hoped everyone else would aspire to. Chalk was in charge. They all respected that and had complete trust in him and what he asked them to do. It was of equal importance for him to learn about these three crucial new people in his team. He needed to try to understand more about them as individuals and how they might respond in different or difficult circumstances. Not that he was expecting such situations, but he did have a faintest nagging doubt.

Splitting Wil off from Emma and Frea for a day was no accident, it had been subtly contrived to allow Chalk to get to know Wil a little better, within a different dynamic. In the past, Emma and Frea had always been present. Phil Chalk liked Wil. Although he could appear to be described as a 'bit of a lad' and laid back, Chalk knew Wil was a smart man, with some backbone and determination.

The two men both said "hi" in unison to the women over the phone, as Chalk began by stating how useful the visit had been. The main reason was that he had not met Tilda before and how he had felt that it was right and important to have chatted with her. He had wanted to reassure her that her box of personal items was in safe hands and they had a genuine interest in finding out more about her family story. It's what Clara would have expected.

In the second part of the conversation, he and Wil knew they needed to drop the 'Christof' bombshell. Chalk explained what Greg Long had told them and described the fascinating CCTV evidence concerning Tilda's recent unexpected visitor.

There was a brief silence down the line.

"We're bloody stunned Phil, well at least I am, I mean what the hell's going on?" asked Frea.

Phil Chalk composed himself and said, "I'm not sure, but I will find out. Guys, I want to reiterate, I don't want you to speak to anyone or do anything you don't feel comfortable with."

Christof had gone away empty-handed so Phil knew there would be a chance he could still be on a mission to do some more digging.

They all agreed it was inconceivable that Alina and her family were involved in Christof's extracurricular activities. The most likely scenario was that Christof wasn't figuring this out for himself, he was involved with other people. He must have decided to share his knowledge with someone somewhere and they were was still blindly trying to put two and two together.

Chalk reminded everyone that Clara instigated this. She had felt the need to do it because other people had started taking far more than a passing interest in her family and family history. She had become unsettled and deeply concerned before she died.

"Guys, someone else is curious but we are in control of all the facts and the information. And we are making progress. Let's figure it out," said Chalk.

"I imagine no one else is aware of the cine films, the camera and the diary?" asked Emma.

"It's only been a week or two Emma since the three of you met Tilda, so it's highly unlikely that anyone knows. They have been with Tilda for decades. Besides, we've made copies of everything, should anything go missing." answered a reassuring Chalk.

They agreed to call it a day and catch up the following day.

Before they went their separate ways, Wil sent a text to another of his local friends who was a mobile locksmith. For months Wil had been planning on upgrading the safe that they had installed at home to something more substantial. He had been given a quote for a hefty second-hand unit half the size of a fridge and weighing more than he did. He told his mate to come around and install it as soon as he was able.

Two minutes later the text came back, "*No, probs Wil how about tomorrow afternoon? Should take me an hour.*"

~

The whole process had been started due to Phil Chalk's close associates at GCHQ in Cheltenham being pinged with the salient information concerning Wil and his rescue of Alina Usmanova which had directly contributed to the formation of the present guise of the Lucidity Team. Therefore, the man they knew as 'Christof' was already on their radar. At that time, he was just a name of someone who had been involved as the intermediary with Wil and was the man that made things happen for a positive conclusion for the rescue of Alina. More information was requested concerning Christof. It took a couple of hours but Chalk was finally in possession of most of the facts concerning the man who was troubling him.

The "G Wagon" was privately registered in the name of forty-six-year-old Christof Sorotkin. He lived in an apartment close to Alina Usmanova, which her family-owned. Using facial recognition software to cross-check, it appeared Sorotkin was identified as a 'retired' member of the FSB Russian secret service. Sorotkin may have been an alias but it was enough to be going on with. He was a regular visitor back to Moscow and still mixed in similar circles to his former colleagues. In other words, he mixed with Russian businessmen and the Russian mafia - the edges were frequently blurred. He was well down the pecking order.

He had been hired following the abduction of Alina, had covered himself in some of the glory associated with her release and was now retained as well-paid additional security for the family. Although, he still fancied himself as a bit of an entrepreneur businessman on the side. Some people are never satisfied with what they have, loyalty is unfamiliar to them - Sorotkin was in that category. But he was well aware of the penalty for disloyalty with the wrong people and knew he needed to be careful.

Sorotkin was aware of all the details concerning Wil's exploits. He also knew the unusual capabilities that he had demonstrated with Alina so was likely, he had decided to share that knowledge. Someone else must have done the same homework on Wil the same as Phil Chalk had and was trying to find out more about what Wil was involved in now. Although Tilda was an elderly lady, she had learnt some basic social media skills and would have been in conversation with her children and friends, she liked to talk. Maybe someone had factored in Wil and combined it with Tilda's history and was doing some digging.

~

A thwarted Sorotkin had been speaking to his shady associates about his unsuccessful visit to The Spires nursing home and his attempt to meet and hoodwink Tilda into divulging some of her knowledge. Sorotkin had been under 'time pressure' to see her before Wil made too much progress. Sorotkin thought of himself as smart, he also thought he had a decent story to tell Tilda. However, he had underestimated her and her resilience and was frustrated by his early exit from the Spires.

Some background details had been provided to him by his backers advising who her late father was. It seemed to be old information and no doubt there were many gaps in it and some parts may have been unsubstantiated. Sorotkin was also told that soon after the war her father had been tentatively exploring possible purchasers of some scientific information that came from the Nazis. Although it wasn't made clear exactly what that information was.

One other critical piece of detail that stood out was that Klaus von der Heyde was said to have died in a boating accident. This was confirmed by Sorotkin's well connected, dark sources, as untrue - and that he had been shot, and fell from his boat into the Atlantic Ocean.

For certain, Klaus von der Heyde had something that had been valuable enough for someone to want him killed him for it. One thing was for sure he died because they didn't get what they wanted from him, or was there another reason for his murder?

Sorotkin wondered, most people would assume that seventy-year-old scientific information would be pretty useless by now. Surely it would have been rediscovered within the last couple of decades. So why would the UK have taken such an interest in it now? More importantly, why would they have 'hired' Wil, Emma and Frea to investigate? Something the UK government should have the resources to do without outside amateur assistance. He concluded, they must be in a big hurry - or desperate.

CHAPTER 13
NOSING AROUND

Montevideo, Uruguay – October 2018

When the elderly Clara came over from Montevideo to meet her younger sister, in Oxford for the final time in 2018, Clara had mentioned to Tilda that some people back home in Uruguay had been 'nosing around' – those were her exact words.

What Clara meant was that her daughter Julia had told her that a red-haired foreigner with a goatee beard had been asking lots of questions. Julia ran a tapas bar in the affluent Pocitos neighbourhood of Montevideo. The man claiming to be a tourist had been in a few times, he may have been American, but she had not been certain. Julia's suspicions were aroused one evening during some regular chit chat that she had with him. He had said on a previous occasion he had been researching his ancestry on one of the popular genealogy websites. He said he was trying to find some German relatives. That was fine, genealogy had become a trendy pastime. Lots of Julia's friends had been discussing their roots and they all had families scattered around all over the world. To begin with, Julia was more than happy and interested in talking to the man.

That evening the alleged genealogist tourist transformed himself into a one-man party. He had racked up a hefty beer, red wine, and cocktails bar tab. His pleasant chit chat had degenerated into him asking her some

99

slurring, unnecessary and specific questions about her family and where had they originated from. He mentioned the name of her grandfather Klaus and her aunt Tilda, enquiring how much Julia could tell him about them. Over the years, Julia had met all sorts in her bar and began to take a dislike to the man who seemed to know too much about her family. Annoying, drunk men were pet hates of hers. Things were beginning to feel most uncomfortable and intrusive. Julia began to clam up and moved away from him as she realised, he was probing her for information which he wasn't entitled to know about.

Two days later, eighty-four-year-old Clara was out meeting her great-grandchildren at a café in the park with her daughter in law who was looking after them for the morning. It was a pleasant regular event. Clara answered her phone to her neighbour who explained that she needed to go home because her house may have been broken into. The toddlers were rounded up in a hurry and the family group headed back to Clara's house. It was unpleasant and distressing news for anyone let alone an elderly woman living alone. Parking tickets and a couple of late-night noise violations were among the worst offences in the suburb of Carrasco where she lived. Clara didn't have an alarm, but she was lucky that one of her attentive younger neighbours noticed a broken windowpane in her door and that the door was open. Her neighbour had walked up to the front door and shouted Clara's name, seconds later, two men in crash helmets rushed out and barged him out of the way before making off on a motorcycle.

The inside of her house looked more like the immaculate 'show-home' she maintained rather than the ransacked property Clara was expecting to find. It had not even been 'untidied'. She was still dabbing tears from her eyes as she looked around. To her amazement, they hadn't taken some of the obvious valuables that should have been easy pickings. Nor had they taken the two thousand pesos that were sitting there on the kitchen worktop ready to pay her gardener when he arrived. Clara sensed the intruders had been looking for something specific.

Clara's Uruguayan husband had died several years earlier. Her daughter

Julia and son Edmund both lived nearby, they were a close-knit family and all pulled together whenever there was a crisis. Edmund owned a specialist car repair workshop which was located adjacent to his home. So Clara, who was shaken up by the break-in, went to stay with him and her daughter in law, who had been with her when she was told of the break-in, for a few days. Her son also had two beautiful ridgeback dogs which were reassuring should any unexpected visitors turn up. They were perfect and made Clara feel so much better about the situation. She also told Edmund about the things Julia had mentioned. That prompted him to double-check his home security, door locks, window locks and the shutters in his garage.

The large garage wasn't part of the main car repair workshop, it was more of a big man cave connected to the house. Edmund worked on cars for a living, but his passion was motorcycles and jet skis, which he kept at the garage. He had two bikes: a speedy Honda Fireblade, a cruisy Honda Rebel, and a Yamaha Waverunner jet ski. Plus, his super-fast accelerating and agile two-seater British racing green and yellow striped Caterham Seven open-top car.

It was standing room only in the garage. He had plans for more vehicles but didn't have a big enough space. He also had an unloved, rusting, flat tyred old Mercedes-Benz 320 classic car at the back of the garage. It had belonged to his father Raymondo and before him, it had belonged to his grandfather Klaus. Edmund kept promising himself that one day he would bring the big old black car back to its former glory. But it was a big, expensive time-consuming job. He didn't have the energy or the enthusiasm for it and sourcing parts would be a costly nightmare. For now, it was unloved and under a big dust sheet, as it had been for decades.

The important thing was that Clara was safe and sound. Edmund's well-protected property in its spacious grounds was not an easy target for anyone.

CHAPTER 14
TUCKED AWAY

Wales - Mid-July 2019

How on earth do you explain to your two grown-up children that you are temporarily diversifying from the 'high-flying corporate world' of running a glamping business? When it's to jet off to South America on a scientific mission on behalf of the British Government.

Wil and Emma had two sons, the eldest Haydn was twenty-six and now running the family farm, along with twenty-two-year-old George who was not long home from agricultural college. Both were now involved full time in the original farming business and had followed in their father's footsteps by playing for the local rugby team. The glamping offshoot was their parent's business, although everyone mucked in, literally, whenever help was required on any of the land. Both lads lived on the Crickhowell farm and Wil and Emma had moved four miles away to a cottage that they had once been renting out. They had renovated it to a high specification and chose to live in it themselves to give the boys and Haydn's young family plenty of space.

Family man Haydn took after his mother with her dark hair and blue eyes, although naturally, Emma didn't have the full Viking look beard that Haydn had adopted. The taller George was the image of Wil. Well over six feet, with a shock of dark curly hair, always in need of a decent haircut and never short of female attention. They both had the same excellent work ethic as their parents.

The boys had a reasonable idea as to the odd things their parents had recently been getting up too. They knew Wil's dreams had been a little more extreme on some recent occasions, although they didn't have the full facts. They had met Frea two or three times but hadn't yet made the big step to becoming yogis like their parents. Joking that one day they might surprise them with a headstand, or a crow pose arm balance.

Emma was still cautiously excited, and when they were emailed the flight details and downloaded their tickets and itinerary, she was more so. The reality had started to sink in. The flight departure date was not long away, and she had been getting nervous and couldn't help asking Wil if everything was going to be OK. It was clear that the Sorotkin affair had unsettled her. Wil said they were going to be far away from him soon so they could forget about the Russian for the time being.

Emma was organising things and double-checking every detail, the weather, flight times, currency connections and hotels. She also had a couple of conversations with Frea and they agreed it was probably going to be chilly so Emma reminded everyone to pack some warm clothes.

Whilst her Lucidity Programme colleagues were thinking largely along the lines of logistics and planning for the trip, Frea was more circumspect. She was listing some of the technical things they needed to do. She reminded herself to ensure she did a software update up on the laptop with the latest version from Phil Chalk's I.T. guys and to check other technical details were all in order.

Chalk's team had created an amazingly intuitive piece of software to capture all of Wil's electrical brain activity data, enabling Frea to have the flexibility of making any required changes to enhance Wil's 'sleep sessions' in an instant. So, making sure everything worked well from an I.T. perspective before she departed for Uruguay was crucial.

She ensured she had enough self-adhesive pads to connect to the tiny transmitters that were placed on Wil's temples whenever they did a sleep session. Spare lithium batteries for the micro transponders, the list went on.

Being a doctor, she had a habit of packing what some people describe a 'go bag', a small emergency kit bag. She often took it hiking, even packing a tick removing tool. She was glad she had never been called upon to use either the tick remover or the 'go bag' in earnest, but it was a good habit to have. As far as she knew no one had a nut allergy, but if it ever happened and anaphylactic shock ensued, she had an epi-pen and many other small essentials. Phil Chalk, 'Mr Thorough', would be proud of her preparedness.

Phil had told them he had arranged for a local guide whose name was Melissa Benitez to meet them at the airport in Montevideo. He had said Melissa spoke perfect English and knew everything there was to know about the area and its local history. Tilda had also been kind enough to arrange for them to call on Clara's children Julia and Edmund. Other details needed to be finalised before they departed and Frea and Wil were due to get into a 'sleep session' the following day, before flying out a couple of days later.

The primary objective for the trip to Montevideo was to try to find more information relating to Klaus von der Heyde and the journal mentioned by Tilda. Did it still exist? Did Clara ever have it? Were there any drawings or specifications written down? What was the secret that they didn't yet have the full understanding of? For sure there was a secret somewhere. They all needed to be in Montevideo, speak to the family and carry out some local research to try to get to the bottom of it. Wil seemed to have a knack of figuring things out from snippets of information he picked up as he went by. He made things happen. Phil Chalk decided he needed to remain in the UK to help co-ordinate and resolve any unexpected requests that the team came up with. It would prove to be a sensible decision.

~

The next day a relaxing yoga session was followed by a 'sleep session' in Frea's studio. These sessions had been proving to have a powerful effect in recent months. Wil and Frea had both been learning from each other, refining their methods after every session. The new portable microtechnology was proving to be incredibly effective. It wasn't long before Wil was in the characteristic relaxed mode and being subtlety led by Frea. She was helping him to check in on some of the unexplored corners of his mind. Wil had spent some time an hour before the yoga started, chilling out, uncluttering his mind, and concentrating on recent events with the lovely Tilda. In his head he was trying to picture her fascinating past and what she had told them about her family. In particular about her sister Clara. It was easy to see, that they had remained so close despite being thousands of miles apart, modern technology had which been a godsend had helped them both immensely.

Clara was the older, more outspoken sister and appeared to have been the most dominant of the two women. It was she who had instigated the sending of the box of items to Phil Chalk. She was the one who had understood the significance of it all and had somehow found out the best place for it to be sent to was Porton Down. Clara had the instincts, perhaps they were heightened because she knew that she was gravely ill. Don't they call it 'getting one's affairs in order?' Maybe, that's what this was all about. Combined with unsettling events at home with Julia's unwelcome customer at the cafe and the subsequent empty-handed burglary of Clara's home.

Perhaps her mother Susan's smart thinking and gritty determination was ingrained and manifesting itself in Clara all these years later.

Wil had also brought the personal items with him to the sleep session that had once belonged to Clara. The fabric sampler, the recorder, and some photos.

Frea could sense that Wil was reacting well to the calm meditative session. His body and limbs were soon twitching as they often did once he was asleep and beginning to dream. She continued softly narrating to him the messages that she hoped would prompt his mind to switch into its much deeper lucid, and informative mode.

Wil was indeed dreaming.

After some confusing images flashing through his mind, he eventually found himself in a cool dark place. There was no noise, no people. He had the sensation he was sitting looking through some windows into blackness. His hands were beside his thighs, palms facing downwards, he sensed a smooth shiny texture and a springiness combined with what he imagined was the stale smell of tobacco. Everything was so dark, he was disorientated. In his eyeline high up to his right, he could see a tiny intermittent red flashing light.

Soon he heard a voice, it was a woman's voice and she knew his name.

"Wil, this is wonderful, you did it, you are here." said the woman in an unusual English accent.

"You are close Wil, it's tucked away, but you can find it." Those were her last words to him.

In his dream, Wil sensed he was alone again, but his instincts told him he was close to whatever it was the woman referred to, close to finding 'it'.

Slowly, Wil drifted back into the real world, a gradual opening of his eyelids, to see a thoughtful Emma looking on from a distance. Frea was disconnecting two or three of the sensors and ensuring his electrical impulses had been recorded. Frea broke the silence, quietly asking "OK Wil, welcome back to reality. So how was that today? How do you feel, what are your immediate recollections?"

"Do I smell smoky?" was the first thing Wil said.

"At first, I had a series of images flashing through my mind at high speed. Old buildings, ships, and dockyards. Like when someone flicks you through a load of holiday pictures on their laptop that you don't want to see any more of, but you feel too embarrassed to say no."

Emma and Frea laughed, Wil had a knack of reducing tension in a room with the fewest of words.

He continued, "There was an empty bed, with curtains around it, I'm almost certain it was in a hospital, but I can't be sure."

Wil paused and said nothing for a few moments, concentrating as he recollected his thoughts.

"Then someone turned out the lights, instant darkness, it felt almost as though I was sat in an old darkened bar room full of smoke, but I wasn't. After a while, I kind of realised I was sat in the dark in the back of a car."

Wil went on to explain he had heard the voice of a woman with an unusual English accent, he described her accent as a mixture. He said it reminded him of Tilda's voice, but it wasn't her. He said for sure it must have been Clara.

"We're on guys, Clara is with us. She didn't say much in my dream, but she said enough." Wil was smiling and excited as he told them.

CHAPTER 15
PROFESSOR BLAKE

Southern Germany - Late 1944

Before she got married and became Frau von der Heyde in the early 1920s, Susan Blake, had been educated as a boarder at the renowned Cheltenham Ladies' College. That allowed her academic parents to pursue their careers as university lecturers. At eighteen Susan was offered a place at the University of Zurich to study languages, choosing to study in Switzerland for a change of scenery and to be closer to her parents. Although she didn't see much of them, she had a good relationship with them, and her father Tim meant the world to her. Switzerland was also a great central location for travel to neighbouring countries and had its own fascinating linguistic culture.

Professor Tim Blake and his wife approved of Susan's relationship with the brilliant German student Klaus von der Heyde. They were more than happy when, after several years, they decided to get married and move to Berlin for him to continue his physics career. Fascism was in its infancy at that time and the great depression, with Germany to suffer more than most, was still a couple of years away.

The Blakes had a home in Oxford which they rented out to a family member for a modest income, whilst they led a nice, comfortable, lifestyle in their second home in Zurich. Living in northern Switzerland was helpful because it enabled them to see their grandchildren not far away across the German border. Although Switzerland remained neutral, family visits became increasingly more difficult when the war broke out. Nevertheless, Switzerland was a good safe place to be in war-torn Europe at that time.

~

In the late Autumn of 1944, in the months leading up to them deciding to leave for South America, Susan and her husband had been planning and making preparations. They were becoming more and more concerned. Neither of them were committed Nazis, but Klaus von der Heyde may have been categorised or scapegoated as one of the much higher profile transgressors if he were ever to be held to account. After all, he was a senior scientist working for the Nazi's. They were not prepared to sit around and take that risk. The truth was, Susan hated the fascist regime, yet her feelings were never discussed in their home. She still considered herself to be British, although she spoke fluent German with no detectable accent and was also fluent in Spanish and other languages.

They agreed during their planning that moving to neighbouring Switzerland would not have been a viable option for them to escape Nazi Germany at the end of the war. It was too close to Germany - and a risk they were not prepared to take.

Due to his important work at the airbase, Klaus didn't see much of his home. Sometimes only appearing at weekends. On one rare occasion, Susan had been allowed to discreetly visit him at the airbase, on a weekend, with the children. He had been away for weeks without seeing his children, so they were given some special dispensation.

Because her husband was not always there it was always lovely when Susan could get the chance to see her parents, and in the university term breaks, they would sometimes visit Susan.

It was during the months of planning and when Klaus was not around that Susan met with her father. He and her mother came on one of their occasional visits to see their daughter and grandchildren.

For months Susan had been desperately wanting to see her parents to break the news about what she and Klaus were preparing to do. Her parents had no inkling of the von de Heyde family's plan to flee. After an emotional explanation, she swore them to secrecy. No one knew they were going, and no one could ever find out where they had gone to. Susan promised she would make contact once they were safe and settled.

They had made their decision to go when the time was right with the minimum risk of being caught by the German authorities. There were also some things that Susan wanted her father to help her with before they departed.

With Klaus being away for at least the next three days Susan took the opportunity to explain the rationale to her parents and more about his work because they were oblivious. However, she didn't tell them all she knew.

In recent months Klaus had confided in his wife everything that he had been doing for the past few years. Including his work on the anti-gravity project. Although, there was something which he had made a conscious decision not to tell her about. Susan was astounded when he showed her the cine film. She always knew he was a weapons and aeronautical expert. For years he had been working on rocket propulsion systems for doodlebugs and supergun ballistics. These could have fired a shell almost the weight of a small car up to a thousand kilometres. She often struggled with to reconcile her husband's work with her family and her home country and it occasionally led to arguments.

Susan's parents were smart sensible people; they knew what she and Klaus were planning to do was the right thing and were convinced circumstances would change in the future enabling them all to be together. Their safety and the wellbeing of their grandchildren was paramount at that extraordinary time.

An hour or so before her parents had to leave to go home Susan's mother was listening to a recorder recital from Clara whilst keeping her other grandchildren occupied. That was when Susan took the opportunity for a private discussion with her father.

Susan told him, "Dad, there's something I need you to do for me. It's important, and it must remain a secret between you and me. But you must do absolutely nothing until you receive a message from me that we are safe. Do you understand?"

"Of course, I understand. What is it?"

Susan explained some details before giving Professor Tim Blake a tiny scrap of paper.

CHAPTER 16
MAKING PLANS

Northwest Spain - January 1945

L ate January 1945 the von der Heyde's 'freedom plane' landed quietly
long before the sun was up in Vigo, north-west Spain.

In the preceding months, von der Heyde had sold almost everything
he owned. Traded in all his money and savings plus some gold rings,
converting it all into US dollars, Swiss francs, and Spanish pesetas. A big
chunk of his bankroll had secured them their flight via a close friend who
had excellent Spanish connections. The friend had needed the cash to
grease the palms of others. The same acquaintance had set them up in a
local hostel for several weeks. Hotels and apartments in the town of Vigo
were considered too risky. There were plenty of foreigners in Vigo, but
blonde children with German accents would be far too obvious.

The journey from the airfield to the short-term hostel was less than
thirty minutes. The building was always closed for the winter, but it had been
reopened for them and stocked up with a reasonable supply of provisions.
In the summer months, it was used as a stopover hostel for pilgrims heading
to Santiago do Compostela. They were safe for the time being.

The next step in the journey was to get to Uruguay. They had decided
that was the safest place for them to start their new lives as fewer Germans

were heading there. Most were going to Argentina. The other reason Klaus had chosen Uruguay was that he was expecting to be meeting an old colleague there as part of his business arrangement.

As soon as it was possible Klaus went into town and made his way to the local offices of the Compañía Trasatlántica Española travel bureau. There he booked a passage on the steamer 'The Habana' which carried cargo, mail, and passengers. It was leaving Vigo in two days and would be stopping several times before arriving in Mexico where he would transfer to another ship for the remainder of the journey. Susan and the children would make the same trip on a sister ship a month later. They had discussed it at length, and both agreed they were mindful of being identified as a family on the run. Klaus needed to settle in and establish things at the final destination. Splitting up and going as separate parties was a sensible precaution.

The key to their future prosperity lay in what Klaus had in his leather attaché case and the secrets he kept in his head. He intended to find a buyer. The prime candidate being the American government or the highest bidder if necessary, for the drawings and the reams of technical documents. Many of which were summarised into note form in his journal.

A black car with a luggage rack, driven by Klaus's trusted acquaintance, came to collect Klaus to take him to the port. Susan and the children squeezed in for the short journey to the port in Vigo to see him off. Susan was insistent they went to the port with him and not stay at the accommodation.

After an emotional send-off, Susan asked the driver to make a brief detour on the way back to their temporary home. They stopped outside the Hotel Palacio. There Susan instructed the driver, whom she knew to be trustworthy, to wait in the car and look after the children for ten minutes. Communications were not perfect in 1945 but Susan was fortunate, after three failed attempts a telephone call to the University of Zurich finally got connected. She found herself speaking to a woman who worked every day with her father. Susan remembered she had met the woman on a previous trip to Zurich, at her father's house and made some small talk with her.

Stressing its importance, she asked for an urgent message to be passed on to him from his daughter. Susan was assured the message would be passed on within the hour.

The message to Professor Tim Blake read: *Hello Father, the family are all well. We had a lovely trip. Please can you run the important errand I asked you do for me before I left? I will be in touch in a while. All my love Susan.*

~

The following morning Professor Tim Blake made a short walk. He took two trams to the British Consulate in Zurich and waited twenty minutes to be seen by the Consul General. They had a brief and pleasant discussion before Tim Blake passed on some crucial information, which was in turn relayed to the 'war office' in London.

The message was originally written on the tiny piece of paper given to him by his daughter Susan. It contained the precise location and some important details of the secret airbase where Klaus von der Heyde had worked.

Forty-eight hours later hundreds of tons of ordnance descended onto the airbase where von der Heyde had not long since worked, destroying it within minutes.

CHAPTER 17
FOOLS GOLD

Hospital Británico, Montevideo – Late January 1945

The full history behind Phil Chalk's self-imposed pressure to resolve the mystery surrounding Tilda's cinematic gifts all started in early1945, in an intensive care hospital ward at the Hospital Británico in Montevideo, Uruguay. At the time it was a modern well-equipped hospital and had been founded by the British seventy years earlier. The hospital had close links to the Uruguayan naval base. In its day it was furnished with state-of-the-art equipment which both naval and medical establishments shared when necessary. This forward-thinking approach had been partially due to the ongoing British influence.

~

Montevideo - January 1945. In adjacent beds were two men suffering from the same condition. They had both been diagnosed with Caisson disease, more commonly described as decompression sickness or the bends.

The men had been admitted several weeks apart. It meant they had received exclusive one to one treatment, first of all from the Uruguayan navy's portable hyperbaric oxygen chamber before being transferred for ongoing treatment at the Hospital Británico. Both men would not have fitted into the small chamber at the same time, so the timing was fortuitous.

The first of the men admitted had been a Russian submariner called Yuri Bubka. The other patient was a German who was admitted wearing civilian clothing and claimed he was an aviator by the name of Lothar *Haas*, Muller had avoided giving his correct surname.

Yuri Bubka had been crewing a Stalinets – S class submarine along with 49 other officers and men in the South Atlantic off the coast of Argentina. Bubka's primary role was as a signalman and communications officer. It helped that he happened to speak a few languages, although not that well. He was also the main designated and trained scuba diver.

His vessel had been redeployed from the Pacific fleet to the Atlantic fleet. One of its tasks was to assist in the hunting down and destruction of Japanese ships and submarines. The crew were interested in Japanese submarines more than anything else. The reason was there had been substantiated reports of wide slow-moving Type C-3 cargo submarines that were transporting hundreds of tonnes of metals and other raw materials to be traded with the Germans in exchange for military technology. The other attraction was that the cargo within the same Japanese submarines had also been confirmed as usually including up to two tonnes of gold bullion as part of the trade.

Bubka's vessel was patrolling off the coast of Argentina's Mar del Plata when their patience paid off. They got lucky and found their prey. They had been searching for a particular sub which they knew had been attacked and severely damaged a day earlier by an American Grumman Avenger torpedo bomber aircraft and was limping up the coast. It was sailing just below the surface to run its diesel generators and recharge its batteries. It also needed to take in as much oxygen as possible through the sub's snorkel device.

To attack another submarine, if they had the element of surprise from a great distance, submariner captains would attempt to adopt the 'end-around' tactical manoeuvre. Essentially, outflanking the target by calculating its speed and direction. The aggressor would then submerge, run until out of visual range before surfacing for maximum speed to gain distance much faster, and submerge once again and lie in wait.

This was exactly what the Russian submarine did to the Japanese sub. The plan was executed to perfection, and they mercilessly sank the soft target in relatively shallow water. When the Russian torpedo struck its target there were huge explosions. The munitions inside the Japanese torpedo room had received a direct hit sending cascades of water hundreds of feet into the air.

Uruguay had remained neutral for most of the second world war, though unofficially supported the allies, before declaring war on Germany and Japan at the back end of the war. If there was to be any contact from the Uruguayan navy, it would not cause Bubka's captain any problems. There was no reaction.

Under normal circumstances, the Russian submarine would have moved on to their next patrol, but on this occasion, they decided to try to find if there was the possibility of any spoils of war to be taken. The potential of finding two tonnes of gold was a huge temptation not to be sniffed at.

It proved a simple task to locate the wreckage of the Japanese submarine on the sonar. As they surfaced and approached a huge oil slick could be seen. Debris and the bodies of several of dead Japanese submariners still clad in their naval white tunics began to pop up from the depths like corks, then floated face down in the chilly Atlantic water. It was surreal and appeared almost as though they were all looking for something under the water.

"We're right over the top of her. Avast," the captain gave the order to stop.

It was Bubka's secondary job as a diver to go and see what he could find, he and his shipmates had seen many dead bodies and had become immune to it. There were some high wispy cirrus clouds in the sky. With not many waves to worry about the sub was stable on the surface and it meant several crewmen had been allowed on deck for some fresh air. The water was just about warm enough, although the depths were questionable.

So Bubka was set to work immediately by his captain, "You can celebrate with some fresh air later Bubka, once you've brought us up some gold."

There would be enough light and decent visibility underwater, but forty-five meters depth was a challenging dangerous dive. Risky, to say the least, if repeated several times in a short period. A safe ascent time-controlled to at least nine metres per minute would have been needed. It would take time and energy and they were sitting ducks on the surface to any non-friendlies. German submarines were a genuine threat.

Once they were in position, Bubka made his initial dive to investigate the Japanese wreckage. Twenty metres down and the body of yet another victim of the attack slowly and serenely passed him on its way to the surface. It was a young man, no more than eighteen years old, with his jet-black hair cropped to a crew cut, his arms were extended, and both his legs were raggedly severed below the knee trailing sinews and ligaments.

As he reached the sunken vessel, Bubka could make out two huge gaping holes in its fuselage and its entire length was bent like a jack-knife. It looked as though it were a toy that someone had cut it open with a tin opener leaving the jagged edges exposed to the ocean for all to see. There were still bubbles and oil seeping emerging from the stern.

Not long before the initial dive, on the surface the excited crew had all been discussing what they might retrieve, hundreds maybe thousands of gold bars. Yuri Bubka had got caught up in the excitement and found himself breathing more heavily than he was trained to do. His heart rate was up, and he hadn't conserved oxygen during the dive. Time disappeared at a rapid pace. Having scoured the surrounding area he found nothing of value and knew that entering the inside of the sub was the next thing he would have to do. His oxygen pressure was low, and he knew he had to slowly ascend, take a twenty-minute break on the surface, before starting again.

Three times he made the trip to the sunken sub, each time he came back with nothing to report.

The Russian captain was becoming increasingly frustrated and Bubka could sense it and hear it, "Sitting on the surface like this is bad news, Bubka."

The science behind scuba diving wasn't exceptionally advanced in 1945. Modern gas supplements mixed with oxygen such as Nitrox to enhance safety wasn't available at that time and more comprehensive knowledge of depths and times to be adhered to were frequently being modified by the experts. The other grey area for Bubka was the frequency of his dives at that depth but he knew he was already pushing his luck. Ascending slowly and thoughtfully is fine but compounding it with the extra depth and the multiple descents was not an equation he was comfortable in being able to calculate and it to be proved to be his mistake.

His fourth dive was to be his longest and his last, he had not rested for a long enough interval on the surface to allow his body to readjust to the gases that were beginning to be created within him.

He dived again, this time when back inside the Japanese submarine he had slowly found his way to the lower mid-section and could see some wooden crates that had been stacked but were now scattered. One of them had split and with his torch reflecting in the pitch back of the mangled steelwork, it was clear enough, he could see several sparkling gold bars. His eyes lit up. He was thrilled. Each bar weighed a kilogram, although four bars was all the weight he could manage to ascend with. Despite the extra weight, in his eagerness he rushed through his ascending protocols, skimming a minute off, taking four minutes instead of five minutes to get to the surface.

As he emerged, Bubka screamed with delight, "Gold. I've found it. Gold bars - crates of them!"

His shipmates hauled him aboard the surfaced submarines deck and relieved him of the four gold bars, his weight belt, and his breathing apparatus. Meanwhile, inside his body, nitrogen bubbles had been forming in his blood, skin, and musculoskeletal system.

When making a dive there is always a small amount of nitrogen present within the pressurised air tank which then gets dissolved into the body when inhaled. Careful dive management at a slow rate will allow the safe reversal of the process to happen.

What Bubka did was foolish. He did not decompress correctly. His body could be compared to a bottle of carbonated cola, shake it up, remove the cap and the bubbles come rushing out. When he was on the surface resting on the deck of the submarine, the build-up of nitrogen began to manifest itself. Having removed his wetsuit huge red blotches started to appear on his torso and limbs and his joints were beginning to ache. Bubka knew he was in trouble and it would soon get worse.

"Captain, I'm in trouble here, I've got a big problem."

The Russian submarine captain made an on the spot, important lifesaving decision and sent a distress message to a Uruguayan frigate that he knew was in the area. The two vessels sailed towards each other and met, well inside Uruguayan territorial waters and a sick Bubka was transferred to the frigate.

Two hours later he was laying inside a hyperbaric decompression chamber at the naval base before being transferred to a hospital bed in Montevideo where he remained for the next eight weeks.

The Russian submarine departed immediately, leaving Bubka and his belongings for him to recover with the Uruguayans. They had not disclosed the location of the Japanese sub nor did they explain what Bubka had been doing to have made such basic errors that almost cost his life.

~

Whilst Yuri Bubka was still slowly recuperating during his lengthy stay in the hospital, aviator Lothar Muller was making what he had intended to have been his final flight from a secret airbase in southern Germany. There was one other person who knew that it would be the last flight out of the base for the anti-gravity aircraft and that was Klaus von der Heyde. Having planned it for months the two Germans had made an agreement. Along with the von der Heyde family escape, Muller was going to join his close friend Klaus in Uruguay, by flying himself there in less than four hours. Both men had become completely disenchanted and disenfranchised with the Nazi regime and agreed they would look for a commercial arrangement to capitalise on the knowledge and incredible asset that they had, making them both wealthy men for the rest of their lives.

Lothar Muller and Klaus von der Heyde had a final discreet meeting at the airbase the day before Klaus's departure. They knew the base Commandant would become suspicious and tighten security as soon as he realised Klaus and his family had vanished. Therefore, Muller agreed he would leave and fly the nine thousand miles to Montevideo in the anti-gravity aircraft the day after his close friend left. His three-hour hypersonic speed flight meant he would arrive at a pre-planned secluded location in the hilly and tree-covered Cuchilla Grande interior region well outside of Montevideo a month before Klaus had completed his long journey. Neither of them had a Uruguayan accommodation location in place making communication with each other impossible, so their secret plan was to meet at the Hotel Carrasco. They would attempt to meet every Tuesday and Friday at two p.m. during the weeks following Klaus's anticipated arrival until they made contact.

The day arrived for Lothar Muller to leave Germany, both his parents were dead, and he was unmarried, so his personal circumstances were a great deal easier than his friend Klaus. Officially, Muller's flight was meant to be a regular long-distance test flight before returning for a debriefing.

It wasn't unusual for Klaus to be waiting in the hanger before one of Muller's test flights. They would often meet in a side office and go through some last-minute technical thoughts and checklists. This time was different. When they met both men had huge smiles on their faces. The darkness that they had been accumulating under their eyes had gone and the mental burden on their shoulders appeared to have lifted. They embraced for a final time - relieved that the day had come.

"Are you ready Lothar?"

"I've been ready for weeks Klaus. It will be a walk in the park. I'll be waiting for you with some champagne."

Susan is nervous, but she's fully committed. We're ready, it will be difficult for the children but they will adapt. We will be wealthy men Lothar in a new and amazing part of the world. A long way away from this strife."

"See you on the other side Klaus," were Muller's final words.

"Yes, I'll see you at the hotel as we planned my friend. Don't forget the champagne!"

It was midday in Germany, people would be having breakfast in South America Muller calmly thought to himself. The hangar slowly doors slid open, he climbed into the aircraft. This time taking with him a full-size kit bag containing his personal belongings, no one questioned it. He went through the usual procedures and seconds later he was silently soaring into the German sky - for the last time.

Lothar Muller's flight duration was going to be three times longer than any previous test flights he had made. The aircraft was in perfect working order, and he was confident there would be no issues. He was going to start by travelling at Mach 5, ascending to high altitudes well over a hundred thousand feet where the air is thinner and greater speeds are achievable. He was an experienced aviator. He had learned to convert his traditional flying skills to navigating this unique object at speeds ten times faster and altitudes ten times higher than he had ever dreamt possible. This trip to Uruguay was going to be the longest he and the aircraft had ever attempted, and he was inadvertently taking medical risks that pilots like him never knew existed. Without realising it, he was gradually developing altitude-induced decompression sickness. After two hours of high altitude, high-speed descents, and ascents his body was starting to ache, and he was becoming fatigued and numb. He was barely able to control the aircraft and so he significantly increased its speed to try to enable him to reach his destination much quicker than he had first intended.

It was a mistake. As he approached the coast of Uruguay the aircraft started to vibrate and slow down. The cabin temperature was rising fast. He was losing control and the aircraft was no longer responding. It was understandable for Muller to be panicking and shaking with fear that the aircraft could break up mid-air. He knew he had seconds left to make his decision. At sixty thousand feet with a small oxygen pack and mask securely strapped to his leather headgear he ejected up out of the tiny aircraft. It continued downwards without him and plummeted towards the Atlantic Ocean shattering mid-air into pieces and sinking once it hit the water.

Muller was still conscious as he floated under his parachute and to his relief, there was no cloud cover, with a little bit of wind. He could see the ocean to his left and land slowly approaching below him. He could see paths, tracks and roads, houses and then a city, Montevideo. The control of the parachute wasn't exact but as he floated slowly downwards it was enough to direct towards an extensive green area within the city, it was a park.

People on the ground were looking up and could see the highly unusual sight of a parachute drifting in the sky and heading towards the park and began to run towards it. By the time Muller landed with a gentle bump he was surrounded by curious locals wondering who he was and where he had come from. They were soon making a heck of a noise. A local policeman took charge and could see that the parachutist was in great discomfort and tried his best to help him, first of all by removing the billowing parachute and its long cords. Four men who were standing watching were then instructed to carefully lift Muller and carry him to a nearby car which took him to the nearest hospital.

When he was assessed at the hospital the white-coated doctor and a small group of nurses who using great care had started to remove Muller's jacket and shirt. By doing so they could sense from his anguished reaction the muscle and joint pain he was enduring. They could also see the same sizeable blotches on his torso that Yuri Bubka had suffered with four weeks earlier. They concluded the new patient, who didn't speak Spanish, could be suffering from the same condition. But how was that possible, he wasn't a diver? Everyone was confused.

After some debating and head-scratching, the doctor decided to make a phone call to the local naval base. The doctor spoke to a senior medical officer at the base who had been trained in the principles of the operation of the hyperbaric chamber. The medical officer immediately explained he had learned in his training there had been examples of high-altitude hot-air balloonists suffering from the bends. He said it could easily be the same problem if the man was an aviator. Muller was then immediately transferred to the naval base and placed in the chamber. His treatment was guesswork as they had no idea what parameters were needed. He was left in the claustrophobic pressurised tube for three hours at a time and received the same treatment every day for two weeks.

Lothar Muller and Yuri Bubka both found themselves as patients on the same ward overlapping for almost three weeks until Bubka was due to be discharged. Neither of them could speak Spanish, but they both spoke a little English and Bubka spoke some German. Between them, they managed to communicate well enough.

Bubka had made a reasonably good recovery from his milder Type I grade of decompression sickness. Muller's symptoms were far more concerning, he had ongoing Type II and suffered from severe pain and discomfort. As his condition failed to improve, he began having regular bouts of confusion, a symptom of severe bends and would often mistake Yuri Bubka for his good friend Klaus.

Bubka listened intently, playing along with it, and managing to glean the real surname of his new acquaintance - Muller.

"Yes Lothar, I'm still here. This wasn't part of the plan was it?"

"Klaus, I thought we were meeting in the hotel, with champagne...?"

And so Bubka's game continued as he formed a picture of the German's activities.

His initial thoughts were of Muller being delusional and with a furtive imagination. The more he listened the more intrigued he became, and he began asking people questions about the day Muller was admitted. What had people seen and what were the rumours? It appeared no German aircraft was recorded as having crashed anywhere within hundreds of miles. Although he said he had baled out at sixty thousand feet, perhaps the conversations with his confused acquaintance had a ring of truth.

It was 06.30 on a Tuesday morning, Muller had been in hospital dangerously ill for four weeks. Bubka was due to be discharged in three days.

A nurse making her early morning rounds came to attend Lothar Muller when she found him dead in his bed. It looked as though he had died in the middle of the night. A doctor was called whose initial reaction was Muller had either choked to death or the seriously ill man's damaged lungs had had enough and failed him. Due to Muller's bloodshot eyes, the medics made a reasonable assumption it was asphyxiation and natural causes, brought on by the bends.

There is another cause of death by of asphyxiation leading to bloodshot eyes - suffocation, and strangulation. Bubka was asked if he had heard any noise or commotion during the night. He explained he had slept soundly all night and he was saddened to hear of his new friend's sudden death. None of the medical staff noticed the scratch marks on the back of Yuri Bubka's hands and forearms.

The following Friday at two p.m. Russian sailor Yuri Bubka walked into the Hotel Carrasco. He was looking for a man who might be Klaus von der Heyde.

CHAPTER 18
PAYDAY

Montevideo – Early March 1945

It was two p.m. on Friday 2nd March 1945 and this was Klaus von der Heyde's second visit to the Hotel Carrasco in Montevideo.

He had come to the same hotel at the same time on the previous Tuesday, as he had arranged over a month ago with his good friend and future business partner Lothar Muller. He would turn up as planned until they met. Both men had agreed if things were delayed by more than three visits after Klaus's anticipated arrival date, whoever made it to the hotel would leave a coded message for the other person with the concierge.

On the first attempted Tuesday meeting date, Klaus had stepped off a boat that morning alone with all his luggage. His night ferry from Brazil had docked two hours earlier than the two p.m. agreed hotel meeting time. He was washed, shaved and full of excitement at the prospect of meeting Muller who should have arrived in town weeks before he had.

After two hours, three coffees, then a small beer and never averting his gaze from the door he realised Muller wasn't going to arrive.

"No Lothar, no champagne reception greeting. Not today." Klaus thought to himself.

He left, trudging out at a far slower pace compared to the brisk, enthusiastic strides of anticipation when he'd arrived earlier. He had been stood up and was concerned.

Klaus had hoped his friend would have arranged some accommodation for him on his arrival. As time went on, he realised he needed to make some other arrangements so after paying for his drinks he approached the hotel concierge.

Klaus's English was excellent, but his Spanish was poor. Like all experienced concierges, his English was almost as good as that of his guest. He was able to make some suggestions for somewhere slightly more private and away from the expensive city centre to stay in. Hotels were expensive and too exposed. Klaus was still in a frustrated and cautious frame of mind. For his first night though, his tiredness and disappointment overcame his caution and he decided to stay at the hotel.

The following day he found and rented a small clean ground floor apartment. A solid stone-built property. It was part of a block of four homes two stories high with some grass at the front and rear. The block was situated next to a park and as recommended by the concierge it was fine, but it was on a busy road. He planned to stay until closer to the date when he expected his family to arrive and then move to somewhere larger and more suitable. The irony of it was his temporary apartment was next to the same park his friend had parachuted into a month before. Yet he was unaware Muller was now dead.

The second rendezvous attempt to meet Muller on the following Friday didn't feel good, he realised by 14.15 things weren't going to plan and sensed he was not going to be meeting anyone. That was until a short stocky unshaved man with cropped hair approached him.

The hospital had given Yuri Bubka the pick of whatever clothes they had available that were washed and folded away, left behind by previous patients. Bubka looked respectable enough but somehow managed to look completely incongruous in the well-appointed Hotel Carrasco.

The hotel was bustling at that time, smoke and Latin American conversation filled the air. Klaus could sense a man was heading in his direction, so avoided eye contact, instead choosing to take a huge pull on his pipe and significantly adding to the thick layer of smoke in the room.

Bubka could see the pipe-smoking fair-haired man was sure to be the only European in the room. Not only that, but he was also the only man who was alone in the room, so he pulled up a chair on an adjacent table and audaciously stared at the man sat opposite him.

He then said in broken English, "Hello Klaus, how are you?"

Klaus's entire body gave an involuntary twitching movement and his eyes widened; he couldn't avoid it. He wasn't expecting anyone to say his name and couldn't avoid displaying the reaction that he did.

He composed himself before choosing to reply in English instead of German, he said, "I'm sorry sir, you must have me mistaken for some else."

"Klaus, we need to talk about your friend Lothar. I have some news for you, let's go somewhere quieter and I'll explain why he couldn't get here to meet you as planned."

Bubka knew he had the right man as a look of anxiety flashed across Klaus's face. The German stood up, placed some money on the table and started to walk out of the hotel lounge.

"Shall we go somewhere more private?" he said to the dishevelled stranger.

The two men left the hotel and walked across the road to the park and sat on a slatted wooden bench. There were two or three people dotted around, some walking dogs, others out for a romantic walk. Although it was sunny it was starting to get getting a little chilly, maybe it felt colder because Klaus felt extremely uncomfortable with the situation as he anxiously wondered what the stranger was going to say to him. Understandably, he was on edge.

Bubka lit a cigarette and offered one to his new acquaintance, which was gratefully accepted, although he preferred to smoke a pipe. Von de Heyde felt slightly calmer, but not much.

In his broken English Bubka then opened the conversation and started by doing his best to explain that he was a Russian submariner and had spent the past seven weeks in a local hospital. The last three of them was in a bed next to a man called Lothar, before discovering Haas's real surname name was Muller. He claimed to have got to know 'Haas', Muller, well during their convalescence.

It was a strange situation, the war was raging on, but it was almost in its final throws, and the Russians and Germans were still at each other's throats. Yet here were these two men, appearing to any passers-by to be like two old friends having a polite conversation on a park bench.

Bubka decided to skip any further chit chat and to lay his cards on the table immediately. He knew his new acquaintance was desperately trying to find Lothar Muller and would be prepared to pay plenty of money to find his friend.

"Klaus, Lothar has left the hospital, he wasn't well, but he insisted on leaving. He is not moving too good at the moment. It's due to the serious head injury he received when he landed, which is much improved now. He refused to tell the doctors where he was going, but I have been looking after him and I know where you can find him."

Bubka could sense the anticipation in Klaus from his body language and by the look of intensity on his face.

So, he continued, "Lothar is very confused these days. Are you interested in speaking to your friend? If so then I will need some money from you, a great deal of money."

Klaus was shocked at this news and said with some uncertainty, "I don't believe you. Take me to Muller first and then I will make it worth your while."

Klaus was becoming more and more agitated by Bubka's evasiveness and his demanding attitude.

"Prove to me you know where he is. Until then will I not discuss any payment," insisted Klaus.

The pugnacious Bubka was unrelenting. He was determined to find a way to fund a search for the Japanese submarine and retrieve the cargo of gold bars. He had a clear understanding of the precise bearings and heading his submarine had taken when they attacked the Japanese sub. He was confident he could find the location. He wanted money as soon as possible.

"You will pay me $1000 tomorrow otherwise you will never see Muller again, and I will also tell the authorities about who you are and your secret plan."

Adding to the pressure Bubka also pointed out he knew about Susan and the children.

"I know they are on their way Klaus, and I can make life painfully difficult for everyone concerned. You need to help me with the money."

This was a new and worrying prospect for Klaus. The consequences of not complying and not paying the money would be devastating for him.

He needed his business partner because Lothar knew where the anti-gravity aircraft was located. Secondly, to be outed as a former Nazi on the run would be dangerous for him and his family, even in Uruguay. He knew he needed some time to consider his limited options and formulate a plan to deal with this unsavoury character. Also, $1000 was a huge amount of money and would wipe out a big piece of Klaus's capital.

He was forty-five years old, unfit and he had never served in the military, Klaus felt sick to his stomach and was beginning to tremble. He had received a privileged upbringing and an excellent education thanks to his wealthy family, before becoming an academic. Von de Heyde could never have been described as a tough man. He knew his limitations and now he was confronted with a penniless, aggressive Russian sailor, who was utterly determined to take a significant chunk of the von der Heyde family savings.

He decided he needed a delaying tactic and by quickly thinking on his feet he said, "I need until Monday afternoon, I won't have the money available until then. And I can maybe manage $500, my wife has the rest of the money."

Bubka considered the response, "$500 on Monday and $500 when your wife arrives. Be here in the park Monday at two p.m.," was Bubka's last directive. He didn't wait for a reply, stood up and walked away.

Klaus stayed seated on the bench; his legs had become shaky. He couldn't believe what had happened. He stared ahead then put his head in his hands. Once he calmed himself down, he stood up and walked the short distance to his apartment.

Bubka had strode off but had kept a discreet backward glance on the perplexed German. When he was out of sight he circled back amongst the trees and at a good distance, he followed his cash cow to find out where he was living. Bubka wasn't going to lose sight of the German now that he had found him.

"Not yet. A little precaution."

CHAPTER 19
GOING IT ALONE

Montevideo, Uruguay – Early March 1945

That Friday evening, after the unpleasant afternoon meeting, Klaus's plans were in tatters. He and his family may become safe if nothing else, but in all likelihood, they were not going to become the wealthy family they had dreamt of. He needed some answers and he couldn't wait a moment longer, his head was spinning.

Donning a hat and a coat, Klaus walked briskly back to the Hotel Carrasco where he knew a man who spoke good English and could give him some clear directions.

The Hospital Británico was a fifteen-minute walk about two kilometres north-west of the Hotel Carrasco. The area around the hospital was a busy place, he thought to himself, as he scanned the signs until he found the one which said "entrada".

The grand foyer area was imposingly designed and displayed a nod back to its British realm founders. The British were still considered as close friends of the Uruguayan establishment with a selection of statuettes of famous British seafarers and some royalty on show. As further evidence of the strong bond, the hospital was erected as a memorial to King Edward VII.

The first challenge was to find a German or English-speaking person to help Klaus find a way to answer his burning questions. After several polite but failed attempts he found a passing nurse who said she spoke a little English but not much. He explained that he was looking for an old friend who was a patient in the hospital. The young nurse asked him to take a seat while she went to find someone who could help him.

The nurse returned minutes later. As she stepped back and wandered away, Klaus stood up to be met by a vast matronly figure dressed in a navy blue dress with huge white lapels, all held in at the waist by a large butterfly-shaped buckle belt. Without a doubt, she was a more senior nurse, who said she also spoke English and asked who he was looking for because she dealt with admissions.

Choosing his words with care, von de Heyde said he was an old friend of a man called Lothar Haas. Someone had told him he may have been admitted to the hospital, several weeks before. He said they hadn't heard from Lothar for a while and were becoming concerned.

The senior nurse's body language appeared to soften, and her matronly facade shifted a little as she said, "Sir, I'm aware we did have a man of that name here until the other day, but I'm afraid to have to tell you he died of his injuries only three days ago. I'm so sorry to give you such sad news. Were you a close friend of his?"

The German resumed his sitting position as his legs felt like jelly for the second time in a few hours.

Composing himself and finding it an enormous challenge in getting his words out, "Well more of an old acquaintance. I was nearby and wanted to come and say hello if Lothar was here and unwell. What were his injuries please nurse, what did he die of?"

The nurse explained he had been suffering from a condition in most cases associated with divers, called the bends. Klaus said he was unfamiliar with the condition, so the nurse explained the severe symptoms his friend had endured. Including bouts of confusion. Until early one morning he was unexpectedly found dead in his bed. Adding it was a shame because he had stabilised and may have been starting to improve.

"We suspect he died of asphyxiation, choking is a possibility, his body was not strong, and we think his lungs had been affected. His body is still in the mortuary if you would like to pay your respects?" said the nurse.

A still badly shaken Klaus responded, "Asphyxiation? My goodness, oh, yes, please, I would like to see Lothar if it's possible."

They went to the mortuary and he was shown the peaceful body of his old friend.

After his initial sadness, he collected his thoughts and then the reality of the situation dawned on him as he contemplated, *"No Lothar, no aircraft, it's me and that Russian bastard Bubka. Asphyxiation? No, he did this, he murdered Lothar."*

The walk back to his apartment was a slow one for Klaus, his brain was scrambled.

"See you on the other side, Klaus." Those were Lothar Muller's last words, Klaus thought to himself, over and over in his mind.

He was also desperately missing his family, most of all the support of his lovely wife Susan. She had always been there when things got difficult. He had plenty of money to pay off Bubka on Monday, but he hated the thought of it and knew he had no alternative other than to risk being exposed. He also knew, from what he had read of them, that blackmailers never stop, they always keep coming back for more and more money.

On the way back he bought some empanadas and a bottle of red wine from a street vendor. The emotional day had exhausted him, and the nightmare was not going to finish for a while. Within an hour he was flat out, in a deep sleep.

All the next day and evening the image of his friend Lothar laying on the mortuary table kept entering his mind. And Muller's final words - *"See you on the other side Klaus."* were still constantly haunting him.

Klaus felt like the walls were closing in on him and someone was stealing his oxygen. He was well and truly on his own, contact with Susan was impossible, she and the children were already on their way across the Atlantic. He was a worried, lonely, man.

It was ten a.m. on the Sunday morning when Klaus was awoken by a loud persistent knocking on his door.

"Un momento por favor," said Klaus, in his limited Spanish.

He pulled on some trousers, combed his hair and still in his vest and braces he answered the door.

Yuri Bubka had woken a couple of hours before Klaus. He had been staying at the seaman's mission hostel near the docks. Basic, cheap, bunk beds, not always that clean, twelve to a room and packed with snoring drunken sailors and warehousemen. His cramped bunk on the submarine was far superior and certainly much cleaner.

Bubka had not slept well and had already had two major arguments that Sunday morning. One, queuing to use the stinking toilets and the other, having to wait longer than he wanted to use the equally dire washing facilities. He had also almost run out of what little money he had and come to the conclusion he didn't believe the German's story. So, he had decided to go across to his apartment and extort the money from him that morning - one day ahead of schedule. Or at least as much of it as he could. Perhaps more than the agreed $500. One way or another some cash was going to change hands.

As the heavy oak door to Klaus's apartment began to open Bubka kicked it hard, viciously swinging it inwards on its hinges, knocking Klaus backwards, almost off his feet.

"Change of plan, today is now Monday," bellowed a hostile Bubka, as he deftly flicked the door shut with his foot behind him and stepped inside the apartment.

A terrified Klaus stumbled backwards on to one of the chairs behind him.

"But we agreed it would be Monday."

Bubka approached him menacingly and towered above him even though standing up he was a good seven inches shorter than the German.

"Like I said Klaus, today is Monday."

Bubka then reached inside his coat and produced a hefty wooden baton which he began expertly tossing from palm to palm in a frightening display of dominance. The baton often accompanied Bubka on evenings out when ashore with other crewmates. The solid piece of wood made its final smacking sound as it came to a halt in Bubka's right hand. It was then pointed no more than two feet from Klaus's chin.

"Go and get it, Klaus, I want the money, now."

Klaus stood up. He was cautious and his instincts made him put his hands and arms upwards in a passive gesture.

"OK, OK, I'm getting it for you."

He slowly shuffled the three paces over to one of his suitcases that was unopened against the far wall on the wooden floor. With Bubka still standing nearby over his right shoulder, the German knelt down, flicked open both catches and hinged open the lid of the dark leather case. It was full of shirts, and woollen jackets.

"C'mon, I haven't got all day."

The light was streaming in through the small vertical gap in the draped window as Klaus began rummaging through his clothes until he found what he was looking for. Head bowed, still kneeling facing the case he reluctantly, slowly, lifted out a grey cotton money belt. Compliantly holding it above his head with his left hand making no eye contact, staring ahead at the wall, waiting for Bubka to take his prize.

In a flash, a grinning Bubka snatched it out of the German's hand. He took a couple of steps backwards to the small dining table giving himself a good couple of arms lengths between himself and Klaus. He placed his trusty wooden baton on the table, thinking it was within easy reach if the pathetic German foolishly decided to make a move on him.

Von de Heyde deliberated as he closed the case and rose to his feet. He turned to face a preoccupied Bubka who was oblivious to the Luftwaffe issue Mauser HSc 7.65mm semi-automatic pointed at his chest. Bubka only looked up when he heard the smooth action of the top slide of the pistol being 'racked' fully arming it. That was the last thing Yuri Buka ever heard. Klaus quickly placed one of his thick woollen jackets over the muzzle of the gun in an amateurish attempt to muffle the sound. He then pulled the trigger, twice in quick succession, killing a man face to face for the first time in his life.

Bubka fell backwards, crashed into the chair, and lay lifeless on the wooden floor. Klaus had never seen the close-up effects of a man shot dead before, he didn't know what to expect. He was shocked by how easy it had been to take a man's life in less than two seconds. However, he had fired his pistol before, he had practised how to load and fire it before he left Germany, hoping, and expecting never to have to use it in anger.

The gunshots had made slightly more noise than Klaus had expected. There was a street not far from the door with some cars and trucks passing, but he had been fortunate. The landlord told him there was no one living upstairs. Being on the end of the block he hoped the solid stone walls dividing him and the other apartment next door would have been adequate to have further muffled the sound.

This dramatic and deadly event was completely unplanned and unexpected. It was remarkable, considering what he had done moments earlier that Klaus's clarity of thought switched in an instant. His first thought was that his extortion problem had been resolved to swiftly reassuring himself that acoustically the soft furnishings in the room would have helped absorb some more of the gunshot noise. His other thoughts then turned to how he was going to clean up the bloody mess and dispose of a dead man's body. His mind was in overload.

His immediate reaction had been to rapidly get dressed and pack his cases in case he needed to get out in a hurry. He then checked outside the door to see if there was any commotion or anyone taking an interest. There was not, although his heart rate hadn't reduced much as a result.

He was satisfied he was safe and for the next ten minutes, still trembling he sat down and poured himself a small glass of rum. With a dead man at his feet, whose lips were starting to turn a bluish-grey colour he went through in his clever mind what he needed to do next.

As his thoughts focused on covering his tracks, he couldn't avoid but look down in contempt at the dead man lying there on his back. Still with the same surprised look on his face that was there ten minutes earlier. He paused as he looked at the pool of blood surrounding Bubka and noticed one of the spent, ejected cartridges must have rolled across the wood floor before getting caught up in the sticky blood. He felt good about what he had done and was certain Lothar had suffered at the hands of Bubka. Poor Lothar, he made it all the way here alive and then it ended when he was murdered by a ruthless Russian chancer.

A walk outside in the fresh air was required. The smell of cordite in a confined space had been strong and unpleasant. So was the smell of fresh blood as he also discovered. He had to get out of that room to clear his head and do some thinking.

A short distance away from where he was staying Klaus could see some stores – a bakery, an ironmonger, a butcher, and a Turkish furniture store. He had an idea.

Continuing with his walk in the warm sunshine the German was trying to gain a better understanding of the topography of the local area. He was on the edge of a park and within thirty metres of what was one of several small lakes. The lake in front of him was fed by the winding Carrasco Creek which gently meandered its way down to the Atlantic.

Most of the Turks that Klaus had met over the years through his business dealings and from travelling were smart business people. Many of them spoke some English, which would prove to be helpful.

Armed with a scrubbing brush, washing soda, a mop and bucket he spent the afternoon cleaning the congealed blood-stained floor of the apartment. He had no idea how much mess a couple of pints of blood could make. Some blood had also splattered onto the furniture which took three attempts to remove. Either of the two .380 rounds which struck Bubka would have been deadly enough. Two did the job with ease, one round had passed through Bubka's body avoiding any bone and had embedded itself in the plasterwork. The bullets had made a real mess and Klaus also had a couple of holes through one of his favourite jackets.

Later in the evening when it was dark Klaus left his apartment. This time he was pulling behind him a four-wheeled 'skate' trolley kindly hired to him for a good price by an English-speaking Turk in return for the German purchasing an expensive big wooden trunk.

Klaus knew exactly where he was going despite it being dark. There was just enough light for him to do what he had planned. He pulled the trolley close to a suitable spot along the creek that he had earmarked earlier in the day. He tipped the trunk on its side and the body of Yuri Bubka rolled like a log down the bank clinking and clanking before splashing into a deep section of water. Bubka's grey-faced body submerged beneath the water in an instant, assisted by an array of heavy chains and shackles. All procured from the local ironmonger and wrapped around the dead Russians limbs and torso.

Klaus calmly thought to himself, this was one dive the Russian submariner would not be surfacing from.

The only evidence remaining was Bubka's wooden baton and his pocketbook, written in Russian, which the German chose to take the risk of retaining should it have any reference to Lothar and the crash site.

CHAPTER 20

REUNITED

Montevideo - Late March 1945

C ontact between them had been kept to a bare minimum, a handful of innocent cryptic telegrams to the offices of the shipping company in Vigo and Montevideo which they both checked in for every other day and felt reassured whenever they saw one.

It was the end of March 1945 and it had been the best part of two months since Klaus had seen his wife and children. He had missed them all desperately. During that time, he had lost his closest friend, their mutual prized asset, and his easiest hope of making his fortune. But he knew there remained other alternatives which were yet to be explored in detail.

He had also murdered a man who had learned of his secret, but he reconciled himself by thinking it was almost self-defence and Germany was at war with Russia. In all honesty, he thought to himself Bubka had it coming because he must have suffocated his friend Lothar Muller. If any man deserved it, then Bubka did.

The German army was in retreat. The war was coming to an end, although Japan was still providing staunch resistance in their war with America. Still, that would be dramatically concluded in six months. Almost everywhere was in chaos. If the reports were to be believed the unanointed victors were already jostling for position to pick over the spoils of war, assets, land, redistribution of wealth and retribution.

Change was a good thing for Klaus's future planning, it created opportunities. He needed to 'keep his powder dry' until the time was right, and he could find the appropriate people to share his knowledge with. People who pay a huge sum of money providing a safe comfortable lifestyle for his family. For now, though, he and Susan had enough money to last them for many months if not years before they got into difficulties. Living in Uruguay was uncomplicated and inexpensive compared to Germany. They had a good back story. They were civilians who were affiliated to the British through Susan and her family. Fleeing persecution, and looking for another life far from war-torn Europe to start over. It wasn't an unusual story.

The Montevideo March summer sun was high in the sky as the steamer came into port. Klaus was waiting, scanning for familiar faces as the ship's propellers trundled to a halt, nudging the vessel up against the rope and rubber buffers. As last, mooring lines were fixed to bollards and passenger ramps were set in place allowing his family to disembark on the port side. The children had spotted him from the ship, and they ran towards their father with scenes joy and excitement, joined by Susan. Smiling, she was relieved to have at last made it to safety, without incident.

"I've missed you. We've all missed you, Klaus." Susan whispered in his ear as they hugged for the first time in several weeks.

"It's so good to see you, Susan. So much has happened."

Klaus had bought a car. It was an almost new black Mercedes-Benz 320. French and German cars were a popular choice at the time in South America, and more accessible than he expected. The children were impressed with the car. It didn't take long before both sons were squabbling over which of them had priority behind the steering wheel. Pretending to drive it as the family luggage was wheeled on a trolley to the car and loaded up. As he watched the porter assist them with the luggage Klaus couldn't help but think back to four weeks earlier. When he had grimly wheeled a similar trolley and trunk himself.

Susan soon snapped him out of his train of thought and asked him, "When did you buy the car and where are we going to be staying?"

He answered by explaining, "I bought it three weeks ago. It's been excellent for driving around looking at suitable properties for us to rent. I've found us somewhere to live, it's a temporary place, on the edge of town not far from the beach with a nice garden. The children will love it."

Susan could feel all the troubles in the world slowly lifting off her shoulders.

As the children sat excited and playing in the back of the car Susan looked at her husband and said again how good it was to see him and that he looked well.

Her next question was, "So how is Lothar, I half expected to see him with you?"

"He didn't make it, there was a problem, I'll explain when we get to the house."

Klaus was right, it was a beautiful property in a lovely location and well within their means. They took in the luggage and had a whirlwind tour of the house and gardens. The children had twin rooms and there was a generous sized master bedroom. Most things had been supplied with the house, including beds and the landlord and previous occupants had left a good selection of other household goods to be getting on with.

There were some chairs in the garden and after familiarising herself with the new home Susan sat down with Klaus. They talked about what had happened to them since they had last met.

Klaus decided he needed to tell Susan the whole sorry tale of what he had seen in the hospital morgue and the aftermath with Yuri Bubka.

"He was blackmailing us, Susan. He had killed Lothar, I'm certain of it, and was either going to kill me there and then or wait until you and the children arrived and continue to pester us and ruin our lives. Besides, he was in the Russian navy, and we are at war with Russia, aren't we?"

"Well, we were Klaus, until we decided to run away. Oh, my God, poor Lothar."

The more Susan listened to her husband, the more she understood the seriousness of the situation he had found himself in. She thought her husband was right, the Russian sailor had pushed him too far, he was terrified. He had then laid his hand on the gun and it was all over in a flash. Things could easily have taken a far different and more painful direction – he could have found himself on the receiving end. Now they had needed to get on with life. Susan consoled her husband and reassured him he had done the right thing for all their sakes.

It was a lovely afternoon so the von der Heyde family walked to the local sandy beach by the nearby harbour. In the previous fortnight, Klaus had rented a small sailing boat to occupy his time. He found the Atlantic Ocean, even on a calm day, a tougher challenge than some of the lakes where he had learned to sail back in Germany. That afternoon they let the children enjoy the sand and the gentle water's edge as the family continued to catch up and talk about the future and their finances.

"We need to wait and see what the outcome of the war will be Susan, nothing can be done until then. It's been made far more complicated now that Lothar and the aircraft have gone."

"But when the time is right, what do you think we should do?" said Susan.

"I don't know who or where yet, but most likely the Americans or the British, or God forbid - maybe even the Russians. One of them will pay me for my knowledge."

He reminded Susan that Uruguay was a safe haven and the country had a long and good relationship with the British. They reassured each other with the knowledge that their children spoke perfect English thanks to Susan's determined and constant use of it in the home. Her husband was also becoming close to fluent. They were in a good position to recalibrate and make a good life in Uruguay. Their medium-term plan, if they had ever needed it, included looking for work either as language or science teachers.

Despite everything that had happened to them, her private message to her father which led to the bombing of the airbase was a secret that Susan would never share with her husband.

CHAPTER 21
FACE IN THE CROWD

Montevideo - 1945

When Susan von der Heyde and her family had disembarked at the end of March, the children weren't the only ones to have had a spark of recognition when they saw their father waiting on the harbourside.

~

It was now mid-May, after six weeks, the von der Heyde's had extended the rental term on their new home. Susan thought Klaus had chosen well, it suited their needs to perfection. The children were excitable and forever playing games together in the garden, always needing to be called several times to come inside. They had also made some friends in the local area, usually when they went to the beach and it wasn't long before they were picking up some Spanish words. Susan was schooling them at home until she and her husband had figured out what the longer-term plan for everyone was going to be.

Things had taken a positive step forward in early May 1945 when the war in Europe with Germany ended. For what it was worth, Uruguay had also declared war on Germany in February 1945. Surely the pressure was off to some extent, thought the von der Heydes.

By early July, the war with Germany had been over a couple of months and Klaus was beginning to get impatient. He decided to move things along with their 'intellectual property' business opportunity as he preferred to describe things whenever he chatted about it with Susan.

He knew he needed to make some contacts that could lead him to the pot of 'anti-gravity gold'. He was first and foremost a scientist and not a businessman, let alone a salesman and he was hesitant about where to begin his commercial quest.

There was so much turmoil in the region, fascism was on the rise in several countries, and America was bleeding South American countries dry with harsh trade deals. Cuba was showing some support for Russia. It was a bun fight, every region wanted to be everyone else's best friend.

During the war, Germany had a huge network of spies in South America based out of Argentina.

"*Where had they all gone?*" Klaus wondered.

He knew he could easily make a mistake by talking to the wrong people and had become indecisive and nervous.

In October 1945, after mulling things over and getting nowhere fast for months, Klaus saw an advertisement in the business section of an international farming magazine. He had been reading whatever he could get his hands on in English or German and this magazine was sitting there in a local barbershop. He wasn't interested in farming, but it did have a huge article and a four-page spread about Expo 45. It was a significant trade show that was going to be taking place in Buenos Aires, in Argentina. It was not just for farming but construction, engineering, aviation, and technology. Manufacturers or their agents and distributors from all over the world were expected to be there promoting their goods and services. It was in three days and an impatient Klaus decided he needed to be there to find out if it would create any opportunities for him.

Argentina borders Uruguay to its south. Buenos Aires and Montevideo are about 100 miles apart as the crow flies. Thirty miles if crossed from Colonia del Sacramento with ferries running several times a day.

It was early on Thursday morning and Klaus was on the first ferry to Argentina. He had not taken any detailed anti-gravity information with him to Expo 45. It was more of a reconnaissance trip to attempt to find a route to market for what he knew and was capable of creating for the right organisation.

The exhibition was taking place at a converted warehouse in the port which conveniently meant a short walk from the ferry. It was an open public area and Argentina was a much different country to Uruguay. The Argentines were a sympathetic friend to the Nazi regime. Thousands of Germans had flooded into the country during and after the war.

After finding a good breakfast Klaus wandered into the tall old building. It had a multitude of windows providing excellent light over its three floors for the exhibitors. He had never been to a place like this before, in fact, he had never been to an exhibition and wasn't sure what to expect. Larger product manufacturers for farm equipment and automobiles were all on the ground floor making it easy for them to get in and out with their latest models. He stopped in his tracks as he watched a salesman in a blue boiler suit from a Swedish milking machine company herd in some Friesian cows. He hooked them up to a vacuum pump device and begin milking them in front of a growing crowd of onlookers. A fifty-litre glass bottle at the end of the row of cows gradually began filling up with fresh milk that had just passed through a heat exchanger to chill it. Avid spectators were sampling paper cups full of the cold creamy milk. Klaus couldn't resist the temptation either.

"How amazing," he thought.

As he moved away from the farming equipment, he began to see signs for Mercedes, Citroen, Renault, and Ford. They were displaying an impressive array of cars supported by an array of over-enthusiastic, smartly dressed demonstrators.

The entry ticket that he bought earlier, included a guide map to find his way around the building. He could see from the list there were some aircraft manufacturers on it whose main purpose was to cater to the farming market. Crop spraying and small commercial shuttle flight airlines were growing businesses.

Klaus soon spotted something which struck a chord with him. The American trade mission offering investment opportunities to and from the USA. They were going to be holding a symposium in an hour, at ten a.m. He thought it could be a good networking and information gathering session and needed to be there.

Arriving for the seminar fifteen minutes early he found himself one row back from the front in a room that had wooden seats for about sixty people. Two minutes to go and the room had filled up and was now thick with various brands of tobacco smoke and there was a noticeable increase in the noise level.

A slick-haired, moustached, and sharp-suited American representative was introduced by the head of the local chamber of commerce to warm applause. He went on to write on a chalkboard explaining the various enticing statistics of the benefits of trading with America, adding some household brand names as an attention-getter. It had become apparent in the weeks after the war the allies, in particular the Americans, were legally confiscating whatever patents or technological know-how ever existed in Germany. The country itself had been divided into four sectors being controlled by the Americans, French, British and Russians.

The event lasted forty-five minutes and at the end, Klaus waited his turn for the opportunity of a brief discussion with the American. Klaus introduced himself as an independent consultant with a strong scientific background. He explained he was interested in getting in touch with American organisations involved in the aviation or defence sectors as he had some exciting new technological ideas to share with them. He added that he had applied for patents, so could not discuss the specific details at the time.

The American was full of enthusiasm.

He suggested to Klaus, "You must join me for a drink at lunchtime. I'll introduce you to some senior executives from potential American partners. It could be a fantastic opportunity for you."

Klaus apologised for not having a business card but graciously accepted the offer.

"Thank you, I'll be there, I look forward to it."

As he made his way through the aisle to exit at the rear of the room, he didn't notice the two men who were sitting over to the far corner of the room who had been glancing in his direction. The men had their visitor name badges pinned to their lapels saying they both worked for "Erneuern Deutsch" (German Regeneration). It was a small business funded by an American investment bank that was looking to squeeze everything they could out of the devastated German regime and find any opportunities that emerged. The truth was they were hired because they had once worked as part of the German spy network that operated in the South American region before their allegiances and skills were taken on by the highest bidders. They had overheard Klaus talking and were interested in him, his name badge had given away the fact that he was German.

Klaus had registered for the exhibition using the alias, *Klaus Schmitt*, it was about as vague as he could make it, or so he thought. He had a back story if he was caught unawares saying he had worked in a laboratory in Germany before the war for a Swiss pharmaceutical company and he and his English wife had moved to Zurich during the war.

The lunch networking drinks meeting with the Americans went well. They were the kind of people Klaus thought he could cultivate. They were also people that had the potential to be just one step away from opening the right door for him to the right organisation, they were well connected. He had made some solid connections that he intended to follow up and then started to make his way home.

The two Germans had also become more inquisitive and had done some digging at the registration area and they left with *Klaus Schmitt's* name and his Montevideo address which he had unwittingly listed on arrival. Information gathering was their speciality, so was information sharing.

~

It was mid-November, five weeks after the exhibition. Klaus had been making tentative written contact and going through a list of follow up long-distance telephone calls. The calls were to some American organisations which were referrals that had resulted from his networking lunch. He told Susan he had not shown his hand to anyone yet, but in fact, there had been some positive correspondence and discussions. He felt he was getting closer to the stage where he would disclose more information to them. He would also need to tell Susan. He had a plan up his sleeve and thought he might have no alternative other than to travel to America for discussions when the time was right, which might be sooner than expected.

Meanwhile, he was continuing to pursue his pleasant lifestyle in the Uruguayan summer sunshine and his yachting skills had improved to a respectable standard. With living costs low and decent finances, he had joined the local yacht club and bought himself a well-used twenty-nine-foot dragon class sailboat which was moored in the local marina. Susan was not happy, she thought it was a frivolous investment and they needed to conserve their money. A bullish Klaus ignored his wife's thrifty words. He was adamant it wouldn't be long before he would make the final breakthrough with some American company that he was convinced would jump at the chance to pay for his knowledge, the Americans were very keen.

~

A fifteen-foot long white pole with its black and red banner fluttering on the breeze had been erected in his garden to indicate wind speed and direction. It suggested it was about five to ten knots, a perfect morning to go sailing. Klaus kissed Susan and the children and told them he would be back by five p.m., asking his wife if there was anything, he needed to bring back for them from the local store. A trip to the baker was her simple request.

He began his usual fifteen-minute drive to the Cuchilla Alta marina. Within minutes of setting off in his car, he passed over a small bridge as he always did to get to the marina. He recalled he was passing over Carrasco Creek where further up, several months earlier, he had unceremoniously dumped the body of Yuri Bubka. It didn't resonate with him that much anymore.

He parked the Mercedes in the marina car park, registered his route in the book at the clubhouse entrance, which was the protocol. He prepared his boat and set off for his trip in an easterly direction towards one of his favourite sailing landmarks, Isla Gorriti. This was a trip he did once or twice a week as the scenery was amazing and it involved an interesting circumnavigation of the beautiful little island.

The north-westerly breeze had picked up to around ten to fifteen knots, but there was no moisture in it. The warmth of the sun was reflecting off the deck and rigging and he could see pin-sharp coastline ten miles each way. Seagulls were also enjoying it as they swirled in and around Klaus's yacht. As he tacked across the slightly choppy water within an hour the old white Punta del Este lighthouse came into view on the famous headland peninsula. This was his target and he decided to position himself to approach and make a clockwise loop of Isla Gorriti before heading for home. This was a manoeuvre he had done on numerous occasions before and in more challenging conditions than on that day.

Rambla General Jose Artigas was classed as a road, although it was more of a dusty track running along the undeveloped headland of the peninsula. It overlooked the little Isla Gorriti that was not much more than 500 metres away across the water from the small pull-in spot which Peter Knecht had expertly chosen for himself.

Knecht was a member of the network of Germans who were in constant communication with each other during the war. They shared information about shipping movements in and out of the British friendly Montevideo harbour and gathered intelligence concerning the comings and goings of passengers at the port. Knecht was with a colleague at the port six months earlier when they were collecting a fellow countryman who was going to be working with them.

The new man arriving was a former high-ranking Nazi Luftwaffe officer who was 'redeploying' to Uruguay. As he disembarked, he thought that from a distance he had recognised a familiar face in the crowd, someone he had met in the past. Although uncertain he mentioned it to his new colleague, Knecht, who noted it down and diligently shared it with his network. What the Luftwaffe officer hadn't realised at the time, he had seen the von der Heyde family, including Klaus as he was greeting them.

As weeks went by the Luftwaffe officer discovered the secret airbase had been destroyed two or three days after Klaus suspiciously went missing. He then remembered the face in the crowd had been Klaus von der Heyde and that he must have been connected to the timely devastating bombing of the airbase. What he didn't know was it had not been Klaus, but it was his wife Susan, who had been responsible for the unexpected and spectacular attack. Peter Knecht had several specialist skillsets and on more than one occasion he had been called on to 'tidy up' some loose ends - thanks to his well-proven ability with a sniper rifle. The war was over but some wrongdoings against his former countrymen still needed to be redressed in the eyes of some.

Knecht had been patient, waiting for his moment for several days, and this was how he had chosen to carry out the simple task. He had been checking the routes registered in the book by the various yacht club members and could see a pattern over the weeks of Klaus von der Heyde's favourite days, times, and trips. That day, Knecht had waited and watched his fellow German leave home and followed him. Not long after Klaus had set off in his boat, Knecht looked in the book checked the trip and knew he had well over an hour to make the fifteen-minute drive to the headland opposite Isla Gorriti and wait for his prey.

He sat peacefully in his black Citroen. He hadn't seen a soul for thirty minutes. The sun was high and behind him and he had a twelve-knot tailwind with a twenty-metre drop in elevation. He then wound down the passenger window and gently rested his Mauser 98K 'byf 44' Sniper Rifle with ZF41/1 Telescopic Sight onto the windowsill. The killing range of the Mauser was up to a thousand metres with the 4 X sights fitted. This was going to be easy.

Peter Knecht had observed Klaus's little boat approaching him from three kilometres away, he was now at a thousand metres. Five 7.92×57mm Mauser rounds were loaded from a clipper cartridge into the weapon's internal magazine. He cycled the bolt action and a bullet was in the chamber and ready to fire.

The boat was no more than 300 metres away when it slowed to less than 5 knots as it changed tack. Knecht took aim at Klaus's head, breathed in, exhaled a fraction, held his breath then softly squeezed the trigger.

He continued to watch the deadly result through his scope. There was a spray of red mist as the wind blew part of his targets shattered head onto the white sail. Klaus then tumbled backwards and was dead before he hit the water. A rope had become looped around his foot and he was being slowly towed face down behind the boat as it continued on its path out into the Atlantic.

CHAPTER 22
THE RUSSIAN CONNECTION

Moscow - Spring 2018

In the spring of 2018, at his beautiful home in a south-west Moscow suburb, having been targeted with sponsored ads via social media and email, senior executive Anton Bubka succumbed, deciding to have his first stab at building his family tree. Several of his friends and family had been having some great fun doing it. Some made outrageous claims to being related to royalty or Rasputin, so he subscribed to a free trial with RussianAncestry.ru. It was a nice relaxing distraction from his long hours as an executive board director for an organisation called Sirin who was one of Russia's biggest private aerospace and defence contractors.

Within weeks, Anton was hooked, he had gone back several hundred years with one of his family lines and before long, he had something to shout about. Ivan IV Vasilyevich the first Tsar of Russia was his seventeen times great grandfather, he was thrilled. Having found some glory Anton then decided to do some investigation a little closer to home, using the Bubka family name. His mother had kept all sorts of old documents and pictures which he had seen when he was younger but had never given much attention to them at the time.

Forty-one-year-old Anton Bubka's mother was in her seventies and was still a spritely woman. One Sunday evening after a family get together, she went into a trunk and pulled out some information to show her son to assist with his family tree endeavours.

She paused at one or two of the pictures. They were images of a young man in his white navy uniform stood on the deck of what looked like a submarine. His mother explained the pictures were of Anton's grandfather, Yuri, taken at the start of the war with Germany. He had died soon after the war. She said he had been staying in South America after an illness and planning to come home, but he never made it.

"We think he'd been spending weeks and weeks trying to find a sunken Japanese submarine full of gold. It's obvious, he never found it, isn't it." she laughed, looking around her smart but not palatial apartment.

She also passed Anton a handful of the letters that were bundled up and said he could keep them.

Later that evening when Anton's two kids were in bed and his wife was watching a reality TV show, he was more relaxed. So he decided to browse through the bundle of letters which his mother had given to him. The majority of the letters were from Yuri to Yuri's older brother for whom he had had great affection.

One of the letters was dated 20th February 1945, sent whilst Yuri was in a hospital, as the envelope clearly showed the hospital postmark. He had mentioned 'the German with the bends' and touched on some of his fellow sufferer's ramblings. With brief details, Yuri described how the German had allegedly claimed to have been a pilot yet there had been no record of a plane crash. The letter went on to explain how the man was getting confused and mistaking Yuri for a scientist friend called Klaus, then talking about an unusual aircraft which had flown him from Germany to South America in just a few hours.

A later letter dated Saturday 3rd March 1945 fascinated Anton. This time Yuri was more animated in his writing, telling his brother the more he had listened to the German the more he had become convinced there was a great deal of truth in his ramblings. Yuri said he had pretended to be

Klaus and played along for hours on end, gleaning Klaus's surname was von der Heyde and had learned details about his family coming to join him in Uruguay on the Habana steamer.

The German in the hospital with the bends, who Yuri named in his letter as Lothar Muller, had also expressed concerns. He was trying to understand how he and Klaus were going to be able to cash in on the knowledge of the 'anti-gravity' aircraft now that it had crashed and lay at the bottom of the sea. He had kept asking 'Klaus' if his journals and the technical information was safe and secure and who was Klaus intending to sell it to. How much was it likely to be worth – and would they become the millionaires they had expected to become.

Also explaining in his letter he needed as much money as possible to fund his search for a Japanese sub that he knew to be full of gold. Yuri said he was determined to find it one day. He said he had an idea to trick von der Heyde into giving him some money in return for information about Lothar Muller's whereabouts.

In his letter, Yuri ended his reference to the German men by saying once he was discharged from the hospital, he went to a hotel in Montevideo. Where Lothar had explained he planned to meet with his old friend and colleague Klaus von der Heyde.

Yuri said he had waited in the lounge of the hotel, at two p.m. on Friday the 2nd of March in 1945. There were a dozen or more people around, but none of them looked European, except for one fair-haired man sat at a table, drinking coffee, and smoking a pipe. Yuri approached him and asked if he was Klaus, he had hesitated, looked uncertain before saying he wasn't but why had Yuri wanted to know. When Yuri told him he knew where he could find his friend Lothar, Klaus's demeanour had changed considerably, his body turned square on to Yuri and eyes became wide open.

It would appear Yuri had not been diplomatic with the persistent, blunt approach he had made to von der Heyde and was rebuffed. Yuri said he felt Muller's ramblings had been right about von der Heyde and he was certain they both had a secret. After leaving the hotel Yuri had followed von der Heyde to his apartment to find out where he lived so that he could get to the bottom of it and to then try and make some money. Yuri also said he was going to bide his time for the time being.

There were no more letters to his brother. Indeed, there were no more letters to anyone.

CHAPTER 23

CHRISTOF

Most Russians like a drink. The truth is most Russians like vodka. As a young man serving in the army posted to some of the more dangerous hotspots in the Caucasus and later in the FSB - the Russian secret service, Christof Sorotkin had developed a serious taste for it. Although it tended to be heavy binge drinking rather than regular daily sessions. As is often the case, his dependencies weren't confined to alcohol and later in his career, he found himself racking up huge amounts of debt through his gambling habits. Gambling is banned in Russia apart from four far-flung outposts and other illegal betting rackets found in most cities.

Sorotkin's heavy drinking, partying and in particular, his gambling activities were flagged up to his bosses in the FSB who considered him as too much of a risk as it could lead to him being compromised.

The final straw came one Friday evening in the fashionable Tverskoy area of Moscow. Sorotkin had been partying in the districts trendy bar area with a male friend before getting into an ugly 'bloody' fight with some doormen who had ejected him.

Before the fight with the doormen broke out, Sorotkin and his friend had been stood at the bar next to a young man who was out with his girlfriend and having a pleasant evening. A drunk Sorotkin loudly passed comment on the young woman's skimpy dress and the ample curves that were inside it. The boyfriend wasn't impressed and threatened to punch Sorotkin, who flipped in a split second into a drunken rage. Launching into a brief but frenzied attack on the young man. It was all over in less than twenty seconds. The young man lay face down in a pool of blood that was pouring from a gash above his eye and a deep split in his lip. The screaming girlfriend foolishly tried to intervene and received a 'straight left' punch which sat her down on to the beer-soaked floor, with a golf ball-sized bump emerging high on her forehead.

Four huge musclebound doormen pounced and dragged Sorotkin and his friend outside the bar. Two more giant doormen joined the melee battering both men with their telescopic steel nightsticks. When the beating relented, covered in blood Sorotkin and his friend managed to get to their feet limped off to find their car which they had parked a block away. A drunk and dazed Sorotkin struggled but drove the car, then minutes later he mounted a curb and crashed into the central reservation of a boulevard ploughing into some small trees dividing the two roads. The car was undrivable. The police arrived in no time, and the two men spent most of the night in a police cell until someone who Sorotkin worked with was notified. Some strings were pulled, and he was allowed to be taken home. That's when his career finished, he had risen up through the ranks and had become a senior officer, but it ended there, he was a liability and an embarrassment. However, he had plenty of well-placed friends and many other people he had "helped out" over the years, so he found an abundance of private security and investigative work in the business world for wealthy masters.

Through his connections, he was one of several people who could be called on to do some dirty work when Russian officials wanted to keep a little distance between themselves and a specific problem. He was called in at short notice to get involved with the Usmanovas when their daughter Alina was abducted and found himself in London.

Most things in his life were back on an even keel. He had learnt his lesson the hard way and his previous problems and risk-taking were at last under control.

CHAPTER 24

GREY DIAMOND

Montevideo - July 2019

After a fifteen-hour overnight flight, including a brief transfer in Sao Paulo, Wil, Emma and Frea were all keen to step into the Uruguayan July winter's morning sunshine. With a four hour difference, after some sleep on the plane then a brief leg-stretch in Brazil everyone was wide-eyed, chatty, and striding along, passports at the ready.

The trio rolled their cases through customs and out towards the arrivals greeting area at Carrasco International airport. One of the first people they saw was a smiling dark-haired young woman holding a printed piece of paper with the name 'Richardson Party' on it.

Wil approached the young woman with a grin and said, "Hi, are you, Melissa, by any chance?"

"Yes, I am. Welcome to Uruguay. You must be Wil...and Emma and Frea, hello everyone." announced an enthusiastic Melissa.

Wil introduced Emma and Frea who were both keen to know what the weather was like at that time of the year. They were pleased with Melissa's response and made a mental note that they had brought the right clothing.

Melissa led them to her vehicle, not knowing how much luggage they might bring or where they might need to go. She had rented a decent-sized Ford 4x4. Her environmentally-friendly Nissan Leaf was never going to work.

She said, "Mr Chalk gave me your driving details Wil, so you are also insured if I'm not around."

"He thinks of everything doesn't he," said Emma as she gazed out the window at the beautiful city trying to catch glimpses of the ocean.

They agreed in the car they would check in to their hotel, freshen up and Melissa would remain downstairs until they were ready to regroup. They also liked Melissa's suggestion of grabbing some breakfast as the hotel's restaurant buffet would still be open.

Wil mischievously asked Melissa how she came to be appointed as their official guide, "Have you got 'best rating award' on trip advisor or something?"

They all laughed out loud including Melissa who diplomatically responded by saying, "A friend of a friend passed on Mr Chalk's request and here I am, at your disposal guys."

It was obvious, the Lucidity Programme team weren't going to get a straight answer from her, not just yet.

It was late morning, the buffet had been a great idea, everyone looked in good spirits and raring to go. Melissa explained she thought they might do an initial familiarisation 'recce' of the city. They could check out its landmarks and surrounding area for a couple of hours to give them their bearings. She also said she had been given some thorough background information by Phil Chalk.

Frea smiled to herself, *"Of course it was thorough, it was from Phil Chalk, Mr Thorough himself."*

Melissa added, "Some of it must be classified information. I haven't been told everything. So, I wanted to hear from you what things are the important points of interest for the duration of your trip? Where am I taking you? What do you need to see? What information are you looking for?"

Emma started by telling Melissa, "We discussed it before we set off and whilst we were on the plane. We need to meet with the von der Heyde descendants - Julia and Edmund. They are Clara's children and they are expecting us. We also want to find out more about Klaus and Susan's lifestyle before Klaus died and in the years after that - before Susan decided to go back to the UK with Tilda. What was the city like in those days? Where did people spend their time? What could Klaus have been getting up to?"

Wil pointed out they also had a diary which once belonged to Klaus which he had also used it as a notebook. In it, he had made some scant reference to places they presumed were in Montevideo at the time.

Wil then said, "Melissa, there were some phrases scribbled in the book for example – 'Hospital Británico?' 'Yuri Bubka, Japanese submarine, Russian submarine?' 'Lothar Haas?' 'The naval base?' 'The bends?' 'Hotel Carrasco?' Do they make any sense to you?"

"Yes, some of them do. Let's take a drive shall we and talk more on the way? I'll show you my city."

The team started with an initial hour-long historical tour of Montevideo's major landmarks and with some cultural explanations of food, religion and demographics thrown in for good measure by a thorough Melissa. Perhaps she was a genuine tourist guide, after all, wondered a still rather sceptical Wil about their chaperone.

Melissa was in her element. Her enthusiasm was infectious and if she ever needed investors for an open-top bus tour business all three would have contributed.

As they circled anti-clockwise passing around the famous 'Fountain Rome to the City of Montevideo' and headed east along Avenue Italia, Wil suddenly shouted, "Stop! Stop! Here Stop. We need to get out."

Everyone in the car did an urgent double take, looking around, inside and outside the car, then back at Wil.

Wil was in the front seat, Emma leaned forwards and asked him "What's wrong? Are you OK? What's the matter?"

As Melissa found a suitable pull in and came to a halt, Wil explained he knew the old building on their right-hand side. He had seen it in his dream with Clara.

A puzzled Melissa was still trying to understand what Wil had said. Something about seeing something in a dream. She wondered if she had misheard him.

All four of them got out of the 4x4 and wandered across to the front of the grand old building. They stood outside on the pavement looking through the railings. Carved into the apex of the façade, under a coat of arms, in big proud letters was 'British Hospital'. Further along at the side of the building was a stone plaque which said it was a memorial built in 1912 to King Edward VII.

"It's now a private hospital. But it has been here for a long time, of course, I think they have a small museum inside. Maybe I can arrange for us to take a look." said Melissa.

Their request was granted and inside they went. The interior of the building was almost as impressive as the exterior, although far more modernised.

The group of 'scientific' tourists didn't know what they were looking for if anything. They were shown around as far as was permissible by a middle-aged lady. She pointed out some of the historical pieces of medical equipment and nurses' uniforms they had retained. Wil wanted to know if they had kept any patient records or other items from the past eighty years. Melissa had been translating and at the end of the little tour, she explained there was nothing kept in the building anymore. But there was a city archives department and her uncle held a senior position, high up in the city council, she could ask him if he could help them.

Melissa made the call to her uncle who put her in touch with someone at the Biblioteca Nacional D' Uruguay. An hour later the four of them were sat in the bowels of a huge old building on Avenida de Julio. There, a man in his late sixties with a bushy grey handlebar moustache called Raul shuffled gingerly along the corridor to meet them. From his appearance, it looked as though Raul had spent his entire life in the building and had never surfaced to see the light of day. His flawless moustache complimented his grey hair, grey trousers and white shirt and double knotted dark blue tie. Although the image that presented itself before them was not enhanced by the unshielded old neon light tube above their heads. The last time it was clean must have been ten years earlier when it had replaced its predecessor.

Looks can be deceptive, as he greeted them all he smiled warmly and there was a definite spark of enthusiasm emerging. It was noticeable as soon as Melissa explained to him what they were interested in knowing. There was a lot of positive gesticulating, affirmative Latin American body language and numerous si, si, si's coming from Raul. It looked as though he was getting excited.

"He said we need to follow him, this way," Melissa led the group.

To his credit, as soon as Raul took the earlier call from Melissa, he had set off on his mission to help. He knew the department like the back of his hand, and the prospect of retrieving documents or items that had not been requested for decades was an interesting challenge for him.

They walked through another door and Raul flicked a switch which triggered clicking and flickering of about hundred more neon tubes. The harsh neon illuminated a thirty-metre long room packed full of steel cabinets and open steel-framed racking which went all the way up to the top of a fifteen feet high ceiling.

A smiling Raul stood proudly in front of a section of racking which had dozens and dozens of boxes all stacked in neat order and categorised with numbers and a familiar coded square sticker on the front of each box.

A triumphant Raul pointed at a typical sticker, stood back with folded arms, and proudly announced, "Si, QR code."

Everyone laughed and Emma couldn't resist a quip, "Wow, QR codes, Raul. Check you out."

They all laughed again, including Raul as he understood the sentiment.

The reason behind it was that a shrewd Raul had learned about QR codes (quick response bar codes) three years ago where they were first developed in the automotive industry. He then got a team of archivist undergraduates to come in for four weeks and transform the document categorisation in the room.

Raul pointed out two boxes in particular that he wanted them to pull off the lower shelves, fortunately, it meant they didn't need a ladder. They extracted the boxes. Each box was the size of about a three drawer bedside pedestal and was placed on a nearby reference table. Raul took out a smartphone and scanned the nearest box.

Melissa explained this section was a selective archive from the old hospital. They didn't keep everything just items of interest or curiosity items as they were described. The items here were from the 1940s.

"Aquí está Senor Lothar Haas," explained Raul.

"That's bloody amazing," said Wil, who didn't understand the first part, but he knew for sure he understood the last second two words. "I think he just said, Lothar Haas."

The dusty lid was lifted off the first box and placed aside it. Inside was a heavy grey woollen jacket, a pair of black leather gloves, and a brown leather 'airman's' helmet.

Frea reached inside the pockets of the jacket and pulled out two or three folded pieces of paper which had some notes scribbled on them.

"It's in German."

She was nervous as she unfolded the papers, wondering what precious facts they might contain.

With an occasional pause to speak out, Frea explained there were names, "Klaus, Susan, kinder, Tilda, Clara."

There also appeared to be various dates, hotel locations and other remarks the team presumed had been noted down before Lothar Muller's condition had worsened.

Emma had barely enough signal due to where they were in the old building. But her phone's travel app managed to translate the German words in seconds, "It says, Bubka, Russian sub sinks Japanese sub and various numbers which don't mean anything to me at the moment. What a find, this is incredible for us guys,"

Wil was excited and decided he wanted to look inside box number two. The lid was removed to reveal what at first glance appeared to be a huge white silk sheet.

On closer inspection and lifting it out of the box it started to unfurl, cords, straps and silk were everywhere.

"Parachute." said an equally intrigued Raul, no translation needed.

The curiosity of all four people drew them to the enormous piece of white silk. They all simultaneously took an edge and then stepping a couple of paces backwards unravelled a long length of it.

Melissa was fascinated but didn't understand the significance of the parachute. Wil, Emma and Frea knew exactly where it came from and who used it. It belonged to Lothar Muller who had been in hospital under the name Haas.

Wil didn't mention anything to anyone, although Emma picked up on Wil's demeanour straight away. He was the one who lingered the most, for ages, gazing at the parachute. Running its silk through his fingers time and again. Tugging at its para-chords and straps. Clipping and unclipping its buckles.

A humbled Wil was deep in thought, *"I'm the reason were are all stood here holding this dead man's parachute. I'm the reason and there's a reason behind it. Let's keep going."*

Wil and Emma exchanged knowing glances and didn't say a word.

There was some further discussion between Raul and Melissa. When they finished talking Melissa explained that Raul had some more information which he had printed off before they arrived.

They all took a final look inside the boxes and went through the pockets of the jacket. Wil grabbed another tactile handful of the silk running it through his fingers for one final time before tucking it back into its box.

Wil was still holding the scraps of paper and asked Melissa if there was any way they could hang onto them. After some further Spanish linguistics were exchanged, there was a satisfying, "Si," from Raul.

As they returned to the area where they first met Raul he disappeared and then returned five minutes later with three printed pages which he gave to Melissa.

She told her new friends that the papers were copies of a scan of old hospital records that had been put on microfiche. They contained details of the hospital admissions from the time and went into detail about Lothar Haas. Dates, notable events and much more. They also explained where he was buried.

None of the group of friends had any idea what they would encounter in the antiquated old building. They all offered sincere thanks to Raul.

A beaming Wil said, "You're a diamond Raul, an absolute diamond."

Melissa shared that with the grey man, and she could tell he appreciated it as he gave Wil a friendly hug and a pat on the back with a big smile.

As they headed back to the car, an exuberant Wil said, "Guys it's nearly teatime, I think we owe a huge thanks to Melissa and we should celebrate by grabbing some tapas and a beer to celebrate our first little piece of Uruguayan progress."

CHAPTER 25
EMERGING PICTURE

Montevideo - July 2019

Their new acquaintance and guide had proved herself to be far more than they had been expecting. She was extremely resourceful and appeared to be more than willing to go the extra mile for them. They found themselves being driven down a dusty, bumpy dirt road before pulling up at an out of town fish restaurant overlooking the Atlantic Ocean. Wil asked Emma to order for him and excused himself to make a call. It was early evening in Wiltshire and Phil Chalk answered the call almost immediately, he was still at work although most people had gone home.

"Hi Phil, it's Wil. How are you? I'm glad I caught you, have you got a couple of minutes?"

"Of course, Wil, nice to hear from you. How was your flight? I hope things are going OK for you all."

Wil gave Chalk an update on the journey, how they had settled in nicely and was quick to point out how helpful Melissa had been in just hours since arriving. He also explained the exciting afternoon they'd had and gave some details to Chalk saying he would be sending images of the archived boxes, scraps of paper and Muller's hospital admission notes within minutes.

"So, this was a brief initial update for you Phil, a pretty thought-provoking one at that, eh? But one more thing, I feel we need to be more open with Melissa, she's integral to this visit and has already been crucial to us... what's the score with her Phil?"

Phil Chalk paused then responded, "Wil I'm glad you asked that, and your feedback has been perfect. Ok, Melissa Benitez, well... let's just say she has signed the 'official secrets act'. She's more of a 'tour guide with benefits' if you know what I mean. Speak freely with her Wil, it's fine, you have my authority. By the way, send me any information you find straight away as it gives me more time to investigate at this end with the time difference. Thanks again Wil."

Wil returned to the bar, where there was half a litre of cold *cabesas* beer waiting for him, with condensation all around the glass. It tasted as good as anything he could ever remember. Emma was quick to point out there was a big selection of tapas *en route* and that everyone could relax.

Melissa had popped to the ladies room, so Wil took the opportunity to apologise to Frea and Emma for going missing for the past ten minutes. He told them about his quick chat with Phil Chalk. They all agreed that it made sense to enlighten Melissa otherwise they would be hamstrung and said it had been pretty obvious she was more than just a guide.

When she returned the three Lucidity Programme team members gave Melissa a full account of events over the past several months and explained at length to her why they had found themselves in Uruguay.

"Amazing. Wow, amazing. How exciting," there was a genuine tone of intrigue from Melissa.

Pointing out she was here to help them, her instructions had been to provide whatever they needed, and take them wherever they needed to go.

"We're all more or less on the same team," said a smiling Melissa, raising her small beer and encouraging a toast over the centre of the table.

"Salud."

"Cheers."

"And I think we need to say a German one for Lothar eh guys? Prost," said Frea.

They sat and chatted, then took photos of Lothar Muller's information and sent it to Phil Chalk.

The conversation came back around to the obscure comments in Klaus's original notebook that Chalk gave them in the UK. It had led to the Hospital and Lothar Muller and it appeared their quest was going to involve looking for more similar information. Maybe more notebooks.

"Everyone seemed to have a pocketbook back in those days, didn't they?" said Wil.

Frea commented, "No mobile phones, not many landlines, no computers, people kept their lives in them, addresses because they wrote lots of letters, birthday reminders, things they saw or needed to remember. Everything."

Emma commented, "C'mon guys, you remember the resurgence of the Filofax don't you. Admit it, you all had one back in the 90s... apart from you Wil."

Wil smiled and raised his eyebrows. "You got me there Em'. No, I didn't."

Emma then used her Google translate app which she would often use for reading travelling information when overseas. This time it came handy for translating more of Lothar Muller's handwritten pieces of paper.

"How cool is that," she said.

Having taken the time to scan and share the images with her companions, they all sat in silence reading through the little notes. Having been so integrally involved with everything for several weeks, more of the earlier writings in Klaus's notebooks contents resonated with the three from the UK, less so with their new friend. But Melissa was no doubt a pretty smart woman and was soon passing some pertinent comments about it.

Emma felt it was good to have Melissa on board, she had been slightly nervous about the 'expedition' before they left, but now she was far more comfortable with everything. Melissa was a good call by Phil Chalk, she thought to herself.

The group ended up having a big brainstorming session, an exchange of ideas and theories. Including lots of corroborated facts, plenty of suppositions and possibilities with a bunch of coincidences thrown in.

Melissa's constant enthusiastic charm suddenly became more focused and 'parked' as she wanted to make a brief point, "I don't believe in coincidences."

She then reminded everyone about one of the pages Raul had printed off regarding the 1945 hospital admission documentation.

Holding it in front of her and translating as she went, "Yuri Bubka, Russian submariner with the bends. On the same ward as Lothar 'Haas', Muller?"

She wouldn't let it go and continued to focus on Bubka's timely departure soon after Muller died. Then she cross-referenced the name Yuri Bubka mentioned in Klaus von der Heyde's diary/notebook.

"Russians, Bubka, Christof, there is your connection guys. There's more, but we haven't managed to figure it out yet have we? But we will," stated the impressive Melissa.

For the time being, they had plenty of facts to go through thanks to Raul's hospital records which identified the name of Bubka's submarine. They agreed to email Chalk to check that out for them overnight and to find out any reference to a Japanese submarine which was described by Muller in his papers.

Melissa gave them all a cautionary note, "The hospital notes said that Muller had bouts of confusion brought on by the seriousness of his bends.

So there was a chance that some information was incorrect."

She also wondered whether or not he may have been physically able to have written any of the confusing notes and numbers after he parachuted into the park.

Frea, with her medical background, suggested, "Clinically Muller could have written the notes in his first days, or at a stretch, weeks. If his illness had gotten progressively worse towards his death, then it would have been impossible. I think what Muller wrote was probably correct."

After a coffee, the group agreed on a plan of action for the next morning. Melissa would pick them up at ten a.m. and they would meet Clara's daughter Julia at her coffee shop. After that, they would go and see Julia's brother Edmund at his garage, leaving plenty of time to slot in other ideas or places of interest throughout the day.

Wil commented, "I'd also like to pay a visit to the grave of Lothar Muller at some point during the day. If it's OK with everyone? There's something remarkable about the guy."

It had been a full-on day, they were wilting and decided to relax for the rest of the evening.

~

The Pocitos district of Montevideo is a smart and trendy area with some lovely shops and cafes. That was where the team arrived to meet with an English-speaking Julia, Klaus's granddaughter, at her café bar. All the staff including Julia were decked out in either black skirts or trousers, black shirts with collars and full-length barista type aprons. Julia was in her late forties, with a blonde ponytail. She appeared to be a fit woman, seeming to be much younger than her years.

They were welcomed in. The breakfast rush had gone and there was a slight lull before lunchtime, so Julia had plenty of time for them. One of Julia's staff took their order for some refreshments and they found a quiet table overlooking the street.

Julia smiled as she told them, "My aunt Tilda has been telling me all about the lovely people that visited her at the Spires in Oxford. Especially you Wil...sorry ladies."

Everyone laughed.

Wil was embarrassed, "Thank you so much for seeing us Julia, I'm pleased that Tilda has spoken so highly of us, especially of me. She is a lovely lady. I like her."

Drinks arrived and they chatted about Uruguay and Europe. Before long they got around to why Clara and Tilda had passed on what they did to the science people in the UK.

Julia explained, in her excellent English, "My brother, Edmund, and I always knew of the stories and myths about Klaus and flying machines and why he left Germany to get away from the war. There had been speculation, but no real evidence about the flying machines, or if there was it was kept a secret. I read and heard a lot about Klaus when I was younger. It was no secret that he had worked on V2 doodlebug rockets and jet engines. So I suppose people always wanted to embellish the truth. Everyone loves a good mystery don't they."

Clara had told Julia and Edmund their grandfather was a scientist and died straight after the war. Clara's mother Susan remarried a wealthy local businessman who went on to become a high profile, right-wing politician but they divorced after several years. Clara was married and stayed in Uruguay. Tilda decided to go back to Oxford with Susan and live in the family home which she had inherited from her parents, the Blakes.

"Then last year things changed," Julia's tone had lowered, she shuffled in her seat and stared at her coffee as she gave it an unnecessary stir. "Mum was terminally ill, Aunt Tilda had a stroke, people were asking me questions here, then Mum was burgled. It was one thing after another. It was a stressful time. So, mum told us she had important family things to sort out and went to the UK to see Tilda. As it turned out it was for the last time, but she knew that was going to be the case."

Emma knew how she must have felt, "We're sorry for your loss Julia, it must have been very difficult for you."

"Thank you, it's OK now. But hey, I know for sure from Tilda that you guys are friends and there is some unfinished business that mum would have wanted us to help you with. So, whatever I can tell you I will," Julia, was now sounding much more forthright and resolute.

Julia continued to explain that Clara was an independent woman and had lived on her own in a nice little area in a single storey house, almost up until she died, before spending her final weeks in a hospice.

"When mum moved to a smaller more manageable house, she gave me and my brother some things to store. I have some of them here to show you which may be relevant."

Julia placed on the table a gold pocket watch on a chain and a small book.

"These belonged to Klaus. The book is all in Russian, with some other German notes, from Klaus I assume, half the pages are blank."

"Another notebook," a bemused Wil grinned.

Frea couldn't resist, "I told you they were popular."

"All the rage by the looks of it. And I'll never forgive myself for not having a Filofax."

They all laughed.

"Please keep the book, it's gathering dust, and who knows, it might help you," said Julia.

Melissa was curious to know more about the man that had been taking an interest in Julia's family last year and wanted to know as many details as possible.

Julia kept talking and explained, "The man had been into the bar several times and he started talking to me and the staff a little bit. We try to be friendly, it's good for business. He was a big guy - a fat man, with red hair and a goatee beard. He always wore a big baggy shirt outside his cargo-shorts. He ate lots of food and drunk lots of beer. He told me he was from LA, but his American accent was mixed up. So I wasn't that sure where he was from. He said his name was Alex Larsson."

Emma was making notes as Julia talked.

"But maybe this can help you. When I became suspicious of him, one evening in the bar I took this picture of his credit card. Let me send it to you."

Whilst they were finishing their coffees Frea received the picture from Julia and shared it on the group WhatsApp, which included Phil Chalk. Emma promptly photographed the little Russian book on her phone and immediately sent the twenty or so double-page images in batches to Chalk. Just as he'd asked it gave him more hours at the back end of his day in the UK to translate and plough through them. They finished their coffees said their thankyous and goodbyes to Julia and set off.

~

It happened so fast. Moments after they had left Julia in the cafe, they were approaching their vehicle when a scooter with two men on board wearing crash helmets mounted the pavement from behind them. Its 175cc engine had revved loudly to get up and over the kerb giving the four of them a split second to turn their heads. Only to see the rear passenger swiftly grab the Russian book that Emma was still flicking through as she walked behind the rest of the group. The man deftly tucked it inside his half unzipped leather jacket before lunging towards the shoulder bag that Melissa was carrying.

As the pillion passenger reached for the bag strap the man steering the bike had to make a slight adjustment. He needed to brake for a street sign that was embedded in the pavement. It gave Melissa the fraction of a second she needed to tussle for a moment with the man on the back before leaning backwards onto one leg and launching a vicious high kick to his face. The man on the front was wearing a full-face helmet. The unfortunate bag thief on the rear was wearing an open-faced helmet with a yellow snood and sunglasses. The sunglasses went flying across the pavement and the yellow snood instantly became a red snood. Melissa's well-aimed kick had landed square on the man's nasal bone just above the bridge of his nose, shattering it. The whole incident had lasted no more than five seconds. The man released his partial grip on the bag and screamed, 'Vamos! Vamos! Vamos!', hanging on to his accomplice for dear life as they revved and sped off.

"Oh, my God. Are you OK Melissa, are you OK?" asked a concerned Frea.

Reassuring her friends Melissa replied, "I'm fine honestly, I'm fine. It's a little graze from my bag strap."

Wil rushed to Emma, "Are you hurt babe, are you OK?"

Emma was angry, "The bastard, he grabbed the book, he didn't touch me, just nicked the book in a flash."

Emma asked if they should call the police. Melissa said to forget it and that they wouldn't be found. She was keen to point out Montevideo was always such a safe friendly city, but at the end of the day it was a big city and 'stuff happens'.

"I think he's gonna need a new snood though," Melissa's voice had a remarkable calmness as she spoke and her face still retained a steely ruthless look.

"And by the looks of it a new nose while he's at it. Did they teach you that move at tour guide school?" Wil asked.

There was some laughter and it broke the ice. Melissa appeared OK and ready to head off almost as though nothing had happened. But it looked as though Emma was shaken up by the incident and there were tears were rolling down her face. They went back into Julia's café and explained to her what had happened and stayed there for twenty minutes. Long enough for Emma to get herself together, feel more comfortable and ready to walk to the vehicle. She kept insisting she wasn't that upset.

"I'm so bloody angry and frustrated that the cheeky bastards grabbed the book while I was still looking at it."

With a hint of a smile, she added that with more luck than judgement, ten minutes earlier she had taken pictures of the pages and sent them to Phil Chalk, otherwise she definitely would have been upset.

Wil knew Emma was tough and gritty, he wasn't too worried about her, thinking, *"She's been through much worse than that."*

CHAPTER 26
BIRD WOMAN

Moscow - August 2018

Two months before the break-in at Clara's home in Montevideo. Peter Brin was the chairman, CEO, and seventy-five percent shareholder in Sirin Aerospace, one of Russia's largest private aerospace and defence contractors. The other twenty-five percent was distributed between various wealthy individuals including some of Brin's family members. No one knew for sure who they were or if the official shareholder percentages stated were a true reflection of where the profits ended up. One thing was certain, they made huge amounts of money, globally. Most of the money was disclosed but a proportion of it was filtered off before it ever saw the light of day to bank accounts and other 'investments' around the world. They were the kind of investments that would be called upon to pay the huge unofficial levy required to win defence contracts in the middle east. In the middle east, this was a 'levy' or a 'tax'. To most African nations, it was more affectionately described as a 'blessing'. Everywhere else in the world it was a bribe. A backhander.

Anton Bubka had not long ago gained a seat at the Sirin top table but didn't have his nose right the way into the main feeding trough. He was highly paid, well regarded and bonuses came his way on a regular basis. Though not always through the official channels. He was almost in the game with the big boys and always trying to impress his paymaster and good friend, Peter Brin with new and innovative commercial ideas. Now he had such an idea.

Tuesday mornings were a regular catch up session for both men. Anton had some commercial ideas he wanted to share with his boss. Brin was aware of Anton's recent interest in Russianancestry.ru and had frequently teased him, often asking him when he and his wife were going to be reinstated as the next Tsar and Tsarina. So, when Bubka brought the conversation around to his occasional genealogy hobby he positioned it a different and more persuasive manner.

"Peter, I think my ancestry research has led me to a discovery that will blow your mind. Nothing to do with Tsars, but everything to do with taking the entire aerospace world by the scruff of the neck and turning it on its head."

"Well, that's not something you hear every day is it! You have my undivided attention for the next thirty minutes anyway, Anton," Brin was fascinated.

Anton Bubka used his time wisely. Referencing his grandfather's letters he explained Yuri's history and back story, sinking a Japanese cargo ship, and trying to retrieve its gold cargo. How he had come to end up in a hospital bed in Montevideo with the bends and the amazing story he appeared to have discovered concerning Muller and Klaus. The test pilot and the designer of an anti-gravity aircraft capable of travelling at twelve times the speed of sound, who both stole it and were never seen again.

He pointed out that to the uninitiated the whole thing would have sounded like farcical science fiction. But then Anton Buka explained how he had done some detailed research into Muller and von der Heyde, confirming they were real people who held high ranking positions in the Nazi regime weapons programme and inexplicably went missing before the end of the war.

Anton concluded, "Yuri had said Muller was dead. Yet we know von der Heyde was alive at some point before the end of the war and living in Montevideo with his family. No doubt he possessed the secrets to a technology unknown to twenty-first-century engineers and with the potential to be worth billions."

"So, where do we start Anton?" Peter Brin was riveted.

"Easy, we find the von der Heyde family or whatever they call themselves these days, in Montevideo or wherever they are, then we find whatever Klaus had to hide," replied Bubka.

Brin didn't get to where he was in life by not recognising a remarkable opportunity whenever he saw it. What Anton Bubka had brought him was exactly that, but they had a great deal of work to do to find the answers. Brin wondered why no one else had found the incredible information after all these years.

Sirin was named after a mythical half-bird half-woman creature that could tell the future and would sometimes lead men to their deaths. Peter Brin had teams of people dotted around all over the world. Many of them were legitimate corporate staff, but a handful of them were hired to do things that needed to go under the radar and leave no paper trail back to him and his organisation.

Alex Larsson had American citizenship and had lived in LA for the past fifteen years since he left the Russian FSB secret service. For a short time, he was married to a wealthy American woman and decided to take her surname. It made his life and travelling much easier than having a Russian name. They divorced and he was left with a bitter taste in his mouth when he realised the more money you had the better the legal advice you could afford. His wife's legal team had wiped the floor with him during the divorce. That led to him setting up his private investigation and security business which retained well-established connections in Russia, the UK, and the U.S. One of his long-standing clients was Peter Brin. Whenever something was too hot to handle, Larsson was Brin's *go-to man*. Brin liked him because he would often get personally involved in the work that was needed and not usually subcontract it.

When the phone call came, the larger than most, red-haired Larsson said to Brin, "Peter, I've never been to Uruguay. I feel as though it's a place I'd like to explore and mix a little business with pleasure."

"Alex, go to Uruguay, have your fun or whatever you're going to do. But don't mess up. Get me what I want. It's important, do you understand?"

"Peter, your work is always important. That's why you hire me, isn't it? Relax it will be fine."

It wasn't long, close to two hours of research before the big man had a clear understanding of the von der Heyde family migration. The Uruguay National Institute of Statistics and the General Directorate of Statistics and Censuses had both for many decades operated an excellent census survey of all Uruguayan households. With a little more effort and some common sense, it couldn't have been easier to figure out which families in Montevideo in the 1950s, 1960s and 1970s had a mother called Susan and four children of a certain age. Two boys and two girls all with the same Christian names as when they were born in Germany. Finding where they and any descendants all lived and worked was just as simple. The UK census and other related websites were also as useful tracing family connections and property once owned by Professor Tim Blake. Tilda was in the UK but everyone else was still in Montevideo. Larsson smiled to himself and wondered why on Earth people paid him so much money to do next to nothing, it was child's play.

The first candidate on Larsson's radar for some observation and discussion was a woman called Julia who owned a tapas bar in Montevideo.

The other slight complication arose much further down the line. It was after Alex Larsson had been monitoring both Clara and Tilda and learned they had met in the UK at Tilda's nursing home whilst Tilda was convalescing from her stroke.

It was amazing how forthcoming with information a Lithuanian cleaner at The Spires nursing home had been for a small monthly retainer. That was when Wil, Emma and Frea first came to the attention of Larsson - thanks to his tip-off from the cleaner who had looked in the Spires visitor's book and made a note of names and car registration numbers.

A regular payment to the Lithuanian cleaner was peanuts. The first time Larsson needed to spend big money for information was to find out more about Wil Richardson, but it proved to be achievable.

The expensive, sensitive information concerning Wil Richardson started to be fed back to him, via his dubious UK and Russian sources.

"I was born lucky." Larsson was chuckling to himself.

Larsson was still shaking his head in disbelief as he read the information on his computer screen, twice, to be certain. He had instantly recognised a name he had come across when he worked for the Russian FSB. Christof Sorotkin. Game changer, Larsson thought to himself.

When the offer came from Larsson, it was considered as business for Sorotkin. He fancied himself as a businessman, almost trebling the initial offer before agreeing on it, paid in advance. For the extortionate fee, he agreed to explain to Alex Larsson what he knew about Wil Richardson and his lucid dream capabilities. Larsson then asked Sorotkin to go and speak with Tilda to try to find out what she was up to. A fickle Sorotkin knew Wil and his friends, but that was history, and this was money.

Wil, Frea and Emma soon found themselves on Alex Larsson's monitoring radar.

CHAPTER 27

KINAESTHETIC

Montevideo - July 2019

Everyone seemed to be back to normal after the incident outside Julia's café an hour ago. Quietly, Wil, Emma and Frea were thinking about how on earth Melissa had reacted with such speed, incredible skill, and aggression. They all agreed to carry on with the day as planned. Melissa drove them for another ten minutes, through the busy Montevideo traffic, before pulling up outside what at first glance appeared to be another of the many parks in the city.

"Wil, you said you were curious and would like to visit the man called Lothar Muller, so here we are, Cementerio Central. This is where he is, I will take you to his grave," said Melissa.

Melissa had made a note from Raul's information of the precise location of the spot where Lothar had been buried in 1945 under the given name of Lothar Haas. She led them through the huge city cemetery passing some truly magnificent statues on the way until they found a less ostentatious area. She explained records showed this was the area where at the time the British Hospital would bury patients who on rare occasions had no family or could not be identified at that time.

Febrero 27th 1945 – Lothar Haas, Alemania

185

They all looked at the inscription on the small stone cross which designated the spot of Lothar Muller's final resting place. The grass in the whole area was mown every week, the cuttings were collected up and the adjacent flower beds well-tended. There were some palm trees and a smattering of other tropical-looking trees which nicely framed the many other simple graves nearby. It was a lovely place, just a sad place.

It was sombre, but it wasn't a strong emotional moment for any of them, as they stood in silence and looked on. Although a slightly distracted Frea was having her private thoughts about the recent funeral of her old friend Ruth.

Wil had wanted to come and see for himself to satisfy his curiosity more than anything else. He liked to visualise things and sensed that he had a connection with Muller, who had been a significant man in the whole story.

Wil recalled Emma many years earlier when she was working in marketing. She once came home full of excitement having attended a 'persuasive communications skills' training course. Using some simple scientific and psychological evaluation tools, the delegates were taught how to instinctively categorise the people they were dealing with, pitching ideas to, or selling PR concepts to. She had told Wil there were three types of people – auditory, visual, and kinaesthetic which was the 'touchy and feely' type. The delegates 'selling process' was adapted accordingly.

Talking to clients and allowing them to listen if they were considered to be predominantly auditory.

More emphasis on visuals and pictures if a client's prominence was identified as a visual type of person.

The Kinaesthetic clients were those tactile people needing a combination of the first two approaches but also needing to touch, feel, smell, or experience a product or an idea.

Wil could remember her saying to him, *"Wil you're predominantly a visual type."* That could have been the reason why he had the lucid dreams or so he thought to himself, and here he was needing to take a look and see for himself the grave of Lothar Muller.

Wil also thought Emma's training course had been a load of highbrow theory that would never work.

Wil's mind was wandering and jumping around, all kinds of things were flooding through his head. Soon he found himself trying to imagine what Lothar Muller must have been like as a man. What was the real depth of his relationship with von der Heyde like? Did they honestly think they were going to pull off such an incredible project and make themselves into wealthy men?

Then Wil thought to himself, *"The sad fact is, they tried and it didn't happen for either of them. They both ended up dead men for their troubles."*

It was strange standing there at that moment. Wil was well aware of the history and poignancy surrounding the man buried at his feet. He felt in a way like a kindred spirit, another adventurer. Somehow, it made Wil feel glad to be there.

He found himself suddenly drawn to the headstone with a powerful urge to want to touch it. He reached out and placed his hand on the top of the headstone for several moments. For some reason, as they walked back to the vehicle Wil felt invigorated and more determined than ever to get to the bottom of what had happened all those years ago and to ensure that things got sorted out one way or another. By the time all four of them were sat in the vehicle and strapping on their seat belts, Phil Chalk had sent them all, including Melissa, an encrypted email. They were always impressed at Chalk's resourcefulness and he didn't disappoint them this time. He and his team in the UK, supported by GCHQ, had spent several hours researching, and hunting for information. His people had been using the information that Chalk had been sent concerning the hospital records and both notebooks that had belonged to Lothar Muller and Yuri Bubka. It had all proved to be an excellent, fruitful effort from everyone concerned.

He explained in his email he had some important information for them all to read and digest and they should have a group telephone call later to discuss further.

There was silence in the car as all four of them were doing the same thing, scrolling through Phil Chalk's email.

The first salient piece that Wil came to read ......*Yuri Bubka: Russian submariner. Signals and communications officer. Trained scuba diver. Born 1910 in Vyshny Volochyok. No death recorded. The last posting was aboard a Stalinets – S class submarine in the Pacific fleet which transferred to Atlantic fleet. Confirmed reports that an American Grumman bomber had attacked a Japanese submarine off the coast of Uruguay. The Russian submarine had been in the area and was then in pursuit of the Japanese. As we know he was transferred to a hospital in Montevideo early January 1945. His submarine was sunk in the mid-Atlantic heading back to Russia, four days after he left it. He had been lucky. As you may have read if you translated his notebook, he refers to the sinking of the Japanese submarine and he was attempting to retrieve its cargo before he became ill. When he was ashore recuperating, he was looking for cash to go back to the sunken Japanese submarine, but he never made it. However, he had written down its co-ordinates, so we know where it is. But in his notes, he appeared to be obsessed with von der Heyde and his secrets. He mentions reminders to write letters to his brother, which he must have done.*

Alex Larsson: Former FSB officer retired and living in LA. Runs a private security company. Records show one of his major clients to be a company called Sirin Aerospace which is a Russian defence company. Owned by a man called Peter Brin. One of the Sirin directors is a man called Anton Bubka, he is Yuri's grandson. Alex Larsson image attached.

We should assume then that a long while ago Anton Bubka had uncovered something about his grandfather Yuri. He may have found some of the letters, which then triggered a series of events.

More to follow. Speak later. Phil.

Emma was the first to comment, "I think I agree with you now, Melissa. I don't believe in coincidences anymore either. That's remarkable. Anton Bubka is Yuri Bubka's grandson. And Larsson works for Anton Bubka's company, it's ridiculous."

"That was big news guys. That's who the competition is, but at least they don't know we know about them. We have a few more things to do and maybe we will have the answers we are looking for?" said Wil.

"Lunch, more coffee, then I think we need to go and see Julia's brother, Edmund, shall we?" said Melissa.

CHAPTER 28

BLINK, BLINK

Montevideo - July 2019

Edmund's car repair business was not exactly what Wil had expected to see. It was on the edg e of town and was more akin to a small ranch than a specialist car repair shop.

There was a long open dusty track leading to the front of Edmund's property with fenced in paddocks either side of it. On the right-hand side were three horses, one of which was a Shetland pony, grazing blissfully amongst a low-level equestrian layout, judging by its size, for smaller children. On the left were about a dozen strange looking animals with long necks.

"Llamas?" asked Wil, hoping his farming background would let him shine.

A more knowledgeable Melissa replied, "Alpacas."

As they got close to the house, they could see a prominent sign which appeared to suggest you could walk with the alpacas for twenty minutes for 500 Pesos.

"How cool is that. I want one," said Emma, taking pictures as she cooed over the lovely animals.

A gleeful Emma continued, "Wil, I've messaged the boys with some pics. We're 100% getting some for the business when we get home."

Then laughing Frea added, "If you do, then I'm building a yoga studio in your field."

They slowed right down to keep the dust to a minimum to be greeted at the house entrance by a man who could have been in his late forties or early fifties. He had long mousey coloured hair down to his shoulders, wore cargo shorts, flip flops, a Black Sabbath T-shirt and a pair of mirror aviator sunglasses thrown in for good measure.

"Wow, living the dream or what, I hate him. OK, I'm growing my hair out," said a rebellious sounding Wil.

They all got out of the vehicle and the man shook hands with Wil first, then the women, saying in good English that he was Edmund and they were all most welcome to his home.

A cheeky Melissa said something in Spanish which included the word Llama and Edmund laughed at Wil's expense.

Frea commented that they were expecting a car repair workshop not a farm. Edmund explained he specialised in exclusive sports car customisations, occasional full-body car wraps and paint spraying and not day to day repairs. All carried out in a separate building away from the side of his house.

"I gave up fitting tyres and exhausts many years ago," Edmund's voice sounded almost as cool as his long mousey locks.

Frea did have a discreet look to see if he was wearing a wedding ring, which he was.

"You have a beautiful home, Edmund. Emma and I have been admiring your alpacas. Maybe we'll get some for our farming business back in Wales," said Wil.

"We export the wool around the world, it's not much but it's OK and it pays for their feed for a couple of months. We love them and the kids have so much fun. Please come inside and let me get you something to drink."

They sat down in Edmund's lounge with its bi-folding doors opened up to expose stunning views back up towards the hillside.

Wil told Edmund, "This reminds me of back home a little bit. Except we've got sheep and cows."

"Maybe we can trade some livestock Wil." Edmund joked.

"Yes, please." Emma was keen.

Everyone laughed including Frea who was beginning to feel left out of the farmyard antics.

"Julia explained to me what happened outside the bar earlier, I hope you're all OK? It was such a shame to come to our city and then that happens." There was a sincere and apologetic tone to Edmunds's voice.

Everyone responded saying they were all good and there was no harm done. Edmund said he was sorry, but he was pleased they still came to see him.

"Julia said you have been helping Tilda with some of the things our mother Clara had asked her to do. I know it was important to them both, so whatever I can do to help I will," said Edmund, now with his sunglasses nestled in the top of his hair.

The group of friends went through what they had said to Julia and that they were simply trying to get a better understanding of the family and anything that would help tie up some of the loose ends. They explained they had been given some items from Julia and those were proving to be an enormous help.

Frea took to opportunity to remind Edmund that although she was a doctor, they were all doing some scientific research and that was the main reason Clara and Tilda had been so keen for things to be resolved. It was unfinished business.

"You're right guys, there was a lot of history in the family and I'm part of it because I'm a mixture of English, German and Uruguayan. Some of the history was a bit mysterious but no one knows for sure the truth about what happened. My mother had some strong views though and that's how you guys are involved."

They all talked for a while, then Edmund pulled out some old black and white photos from a folder that was on the floor beside the sofa and laid them out on the coffee table. The British friends had not seen these images before.

Edmund narrated as he flicked through them. In one image, he pointed out a man who was obviously Klaus when he was working during the war. He was stood next to another man, arms draped around each other's shoulders almost like a modern-day selfie. He then turned it over he read out loud what was written on the reverse side. The handwriting said it was *Klaus and Lothar, October 1943*. Wil asked if he could take a picture of the photo, which Edmund agreed was fine. That was about it, there were no other notable pictures other than more of Susan, Clara, Tilda and their two older brothers, now both dead.

Wil passed comment on a picture on the far wall. He stood up, walked over, and took a closer look. It was a motorcyclist, in full race mode, green leathers, sponsors logos and a number four on the bike panel. He was banking around a corner on a racetrack hanging off the side of a huge lime green motorcycle with a left knee almost scraping the tarmac. It was a cool and super professional action shot, and well worth its place on the wall.

"That was me over twenty years ago, I was sponsored by Kawasaki and some other big brands back then. But I've always loved Hondas," said a smiling Edmund.

Edmund asked Wil if he was into motorcycles. He replied saying he used to ride motor cross bikes for fun and his two sons Haydn and George still did, but it was mostly quad bikes for chasing sheep and cattle these days.

Edmund had a thought, saying, "Come with me, I'd like to show you something."

The two men walked ahead followed by the three women, through the kitchen along a darker corridor until they walked through into an even darker room.

There were several moments in the darkness whilst Edmund rummaged around in his pocket to find a key fob to turn off the localised alarm in the room.

"That's it. This was where it was," said Wil out loud.

"Are you OK Wil, are you afraid of the dark or something?" asked a curious Edmund.

He then turned all the lights on and then opened up the electric roller shutter door to his man cave, letting in some natural light and some welcome fresh air. This was Edmund's private garage and not his paint shop. As Wil had stood there in the gloomy light ten seconds earlier, he had spotted something out of the corner of his eye, high up. A blinking red light. It was the same one he had seen in his dream with Clara three days earlier. The intermittent light was the zone burglar alarm indicator.

The group stood amongst a collection of motorcycles, a jet ski and a super seven sports car.

"What do you think Wil, can you be converted from quad bikes."

"A stunning collection, do you ride them all regularly Edmund?"

"Whenever I can unless work gets in the way."

"What's under the dust sheet?" asked a curious Wil.

Edmund squashed himself sideways between a couple of gleaming Hondas. Breathing in, and explaining as he went, that what Wil had been referring to was a work in progress. Adding, that what he meant was it was more of a work never in progress.

As soon as both men had wriggled alongside the dust sheet covered object, Edmund tugged at the sheet, pulling it off to reveal a sorry-looking old black car.

"It's a 1943 model Mercedes-Benz 320. It belonged to my father and before him, it belonged to my grandmother Susan. Or to be correct, the family have always said it was bought, to begin with by Klaus six months before he died."

The car had been passed around because Edmund and his Uruguayan father before him were always into cars. It was one sentimental piece of history that always hung around, there was no question of it ever being sold, scrapped, or renovated.

"One day I keep promising myself I'm going to bring it back to life."

"Does it run?" asked a fascinated Wil.

"It did ten years ago but now it needs some love, some fuel, a new battery and some new spark plugs. Oh, and a new condenser. And then a couple of hundred hours of work."

The old Mercedes was unlocked. Wil tugged a rear door handle and with a loud, agonising squeak, he found himself looking inside the vintage vehicle. Many years of stagnant air exited as Wil stepped inside. He didn't have to duck too much which was a novelty for him. He found himself sitting inside, on the rear bench seat.

He closed his eyes for a moment as he sat there, *"Is it possible I can smell tobacco smoke after all these years. Or am I imagining it?"*

Wil's eyes remained closed as he placed his hands beside his thighs, he sensed the smooth shiny texture and the springiness of the old leather bench seat. He cast his mind back to the dream that he had before he left the UK a week earlier. It had been Clara in his dream, he was certain of it. He knew he had been sat in that spot, just as Edmund's dead mother told Wil 'he was close' and 'it was tucked away'. Whatever that meant.

"Tucked away where?" Wil wondered, *"What's tucked away."*

Edmund asked Wil if he was OK in there. Wil said he was fine, but he had an idea they might find something helpful to them in the car.

Wil had an idea, "Edmund, do these rear seats move or come out easily?".

"I'm sure they do Wil, think German efficiency, advanced design ideas and all that stuff. Please hop out. Let me take a look." Edmund commented, "I've never taken these seats out before, but I've done similar work on some old Porsches with torn leather, let's see what I can do."

Wil was assisting from the other side of the car and in less than a minute Edmund had released a couple of old catches and the heavy leather bench seat lifted away and out of the car. The empty space where it had come from revealed a pile of old yellow looking Uruguayan newspapers from the 1940s. Whilst Edmund was stowing away the hefty leather sprung seat so that it didn't fall and scratch any of his precious Hondas, Wil delved in amongst the newspapers.

What he found, to begin with, was a scuffed piece of wood about 12 inches long, it was round with a knurled grip, like a policeman's truncheon. The name Yuri was scratched into its butt. Alongside the baton, was an oily-looking rag which had something heavy wrapped inside it. Wil unfolded the rag and in the palm of his hand lay a pistol. Before then, Wil had fired nothing other than double-barrelled shotguns on the farm or at posh friends' grouse beats. Wil knew, that from the glinting in the artificial light, he was holding a semi-automatic pistol. It had a wooden grip and the word Mauser embossed onto its body. He also noticed the safety catch was on before carefully handing it to a surprised Edmund.

"How on Earth did you know that was in there?" asked a bemused Edmund.

"Educated guess," said Wil, before stepping out of the car with something else in his hand, adding, "I've found this as well, it's a book."

The five people returned to the lounge by which time Edmund's wife and two young children had arrived home from school. The children said hello and disappeared to their rooms whilst Edmund's wife made them all some more coffee.

"It's been a long time since I handled a weapon. National service thirty years ago to be precise," commented Edmund.

He then pointed the pistol towards the ground urging its tired old spring to operate as it should and release the magazine from the pistol grip, before racking its top slide a couple of times to ensure it had nothing left in the chamber.

"OK, it's safe now, should be seven rounds, we've only got five. Someone has fired the other two."

"Maybe that's a message and it's time for you to fix the car Edmund," said Emma.

Wil hadn't heard a word, he was too busy flicking through the old book, yet another journal he thought to himself, surely this is the last one.

"Maybe it's the best one?" he thought, and reminded himself of the mantra from the day before that no one had mobile phones or computers or landlines back then, notebooks were commonplace and where everyone kept their day to day information.

Some of the pages were torn out, others had calculations and formulae and lots of notes and some crude pencil sketches. It was written in Russian.

Wil asked Edmund if he would mind if they kept the book to study back at their hotel.

"Sure, no problem, but I'll keep the gun if it's OK. Police catching tourists with a gun - you might never see the light of day again. And next week the Mercedes project begins for certain."

It was time to go, so the friends said their goodbyes to Edmund and his wife and headed back to their hotel.

As they drove back to their hotel Emma had been thinking and speculating and said, "So, Klaus has managed to obtain Yuri Bubka's precious Russian notebook and a wooden club with his name on. I'm sure they weren't gifts, were they? Lothar Muller must have been killed at the hands of Yuri Bubka. Yuri is never heard of again, and two out of seven bullets are missing from Klaus's loaded gun. I think we know what happened – our friend Klaus shot and killed Yuri didn't he?"

CHAPTER 29
TAKING STOCK

Montevideo - 2019

It was late afternoon and back at their hotel in Montevideo the Lucidity Programme team and their newly adopted local member had regrouped in the lounge.

"If ever a beer was needed or had been earned this was the moment," thought Wil.

They were in a celebratory mood, apart from the tussle on the pavement which 'the find' under the car seat in the garage had helped put behind them, it had been a good day. To the best of their knowledge, they had obtained as much of the available information. They had come looking for some key information and they had found it. The next task was to figure out its relevance.

Clara's two children had been the custodians of significant items plus a couple of other items which were either uncovered or had been gifted to them. Now all the three friends needed to do was translate the information and understand what it meant - or least some smart people back home in Chalk's organisation would figure things out.

Did Klaus's latest journal hold the final secrets that Chalk had asked them to find? There had been a slight problem though, several of the pages in Klaus's notebook from the Mercedes were missing, they had been torn out. Nevertheless, there was a great deal of apparent technical detail in the book. Some mathematical formulae, and scientific sketches, though nothing which resembled the aircraft as they had seen on the cine films.

Lines of German text some of it obscure, memory jogs to himself read, *"only some new material combinations proving successful, others wasting days, weeks of time and effort.........Persevering with these new alloys, they may have some potential........the marriage not made yet made for heaven........significant performance improvements..........Lothar's feedback was very harsh he doesn't appreciate the challenges we face....... Elevation and speed achievements remarkable yet so simple, control and navigational issues remain the biggest threat to us."*

Towards the end of the journal there was a reference to the expo 45, *"......must not forget to ask Uncle Sam to help me complete the puzzle....... yachting venue proved very fruitful will need to consider full demonstration for northern journey soon."*

"Surely he was referring to America and meetings that either he had or was planning to have following an exhibition," said Emma

There was a note at the rear of Klaus's notebook, in different handwriting, and written in English.

The line read, *"The Earth is a Realm"*, then written downwards on the other side of the same page another line of text read, *"rare earth"*.

Frea was the only one among them who could be considered the closest thing to a scientist and she was the person who said, "Rare earth? Might have something to do with rare earth metal and materials. Klaus was a chemist and metallurgist perhaps he was already using those materials with his previous projects on jet engines and rocket propulsion systems?"

"What about Earth is a Realm?" asked Wil.

Emma Googled it and said, "It's a line from a quote well over a hundred years ago from a famous chap called Nikola Tesla - yes like the car.

He had said something about gravity being disproved by levitation using electromagnetic force. Ring any bells guys?"

They asked each other who wrote the English words in Klaus's notebook. Concluding it may have been Susan, but if so why? Had she simply been doodling? Did Susan put the gun and the book under the seat or was that somewhere Klaus kept them for safekeeping? And why keep the baton? They wondered if the vertical wording of 'rare earth' was something to do with upwards and downwards movement?

Frea had noticed something, "English wasn't my speciality in school. But maybe it was Susan's, she was the linguist. Can you see how 'Earth is a Realm' is spelt with a capital 'E' and rare earth lower case 'e'? Earth the planet and earth the mineral or metal. That's what he is referring to."

Emma did the formality of photographing the latest book found in Edmund's garage and sending the images to Phil Chalk. She also explained they'd had the Russian book stolen but fortunately had images of its pages. Emma reassured Phil the theft was a minor blip, a moped bag snatch and nothing to worry about, no one was hurt. At least none of Phil's team because Melissa had taken care of the thieves single-handed.

Not that the efficient Chalk was ever likely to get confused, she reminded him they now had three books - Klaus's original diary which Chalk gave to them with the cine films and cine camera - the Russian notebook, although only images of it now, belonging to Bubka that Julia gave to them which Klaus had 'obtained' in 1945 - and now this one of Klaus's from the old Mercedes. Not to mention Lothar Muller's pieces of paper which Raul gave to them after Frea found them in the jacket pocket in the archives. In her email, Emma also told Chalk about the pistol, which had been recovered from the old Mercedes, and was now being proudly retained by Edmund. She told him they all agreed it was a murder weapon.

Wil had been a little quiet for ages and said he was sending a couple of WhatsApp messages. Twenty minutes later, after Emma had nudged him to stop playing with his phone, it pinged a couple of times.

"Brilliant, just brilliant," said Wil.

"What's suddenly so brilliant?" asked Emma.

Wil explained that half an hour ago he'd had a recollection of something he'd seen in Tilda's box that came from Phil Chalk, the cine camera items. He had remembered when he took the cine-camera out of its case, at home in the UK, that there had been a couple of small rolled up balls of newspaper, in there as packing. "They didn't have bubble wrap in those days did they?"

He didn't pay much attention to them at the time but did recall the old newspaper appeared to have been Spanish and he had begun to wonder.

"I messaged George and asked him to pop over to our house and look in the safe at something for me," said Wil.

George had done as his father had asked, he'd gone into the safe, opened the cine camera case and unrolled the balls of paper. Then he took a couple of pictures and sent them back across to Wil.

"Is anyone any good at crosswords?" asked a smiling Wil.

~

It was seven in the evening in an unusually balmy St Petersburg on the Baltic coast of Russia, when Peter Brin's mobile rang, vibrating on its silent setting. He was wandering around the outdoor Geek Picnic Festival of Science Art and Technology, which was an annual mid-July pilgrimage for him and wife. Although Brin never needed much of an excuse to visit the beautiful historic city of St Petersburg despite the renowned frequent wet weather of the region. A respectful Brin excused himself from his wife, moved to a quiet spot and answered the familiar number he had stored in his phone, "So, what have you got for me today Alex?"

"Well Peter, let's say positive news overall, some good, some not so good, though all of it is interesting," replied Alex Larsson having just completed a huge lunch in Montevideo.

Larsson explained to his important client that 'his people' had managed to obtain a pocketbook once belonging to Yuri Bubka.

"Most of it's in Russian, I've read it. It contains corroborating information concerning Klaus von der Heyde and Lothar Muller. It validates the letters sent by Yuri to his brother, but with more details. It's dynamite, Peter."

"That's excellent news, it makes up from the debacle that another of 'your people' managed to contrive in Oxford eh?"

"Yes, point taken Peter, we all make recruitment mistakes from time to time, don't we? But relax Christof Sorotkin is no longer on the payroll. Though the cleaner at the Spires still is."

A narrative summary of the contents of the notebook was relayed by Larsson, explaining more about the sinking of the Japanese submarine and its approximate location. Yuri, being stranded in Montevideo and believing that the anti-gravity aircraft must have existed. But that Muller had watched it break up in mid-air and then head in bits towards the Atlantic Ocean. That was the not so good news. Adding reassuringly, he was certain Klaus von der Heyde had the knowledge and secrets for sale at one time, so they must surely still exist somewhere.

"The British are looking for the same thing that we are my friend, they hold the key to unlocking the secrets. We will do our best to take the key from them," said Larsson, adding that he would send images of Yuri's book across soon.

"OK, Alex, keep working hard for me. So, we continue to observe the British and for now, we must implement our contingency plan. Make it happen tomorrow. I have to go now, goodbye."

Alex Larsson knew exactly what the contingency plan was. He had already lined up the resources and the manpower. Meanwhile, he sent across Yuri's book images to Peter Brin's mobile phone in St Petersburg.

CHAPTER 30
FOUR ACROSS

Montevideo - July 2019

Wil told his friends that the note written in English at the back of the notebook found at Edmund's garage had given him an idea. It had been written like a crossword clue answer across then down. 'Earth is a Realm' across and 'rare earth' was downwards although not connected to each other.

His son George had sent through images of a couple of unrolled paper balls that were inside the cine camera case. They contained part completed crosswords with a jumble of words that weren't necessarily in Spanish, but they were scientific words from what Wil could see.

Moments after he saw the images on his phone from George, Wil made an urgent phone call.

A quietly spoken Edmund answered, "Hi Wil, how are you?"

Wil said, "You sound like you're out walking Edmund. I hope I haven't interrupted anything?"

"A little bit of business Wil. We're hosting a young girl's birthday party and leading them on llama walk. To be honest it's more like fun than a profitable piece of business."

Wil laughed saying "Nice try at catching me out, but I'm now a lifelong alpaca aficionado, and I need a favour."

Wil needed to know if the old newspapers in the boot of the Mercedes were still safe and sound. Edmund reassured Wil and said he had put them to the side ready to go into his biomass boiler, but he hadn't burnt them yet.

Forty minutes later in full premium black leathers, Edmund 'squat walked', as motorcyclists in full racing pants tend to do, into Wil's hotel. Looking most peculiar as his top of the range leathers typically prohibited the straightening of the knees. He said that he couldn't stop, he joked he had to get back to light some candles and handed over the bunch of yellow-tinged old Uruguayan broadsheet newspapers.

Wil thanked him once again, said goodbye and hunted for the crosswords and there they were, completed in a similar way to those he had seen earlier sent by George. Part completed with lots of strange scientific words, maybe they were some atomic letters. Fantastic he thought to himself as he heard a factory-tuned 1000cc Honda Fireblade rev to 12,000 RPM and scream up the street outside the window.

Melissa had thought they were done for the day but hung around when she heard the new and surprising theory. It appeared to have some substance and before long the four of them spread the old newspapers out on a long rectangular table in a quiet corner of the hotel lounge.

"Nothing notable other than for the crosswords, no other notes as far as I can see," said Emma.

Frea had spotted something though, "But can you see what isn't on there, guys, something is missing."

Everyone looked blankly before she said, "When was the last time you did a crossword and didn't scribble little notes or first attempts somewhere else on the page near to the crossword, or cross off your completed question unless you're a crossword genius. There are none of those markings on these papers."

"Yeah I can see what you mean," said Wil.

There were so many words in such a random arrangement no one could comprehend what they meant. Although they wondered if the crosswords were related to the torn-out pages of the book. Perhaps the information had been separated as an extra precaution.

Everyone gave a Wil some extra kudos for his ingenuity leaving him with a pleased and satisfied look on his face.

He then said "It's been a strange day. Although I didn't mention it earlier, one of the highlights for me was visiting Lothar Muller's grave."

Explaining he felt a strong connection there for some reason and had been compelled to touch the headstone. It was a sobering comment after the elation and fun of the 'crossword solution' as they had all described it.

"Frea, maybe later we should do a sleep session before dinner and see if something happens," Wil said calmly and confidently.

Phil Chalk had booked them all generously sized suites in the hotel as he knew they would be working together as a private group at some point. Frea suggested she go and tidy her room and they should all join her in fifteen minutes. Wil agreed and invited Melissa to sit in. It was noticeable from the things he had been saying to the group, his calm body language and chilled attitude, that Wil was relaxed. Although they had roughly explained the process to her the day before, Emma briefed Melissa in more detail about what the sleep session would entail. Sit quietly and observe was the final comment.

Frea had readied her room and arranged a couple of well-positioned seats for Emma and Melissa. Wil and Frea had done these sessions more than twenty times before, each time they had learned a little bit more than the last one. On the previous occasion, the gong bath had been a great success and was a session that they hadn't reproduced since but was about to be reintroduced digitally for this session.

As always Frea serenely switched into doctor mode and with politeness and authority, she took control of the session. It relaxed Wil immediately. She was the trusted knowledgeable one, in charge and always selecting the correct approach and process. Wil never interfered and Emma always stayed calm and let them get on with it. She had heard enough of Wil's lucid dreams for over twenty years so and was never fazed by it. Melissa's eyes were wide open, taking it all in. She was fascinated and transfixed.

The lights were dimmed, the two small unobtrusive micro tech attachments were attached to Wil's temples and then connected to Frea's laptop. She wore a small voice-activated headset. Wil was not a showman or an extravert, and he wasn't the slightest bit perturbed by the new dynamic of Melissa sitting in. He was focused and intent on doing what was necessary.

Wil lay on the bed with his head at its base and closed his eyes. Nearby on the bed were some of the objects they had found or had been given by Raul. Frea began massaging his head and had touched some essential oils around his forehead. Soon the room had a beautiful warm smell of rosewater. Frea's phone was synced to the laptop which meant she didn't need to move far away from Wil as she touched her phone and started the gentle humming sounds of the early stages of the gong bath.

Part of her meticulous preparation on leaving the UK also included the addition of a mini Bang & Olufsen wireless soundbar which kicked in and provided a highly authentic sound bath experience. Emma and Melissa could feel the subtle vibrations almost as clearly as a genuine gong bath. Melissa was staring, deep in thought, reluctant to attempt to even blink an eye for fear of missing something. Emma may have appeared nonchalant, but she was always interested and took immense pride in what Wil was doing.

Before long Wil's body started to demonstrate some tell-tale twitching signs suggesting he was fast asleep. All Frea needed to do was keep opening the doors for him inside his head and let him take whatever path he needed to. Frea would make some quiet comments as she monitored the feedback on the laptop's software, she was never entirely sure if Wil had understood or heard all of her comments after a certain point, but the reactions and outcomes were always positive. Wil once described her as akin to an air traffic controller.

Wil's brain was making a connection, things were swirling before his eyes, he was dreaming, lucidly.

In Wil's mind's eye, he was seeing a series of staccato images flashing past, of what appeared to be an airbase. Then, high snow-capped mountains, blue sky, clouds, more blue sky, oceans, landmass and then gradually the mental film reel slowed down. He sensed that he was immobile, inside a confined, almost claustrophobic space with small portholes and sunshine blinding him to the extent he wanted to put his hand in front of his eyes to shield them.

The smooth almost silent purring noise he could hear was becoming more pronounced, at which point he heard the heavily accented voice of a man, unmistakably German but speaking in English.

He immediately sensed it was Lothar Muller, "This was the moment Wil. Can you hear it coming Wil?"

The confined space was starting to vibrate, the clouds were shaken to a blur through the porthole. Wil looked at his wrist and recognised something unusual, something he had seen somewhere before. It was a modern-day GPS wristwatch - it was Frea's.

For a few moments, he lost his concentration because of the watch wondering, *"What is Frea's watch doing here?"*

"One day Wil, follow the watch, one day, eh," said the frantic German voice.

There was a blinding flash and suddenly Wil was surrounded by a bright blue vista, the ocean and the sky meeting way in the distance and a huge white billowing silk parachute above his head.

Way below him he saw the aircraft, that moments earlier he had been inside, breaking up and then spectacularly exploding mid-air.

"That was oxygen, hydrogen and a couple of other explosive gases. Listen to me Wil, Susan has what you need to stop the Americans, go, and find it. Remember this - the secret is within your grasp Wil. Bubka doesn't have the answers," were the final comments from the German, then he was gone, it was over.

The whole sequence of events was so different from some of the other dreams Wil had experienced. These were short sharp bursts of commentary in a dangerous and intense situation for a short period. Wil was certain the narrator had been the pilot of the craft, Lothar Muller.

Frea changed the dynamic and started speaking with more conviction. The rhythmical pulsing tones emanating from the soundbar had passed the crescendo. Melissa was reluctant to move a muscle or say a word and wondered what was coming next as a spellbound Wil gradually opened his eyes. Frea helped him up into a more sociable seated position.

Turning to face Emma and Melissa, with Frea listening as she concluded the session, Wil smiled and said, "Wow, so that's what Mach 10 feels like."

Wil knew from experience that he needed to recall as much information as close to the end of the session as possible, whilst it was still vivid and in the front of his mind.

Recounting what he saw and experienced, Wil was highly excited to have made the lucid connection with Lothar. He had sensed earlier in the day it was likely to happen and that's why he instigated the sleep session – he'd known it. Although Frea was instrumental to the sessions, nothing would ever happen without Wil, he was the lightning conductor, every time.

The GPS watch was something Wil had noticed in Frea's hiking 'go bag' when she'd needed to find some antiseptic cream to soothe Melissa's bag snatch friction graze. It had stuck in Wil's mind as strongly as all the other weird things he had seen in the dream. Frea's watch had been transposed into the dream and on to his wrist. Wil didn't know why.

No one knew what the message meant concerning the Americans and that Susan could 'stop them'.

"He was categorical about Susan, so I have to go and find 'it', whatever that means," said Wil.

~

Whilst the sleep session was taking place in Montevideo, Phil Chalk's boss had messaged him. It was late in the evening in the UK and it was rare for him to leave it so late unless it was important. He asked Phil to give him a quick call about a new, urgent meeting they needed to schedule for first thing in the morning.

Chalk rang him straight away and was told moments earlier he had come off the phone from a mutual associate in the U.S. The Americans claimed the British may be about to find historic information which legally belonged to the U.S. and they expected to be kept abreast of all new developments.

Then there had been a sequence of messages from various senior UK stakeholders suggesting the shit was about to hit the fan the minute there was a satisfactory resolution of the current Lucidity Programme project – the search for the anti-gravity aircraft or information relating to it.

"How the hell did they know, and who or what gives them the right to come barging in?" said a furious Phil Chalk.

"Who knows but remember those red flags and algorithms you once had for Wil? My guess is whatever you had the Americans must have had three times as many - and they've been watching with great interest and anticipation from afar. Now they know something is kicking off they think they are entitled. I'll see you in the morning, Phil."

CHAPTER 31

PLAN B

It was the team's final day in Montevideo, they were flying back to the UK after lunch. Melissa met them at nine a.m. after they had taken an early breakfast and checked out. She said it was a beautiful sunny day and asked them if they wanted to see some of the coastline before heading off to the airport. Knowing they would all agree, Melissa drove them east along a stunning coast road giving them time to watch and photograph the waves rolling in off the Atlantic Ocean and crash on the beaches and coves. They headed towards Punta del Este with its tiny peninsula and exclusive little marina. The nearby trendy beach bars were mostly dormant at that time of the year, then in the distance, Isla Gorriti came into view, almost a stone's throw away from the headland.

"How lovely," said Frea as she gazed at the tiny little island.

"Hundreds of years ago they used to bury sailors from faraway places there," said Melissa.

As Melissa approached the peninsula, which was not much bigger than about a dozen football pitches, she explained to the group that with the help of Raul she had done some historical research. She had purposely driven them in that direction for two reasons; beautiful scenery and secondly, it was a road which mirrored the final scheduled sailing route that Klaus took before he was lost.

"From what I discovered this was one of his regular sailing journeys and was where he went the day he disappeared. Around this island and then back - but something went wrong and he never made it back."

As many tourists do, they drove to the tip of the peninsula and looked across at the island. The same as assassin Peter Knecht had done many years ago. Watching, and waiting with his rifle, ready to kill, sitting in his Citroen less than 100 metres from where they were that day.

~

Before Wil and his friends had been having breakfast, Alex Larsson, who was not far away from them back in Montevideo, had made an early start, which was unusual by his standards.

He was following his backer Peter Brin's instructions. Before he left LA, and in anticipation of needing to go to the contingency plan, Larsson was on board a fifty-foot, state of the art salvage vessel. It was equipped with sophisticated proton 5 magnetometer seabed sonar scanning technology.

Peter Brin prided himself on having the ability to usually stay one step ahead of the game. He was desperately hoping to find the secrets to the anti-gravity aircraft, but he had no idea where or what, if anything, was left of it when according to what Yuri Bubka had discovered. It had appeared to have disintegrated in mid-air.

But now that he had Yuri Bubka's notebook he did know where to find two tonnes of Japanese gold worth well over $100M. Brin hoped Yuri Bubka's navigational skills which recorded the precise location would prove better than his diving abilities were. They had almost got him killed. Electronic navigation was crude at that time with navigators relying on various devices such as a gyrocompass, but they were reliably accurate. Bubka's sketches and notes were about to be put to the test, but with modern-day diving experts and equipment.

The short notice chartering of the specialist salvage vessel and its Argentinian crew had cost Peter Brin the best part $40,000, less than he earned in a couple of days, it was a bargain.

One hour southeast of Montevideo the skipper deployed the proton 5 magnetometer - the glorified metal detector. At first glance, it looked like a yellow sit on inflatable banana, often found in beach resorts towed behind a jet ski. But the best part of a quarter of a million dollars provided much more than that.

The ship's sonar was getting a basic heads up reading, and the skipper decided to submerge and drag the proton 5 to capture a precise profile of what they had found. It wasn't long before they had identified what it was - without doubt, a sunken submarine laying on its side on the seabed. The device had also picked up the shape of some of the ragged carnage that had been inflicted by torpedoes on the vessel's hull. It couldn't have been anything other than the remains of the Japanese sub.

The crew knew what they had been hired for. The skipper had signed a bonus agreement with Larsson and Brin. Everyone was excited and optimistic because the information concerning its whereabouts had been accurate - so far.

Two experienced professional divers were ready, prepped and in the water. The forty to fifty-metre depth range was technically classified as a 'deep dive'. A calibrated dive line was deployed to help the divers descend providing a 'pony', a spare air supply mid-way if needed, to assist them with the ascent. Always working in pairs with voice communication there were no risks or errors of judgement. They had done this relatively simple dive hundreds of times.

They followed the dive line and entered the sunken Japanese vessel. Bubka had tabulated his notes as a reference for himself for his future dive which was never to be. But the notes provided an excellent route map for the modern-day divers. They knew where they were heading and which bulkhead doors they needed to pass through. Dodging two-metre eels and swarms of small fish, trailing a line, and counting off the open rusty doors, one, two, three, four. Their LED lights made it appear like daylight inside the dark but clear water of the steel wreck. After six minutes they reached an area designated for cargo, which was, where according to Yuri Bubka, where 'X' marked the spot.

"Nothing here, rotten wood, empty rusty steel racks. Nothing, no gold, it's gone," said the experienced lead diver with confidence.

"Are you 100% sure you're in the correct location?" asked a bitterly disappointed sounding skipper.

The lead diver's synthesised sounding voice interspersed with breaths of air responded, "This is the place. It's opened up into a dedicated storage bay area, that Russian diver's description was accurate. The steel racking welded to the bulkhead is still in place just as he sketched. We've even got the steel strapping bands that bound the wooden crates laying on the floor here. Taken some pictures, coming up."

Thirty minutes earlier Alex Larsson had been sat on the salvage vessels bridge smiling and drinking beer when they'd located the Japanese submarine. Now he was looking deflated, pissed off and to make matters worse he knew he had to let Peter Brin and Anton Bubka know the outcome of the wasted investment. It had not been a good day for Larsson, he felt like crap.

Brin had flown back to Moscow on his private jet, he and Bubka were together at their office when Larsson called mid-afternoon to explain the non-event. Ultimately, it was Brin who had made the evaluation of all the previous facts and evidence and it was he who made the wrong call to go treasure hunting. But that didn't stop Anton Bubka averting his gaze, and having far less to say for himself than he did as a rule. Larsson knew he had been paid handsomely and there was no skin off his nose whatever happened, but he sensed he needed to start producing some results. He apologised explaining that the skipper thought the Japanese sub could easily have been stumbled upon several times over the years and it would have been potluck if the gold had still been there.

The skipper was an experienced local man, he knew that the area and location were not ones that had ever come to his attention, or anyone else's. There had never been any rumours, which usually circulate if there had ever been a successful find.

Brin was annoyed, bluntly saying, "Alex, I think you need to get yourself on a plane to England and find out why everyone is making a fool out of me. I'm not impressed, you get well paid to get me results."

The call ended abruptly. Larson booked himself on a flight to the UK - he would be arriving twenty-four hours after Wil, Emma and Frea who were about to head for the airport.

~

After admiring the beautiful coastal vista and providing a thoughtful history tour of the area Melissa decided to take the team for a goodbye lunch to one of her favourite steak restaurants in the area.

"Uruguay has the beef that Argentina thinks it's got," said a smiling Melissa, dismissively referring to the neighbouring country's famous reputation for steaks.

"The red wine isn't bad either," said Wil, raising his glass and encouraging a toast for their superb host.

"It's been an amazing thought-provoking three days Melissa, you've made it an amazing success for all of us," said Emma.

"Thought-provoking for you, mind-blowing for me, I can tell you," Melissa's voice was full of sincerity.

She was right, the steaks were amazing, and the wine was better than good. They all agreed they would continue to work together and keep in touch from several thousand miles away until the mystery was resolved.

Frea had managed to find a thoughtful gift and presented to their new friend, "A sincere token of our appreciation for taking good care of us. And for unlocking some doors."

It was a beautiful Hermes scarf. Melissa was stunned, she put it on and didn't say a word. The look on her face said plenty about her gratitude and affection.

Frea quoted some marketing blurb saying, "Hermes was the messenger to the Gods. They say he was also the god of interpreters and translators. Oh, and allegedly he did something with the souls of the dead because he was the also the god of sleep. Therefore, he was the perfect choice for Melissa."

They all laughed.

Even Wil knew what a Hermes scarf was and quietly asked Emma how much it cost, "Don't worry, Frea will get the duty back on it at the airport. It worked out at less than £200 which Phil Chalk had better be reimbursing as money well spent - Melissa has been incredible for us."

They said their final goodbyes at the airport and passed through check-in and passport control. The adrenaline of the last few days was leaving them as they sat in silence, relaxing and looking at the screens waiting for their boarding gate number to appear.

Frea broke the silence, "Wil, you never explained in any detail what you meant when you said you saw my GPS watch on your wrist in the dream. You were a bit vague about it at the time. What was all that about?"

"Well, it's complicated, but what Lothar showed me was a GPS location on your watch, I've written it down, so I don't forget it. Then he and my dream led me through some deep dark murky water. That's when I saw a red star painted on the side of something. I realise now it was a Russian submarine. Yuri Bubka's old submarine, which got sunk a couple of days after he was put ashore. Inside the submarine, I saw crates of gold. The Russians went back to the Japanese sub and got it all before they got sunk themselves soon afterwards. And I know where it is, thanks to your imaginary watch, I've got the GPS coordinates written down."

Emma realised something else, "So, Yuri Bubka would have wasted his time. Even if he had gone back and found the Japanese sub, the gold had already gone with his Russian shipmates. They had done the right thing in the first instance when they left him in hospital in Montevideo to recover."

Wil added, "As Lothar said to me, 'One day follow the watch Wil,' so one day we will, and when the time is right maybe we can give Melissa a call."

CHAPTER 32

INTERFERENCE

Porton Down, Wiltshire - July 2019

Phil Chalk was in work earlier than usual. He wanted to clear his urgent emails before sitting down with his boss at nine a.m.

Chalk and his boss had a good relationship, they went back with each other many years. As soon as Chalk walked into his boss's office, his boss avoided the regular morning small talk getting straight to business. Speaking at a much quicker rate than usual and grabbing at pieces of paper that were strewn all over his desk.

"What's going on, any developments overnight?" asked Chalk.

"Well, I've had some emails and I'm on a conference call later this morning with an American guy who is based in the UK. Take a look at this."

Chalks boss slid across the table several pages which had been printed off two minutes ago. Chalk sat there quietly reading through all of them.

"They're taking the piss. Are you kidding me?" Chalk was furious.

The first page was an email that had been sent to Chalk's boss from his counterpart in the U.S. Government. It read:

CLASSIFIED

Dear Sir

Further to our telephone conversation earlier today I can confirm that the U.S. government has the legal rights to the intellectual property that you are pursuing. This is something which had been lost to us for decades after the sudden demise of our associate Klaus von der Heyde.

We have evidence to prove that following discussion and subsequent meetings we procured the rights in 1945 from Klaus von der Heyde to his anti-gravity technology. He and his family were about to join us to live and work in the U.S. before his sad and unexpected death.

I have attached a letter of confirmation of acceptance of the check that was sent to Mr. von der Heyde.

Best wishes

The second piece of information was the essence of a scanned document of a letter sent from von der Heyde with some of it redacted.

20th November 1945

Dear

Thank you for coming to meet me. I'm pleased that you had other business in the region which enabled us to meet. It was good to meet you after our series of cautious phone calls which are always complicated and never without risk.

I'm delighted that you enjoyed the yacht club and my 'cine film' demonstration. Your offer is a generous one and my family and I will be making plans in the near future to join you in Virginia. We are grateful for the cheque advance of a $1000 which will be most helpful to us.

I will contact you again when we have made final preparations.

Yours sincerely

Klaus von der Heyde

"Phil - the thing is von der Heyde was killed in a boating accident two days after writing the letter."

"Does that letter constitute a legally binding arrangement? He hadn't even gone to work for them. It's bullshit and the Americans are taking us for complete idiots. There's not a patent let alone 'a legal right to the intellectual property'. They can whistle for it," Chalk was adamant - his face and bald head were bright red.

His boss said he tended to agree with his colleague Chalk, but they had to be seen to be squeaky clean and not leave the door open for the Americans.

The normally impassive Chalk had calmed down. It was unusual for him to get rattled. Those messages had irked him. He switched his phone back on and saw a missed call from Wil and was annoyed with himself for missing it. The voice mail said they had landed on time and would speak with him once they got in the car.

~

In Moscow, Peter Brin and Anton Bubka were running out of ideas and felt they might also be running out of time. If they were going to get anywhere with the anti-gravity project, it was going to be from whatever they could uncover in the UK.

"It's the daughter in the nursing home - she has all the answers, but she saw us coming, didn't she?" said a philosophical Anton Bubka.

"Larsson needs to raise his game, I've told him this is serious business and not to pussyfoot around anymore and crank it up," Brin was emphatic.

Larsson had responded by telling Brin that his cleaner in the nursing home was making some progress for him. Not exactly described as 'cranking it up' but it could lead them somewhere.

It occurred to Larsson, she was forty-one but looked fifty-something, that's what sixty hours a week, three kids and no immediate family in the

UK for childminding duties can do to you. The Lithuanian woman was called Kristina, she was surprisingly well educated and was doing two jobs to pay the rent and keep her family afloat since her husband had vanished with their savings over a year ago. She was smart, engaging and had been following instructions by making a friend of Tilda. Kristina was also on a bonus from Larsson if she was able to uncover any more useful information and pass it on to him.

~

The Ford pick-up truck had stopped to give its passengers a comfort break at the services well along the M4 motorway heading west. There had been emails, messages, and a couple of phone calls, as Wil wanted to keep Phil Chalk abreast of things. To be fair Chalk expressed sincere concern when he had been informed of the bag snatch incident and wanted to know if everyone was OK. He knew had made a wise decision by bringing Melissa on board. But he didn't know it was going to cost him another £200 for a scarf yet, that was going to be Frea's job to tell him.

"Frea and Emma are taking a break, Phil. We had a good flight and as you know a worthwhile trip, but it's good to be back."

"Glad you're all back safe and sound Wil and thank you for keeping me updated as you have been doing. We are still scratching some confused heads here and in GCHQ over the crossword puzzles."

Chalk explained that they understood the words but the context and the relationship between them all was so subjective, and they were perhaps more of a reminder or a to-do list than a specific sequence.

"Understood Phil. Listen, mate, with the time difference, the travelling and all that stuff there was something I forgot to mention to you yesterday. In my dream, 'Lothar' said something which didn't make much sense. He said, 'Susan can help you stop the Americans', and that I have to go and find 'it', that's all. Whatever 'it' is."

Chalk was never lost for words, as the silence continued on the other end of the phone Wil wondered for a moment if he was still there.

"Are you OK Phil?"

"I'm terrific Wil, trust me, that's brilliant news about Susan and the Americans. Impeccable timing."

Wil explained they needed to get home to sort some things out and he intended to pop up alone in a couple of days to see Tilda again, "I can tell her about the trip and I might take her some flowers. She may have forgotten to explain a few things and with any luck, I can jog her memory."

Chalk agreed with his plan before telling him the story of the U.S. agreement. Wil knew then that he was well and truly on a mission to uncover something else in Oxford, whatever "it" was. Later, he telephoned Tilda, to arrange to go and see her, and when he did, she was thrilled to speak to him.

CHAPTER 33

OXFORD REVISITED

Late July 2019

It felt good to be back home in Wales, Wil and Emma were both in agreement. They had spent an intense few days with their 'pseudo-scientist' hats on in a far corner of the world. It had been an exciting adventure, although a bit more than they had bargained for. Montevideo was somewhere both of them knew they wanted to return to one day. Although, Wil would proudly tell anyone he met, the Black Mountains and the Brecon Beacons can be a match for anywhere in the world on a good day.

They had finished a fabulous dinner with their sons and families at the farm in Crickhowell, the boys Haydn and George both loved cooking. Wil sat outside on the lawn waiting for Emma to join him. Not a cloud in the sky, no noticeable road-noise, the faintest hint the River Usk was running somewhere nearby. Wil could hear it and thought to himself of the time when Emma was once close to ending up in the river.

He wondered had it all been for some kind of inexplicable or spiritual reason. He thought of Emma's mother Maud and all the other individuals who had unexpectedly appeared in his sleep since then. As Emma had once said, 'they were not getting off the bus yet'. Wil was resolute, he passionately wanted to finish what they had started. He was a bit of an adventurer at heart and was driven and excited by everything that had happened along the way so far. He paused and gave himself a reality check, some people had made huge sacrifices over the years, some had lost their lives, and all because of those bloody cine films. Wil also thought that he had been singled out, he felt like he had been tasked to do all of this.

~

A determined Alex Larsson had also arrived in the UK although he had chosen to base himself several miles east of Oxford within easy reach of Heathrow and close enough to any developments with Tilda at her nursing home.

There had been significant developments with Tilda. She was so excited because she was looking forward to meeting Wil Richardson again the following day. He was coming to the Spires to tell her all about his recent trip to Uruguay and how he had met several of her late sister's family. He had said he had lots of things to chat about, photographs to show her and wanted to know some more about her mother Susan and where they had lived nearby. It was still Tilda's home, although it was now empty and for sale.

Tilda's lovely new acquaintance Kristina, the cleaner, had been listening intently to Tilda sharing her news with her. Kristina said she was thrilled for her and that she would have to tell her all about it after her visitor from Wales had gone.

"I love hearing about peoples holiday stories, I must be a born traveller Tilda, or maybe I should have been a hairdresser," said an overly enthusiastic Kristina.

~

A familiar face greeted Wil at the entrance to the Spires, Greg Long.

"Great to see you again Wil. How was South America? Tilda hasn't stopped talking about you and your friends, you won't be able to keep her quiet today."

Wil couldn't help but show his enthusiasm as he replied, "Greg, to tell you the truth it's a fab place to visit, you must go there some time. It was business and pleasure; I'm sure Tilda did her best to explain some of the story. She may have got her wires crossed and a little bit confused with other parts of it though, eh."

Wil signed in and was taken through to Tilda who must have been clock watching as she was already waiting for Wil in the lounge. She greeted him as though he was a long-lost son and couldn't wait to get him seated and poured him a cup of tea.

"Well, I've spoken to Julia and Edmund and they were thrilled to meet you." Smiling, she added, "Tell me Wil have you and Emma bought your alpacas yet?"

"News travels fast doesn't it Tilda."

Wil smiled inwardly and thought Greg had been spot on and Tilda was 'going for it' already.

The next twenty minutes were a Montevideo narrative. Where they went, who they saw and what they did, but with several pieces of the story left out. Wil embellished a little bit in places which kept Tilda on full concentration. Then he managed to cleverly filter in a handful of relevant questions. Attempting to get Tilda to recall whatever she could remember or was told of her time in Montevideo before her father died and in the intervening years and before she returned home to the UK with her mother.

He specifically asked her, "As you got older Tilda, did you ever go to the yacht club where Klaus was a member? What can you remember about it?"

Tilda explained, "After my father died, I think I was aware that my mother had tremendous support from the people at the club. Although they hadn't known our family for a great length of time. My mother once said they rallied around and helped her. As it happened, that was where she met her second husband Jorge Rodrigues. He was a wealthy man in the shipping industry. He was a nice man as I recall."

Tilda said as Wil could see from the pictures and the cine film, Susan had been an attractive woman, a real head-turner. Adding she was too young to remember it, but her older brothers had told her that Klaus could get quite jealous of her, especially if he had been drinking. She knew Susan had also mentioned this to Clara in the past.

Tilda continued and explained that Jorge appeared on the scene not long after Klaus died, and when they married, they always had the best of everything including a good private education. Jorge also had a big yacht which Susan loved. Although she was said to have hated the idea when Klaus was alive and was sailing.

"He was a good man, he looked after all of us and treated us well. He was good enough to sponsor Edmund early on in his motorcycling career. But my grandparents, who had long since moved back to Oxfordshire from Switzerland, were ill and Susan wanted to return to England. Jorge was never going to leave so Susan returned home alone and a few years after they were divorced."

"Did Susan ever talk to you about the Americans and Klaus? Was anything ever mentioned?"

"Now you mention it Wil, I can remember something that was said when I was younger back in Oxford, living with my mother. We had some builders in, and they were knocking walls down upstairs, changing the boiler and the plumbing and she had a few things hidden in secret places like many people do."

Wil was listing intently, he didn't interrupt and just let her continue speaking.

Tilda paused for a moment visualising something in her mind's eye, "Yes, under the carpet, upstairs, there was one loose floorboard in one of the rear bedrooms. She used to keep a tin, with letters in, maybe some premium bonds, I can't be certain, to be honest with you. I'm sure she said there were important papers from America in there. We had to move it to keep it safe from the builders."

Wil, fleetingly thought to himself even he had a safe, a much better option than under floorboards.

Tilda continued talking and reminiscing and said she had forgotten all about it, and the tin was certain to be still there, pointing out that her house was empty and for sale. She said the Americans were mentioned in some conversations many years ago when she was told some stories about Klaus meeting people after the war because he was a scientist and he thought he could make some money with his ideas.

"It was mentioned that we could have gone to America to live but my mother was dead against the idea and it was the cause of a blazing row between them, so my mother had said. My father had told her he was going to take the family there whether she liked it or not. But it never happened and then, well, he 'died tragically', and things changed for us."

Wil thanked Tilda for filling in the gaps and told her that her family in Uruguay were marvellous people. He joked that Emma hadn't joined him today because she was too busy trying to find someone to buy some alpacas from. It greatly amused Tilda - but the joke was wearing thin on Wil, he was ready to strangle one of the creatures.

Tilda reached out and grasped Wil's forearm as she shared an idea, "Wil, I've just thought of something, why don't you go to my home and have a look for the tin? I'm sure it's still under a floorboard, I'd forgotten all about it. There might be some information inside it that will help you."

"Are you sure Tilda, that's so kind of you, it might be helpful."

"Yes Wil, you must, please give me a moment."

Having wandered off to her room Tilda returned with some keys and a small fob, giving it Wil for the alarm. She gave him the address saying it was about twenty minutes away and he could bring the key back later or on another day.

Wil was touched that Tilda had wanted him to go to the property and have a look for the tin. It crossed his mind what Lothar Muller had said about Susan and stopping the Americans and then Phil Chalk mentioning Americans almost in the same breath. It kept getting crazier and crazier he thought to himself.

Wil said his goodbyes and got in his car and set his sat-nav. He had a small audience when he set off, Tilda had joined Greg in the doorway. Kristina wasn't far behind them looking on.

CHAPTER 34

REACQUAINTED

Oxfordshire - Late July 2019

The sat-nav said twenty minutes and Wil set off, his truck's chunky tyres crunching away from the Spires gravel entrance. Tilda had described the house that had once been home to Professor Tim Blake then later Susan and Tilda. It was on the edge of a nature reserve not far from Bicester. It sounded more like a small estate than a house set in three acres. No wonder Tilda couldn't manage the place on her own. Susan had left Uruguay with a generous settlement from Jorge and that's where she lived out her days.

Having left the main road Wil found himself cruising down back roads in the Oxfordshire countryside. Horses, cows and crops in the fields, a landscape artists dream presenting itself on either side of him.

"You are approaching your destination on your right," said the synthesised female voice from his dashboard.

He slowed down, then realised he had arrived at Tilda's home and pulled up in front of the large property with its bright green for sale sign still displayed proudly on the thirty-yard curved front driveway. Nice place, Wil thought to himself, tucked away behind some hedgerows with tall rhododendron bushes which all needed a good trim. Farms and other neighbours were not too close, it was quiet. The tiled roofed stone property was at least a couple of hundred years old and worth well over a million pounds was Wil's guess. He thought at one time it may have been a farmhouse that had relinquished some of its land over generations. But it was a lovely, reasonably well maintained, and secluded property.

Wil stepped out of his truck and fumbled with a bunch of keys until he found the most obvious one. Burglar alarm fob in hand he entered the front door and disarmed it. One of Tilda's nieces and her family had been living there for a few months until they bought their own home closer to Bicester. Piles of mailers had been stacked up to the sides of the door and almost as many more had arrived and remained on the floor. Wil tidied those up putting them with the others. He was curious and had a quick nose around the ground floor to check out the kitchen, the views, and the rear garden. He knew if he was going to find anything it was likely to be upstairs under the floorboards, hopefully, just as Tilda had suggested. He had brought in a small toolbox from his truck in case he needed a screwdriver and made his way up the tired-looking red Axminster carpet held well in place by its original brass stair rods.

The house was "L" shaped and a back bedroom was the suggestion from Tilda as Wil recalled. There were two spacious double aspect back bedrooms, straddling a modernised family bathroom with a big walk-in shower room. At the top of the stairs, Wil stood on the landing and chose to turn to his left and walked to the end of the short corridor. More Axminster, this one was blue and looked almost new. The end room was one of the spare rooms and looked as though it had never been used, he thought to himself. As luck would have it, the room had fitted wardrobes, far better than free-standing wardrobes which would have needed shifting. The carpet was fitted up to the plinth of one of the fitted wardrobes and he used a pair of pliers from his toolbox to start peeling it and the underlay back. He had exposed two metres of wooden floor and looked for a loose floorboard. All of the floorboards had some old traditional looking narrow-headed nails holding them down. In some case not that successfully by the sound of the squeaks when he walked into the room.

Then he noticed something of a contrast. In front of the main window, one floorboard in from the wall had some screw heads, not nails. Wil unscrewed the length of wood and looked underneath. Nothing obvious, but on closer inspection, with the light of his iPhone, he put hands on a small rectangular tin. He pulled out the red dusty scuffed old tin, which had 'OXO Cubes' emblazoned across the front and was about the size of a small cereal box. Wil sat on the nearby bed and prised the lid off. He struggled to open it, for all he knew it may have been fifty years since its lid had last come off. He wondered what he might find and felt a genuine buzz of excitement at the prospect.

No jewellery, he thought to himself, slightly relieved, as he wasn't expecting to find any, but it was full of letters and papers. He flicked through some of the letters without looking inside the envelopes, but one or two stood out from the rest. They had red postage stamps that said - "U.S. Postage" with the face of a man and the name "Roosevelt" below the image.

As Wil started to slide out the contents of the first of the U.S. letters he almost jumped out of his skin as the doorbell rang.

He wondered who it could be, *"Concerned neighbours? Or maybe estate agents?"*

Wil walked downstairs to the hallway and opened the front door. The last thing he could remember was seeing a huge man with short ginger hair wearing sunglasses and a fancy looking surgical face mask, like those worn by car paint sprayers, before a cold hazy mist sensation hit him in his face.

~

Alex Larsson had arrived in the UK one day after the person he was interested in - Wil Richardson. That gave him a day on the ground to make his plans. Larsson had received information from Kristina that Wil was going to be meeting Tilda, two days after returning from Uruguay. The suddenness of the visit made it significant. Larsson was going to be watching, waiting, and following.

There was a sense of urgency from Peter Brin that Larsson had never experienced before on all the previous dark projects that he had carried out for him. This was not the project to take anything for granted, it needed to be full-on and hands-on. Maybe someone was going to get hurt, which was irrelevant. Larsson had shot, tortured, and killed dozens of men and women all around the world throughout his murky career in the Russian secret service when he was a younger man. He was still a ruthless, dangerous man.

Larsson had called in the support of another fellow Russian. The man was reliable and had worked with him before on an assignment in Paris. The two aggressors had intended to follow and wait, not knowing what would result from Wil Richardson's meeting with Tilda. They might have assumed that Wil was going back to Wales and would let him set off. Their initial plan was to cause a minor road shunt on a quiet stretch of road to grab him. That would not have been ideal, but as things turned out Tilda's property had been a perfect location execute the abduction, secluded from all of the neighbours and any passing traffic.

Moments after opening the door Wil collapsed unconscious on the hallway floor. They had used an enhanced aerosol form of a drug similar to Rohypnol. Hence the need for the ventilated surgical face masks until it dispersed. The front door was slammed shut whilst Larsson looked around the building to ensure they were alone. He was delighted with himself when he found the back bedroom, and its exposed floor, where Wil had been rummaging around. He put the spare bedroom carpet back down, retrieved the letters that were on the bed, the keys and Wil's toolkit. Then with the help of his associate, they zip-tied Wil's hands before bundling him into the back of a white van. They armed the house alarm and for good measure, they removed the battery from Wil's mobile phone so no one could track it that way. Larsson drove the white van whilst his accomplice followed him driving Wil's truck. A few miles further down the road, before hitting any major roads and the risk of an ANPR number plate recognition camera, was a low-key rugby club car park where they left Wil's pick-up truck. They were done, it was an efficient and highly professional job.

~

Wil had been gone half the day and Emma had sent Wil several messages with no response. She tried ringing his mobile phone, but it went to voicemail. Had he taken his power charger? Maybe not she thought to herself.

~

All he needed was twelve hours absolute maximum, thought Larsson. An hour or so drive towards London, then a two or three hours maximum before Wil became aroused and alert. Plus as long as it took to find out from Wil as much information as possible. Not much more than fifteen minutes on previous experience. Then, hold him restrained while they checked out the information if that was even necessary, inform Peter Brin then clean up and go. Wil Richardson would still be alive. That was the plan. In the meantime, they couldn't get into Wil's phone until he was awake as it used passcode security, rather than fingerprint entry and he was still out of it.

The destination was a cottage with front and rear access, not far off the M40 motorway, a short drive to the M25 and rented under an alias for a week. There would be no accidental visitors. They reversed the van up to the cottage's double garage, unlocked its door and flipped it up. Wil was then dragged through the garage and into the kitchen before being tossed onto the sofa in the lounge. He was still sedated, although murmuring to himself. Larsson began to wonder if the aerosol had been overcooked. It was a military-grade supply from Russia. He would have to wait, knowing it could be another hour.

He had sent Peter Brin and Anton Bubka a couple of WhatsApp messages to update them with progress, including a couple of gratuitous images of a bound, drugged, and gagged Wil Richardson. Bubka felt way out of his comfort zone when he opened the messages. It was though a wakeup call to remind him who he was working with and what he was getting into. Although he knew was committed and sensibly kept his views to himself. Conversely, Peter Brin's gleeful response had been to state simply that it wouldn't be long now, and he had appreciated the images.

Physically, Wil Richardson's body was temporarily paralysed, his mental senses were in some kind of a coma. Spiritually, lucidly, something inside him was trying to be cognitive. Something inside Wil Richardson's head knew something was wrong and that he needed help, fast. His subconscious was coming alive.

Larsson's Russian accomplice was an experienced professional, but he was getting bored. It was a little after two p.m. and had been almost four hours since they tracked Wil Richardson to Tilda's cottage and incapacitated him. The man had been outside seven times and was almost half-way through his first pack of twenty Belomorkanal Russian cigarettes. He went outside once again, around the corner to the wood burner log pile and turned his back to the wind to light up cigarette number ten. As his disposable lighter flickered into life, he was viciously smashed over the head from behind with a baseball bat. He fell to the floor lying face down in a pool of blood which was oozing its way and spreading through the remnants of some wood chippings and a broken, unlit, Belomorkanal.

As the assailant stepped over his unconscious victim, he uttered the words 'amateur' to himself and silently headed towards the back-kitchen door. He had observed that his second target was oblivious to what had happened. He hadn't been paying close enough attention either.

The extra-large Alex Larsson had brought with him a huge stash of food even though he was never going to be at the hideout cottage for more than a few hours. He was busying himself at the island kitchen counter having retrieved a ready meal lasagne from the cottages micro-wave oven. With his back to the door, Larsson sensed it quietly open. He wrongly assumed his accomplice had returned from having a smoke and was stood behind him.

Larsson slowly turned, holding the lasagne, asking his partner, "Are you having some of this...Christof!"

When you're holding a hot lasagne and someone holding a heavy wooden baseball bat, parallel to the floor, rams the blunt end of it straight into your mouth, it's difficult not to drop the food.

With one ferocious ramming blow, Christof Sorotkin had broken Alex Larsson's jaw and cracked or removed eight teeth in the process. Both his lips had split, and he had an understandable look of complete shock on his face. He cupped his now empty hands and raised them to his face to see them filling with streams of blood. Larsson was so stunned that his legs gave way and he slid down the kitchen unit door until he was sat forlornly on the kitchen floor tiles, looking helplessly upwards at Christof.

That should have been enough, but Christof Sorotkin was a violent, angry man and couldn't help himself from kicking Larsson's head, just once, like a football, backwards into the kitchen unit door.

Managing to restrain himself from dishing out any further brutal punishment he went through the semi-conscious Larsson's pockets removing his phone, keys, wallet, and a lock knife. It was then Alex Larsson's turn to be zip-tied. The other bloodied man, still in the log pile, was checked. He happened to be still alive and was also zip-tied as a precaution.

Sorotkin could see his former acquaintance, Wil Richardson, comatose on the sofa. He cut him free, removed the hood that was pulled over his head and peeled the gaffa tape off from around his mouth. Using extreme caution, speed, and efficiency Sorotkin moved through the rest of the cottage in case his earlier observations had been incorrect. He confirmed to himself they were alone.

~

Three hours before Christof Sorotkin had reacquainted himself with Alex Larsson, it had been five a.m. eastern standard time, in New York City. Alina Usmanova and her parents were in New York a few days ahead of the wedding of one of Alina's first cousins. Alina was asleep and dreaming.

She knew she was blessed with a similar gift to Wil Richardson and was aware her dream capabilities had not developed or expressed themselves to the fullest extent, not compared to Wil's. She couldn't explain the desperate connection she once made with Wil, neither could he. Somehow or other that day when she was trapped in London, Wil had found himself receptive to her plea for help. On some kind of similar wavelength, they had been able to connect with one another, and Wil had ensured her rescue in London. In New York, Alina had made another important connection with Wil.

CHAPTER 35

ONE GOOD TURN

Late July 2019

Greg Long was pleasantly surprised to hear from Emma, although he could tell by her tone it wasn't entirely a bright and breezy social call.

After some brief pleasantries and trying to avoid sounding concerned Emma asked, "Greg, I'm trying to get hold of Wil, but he's not answering his phone. He must have left his charger at home. What time did he leave Tilda, do you have any idea?"

Greg explained Wil had left a few hours earlier, but he thought he may have been going to Tilda's house before going back to Wales, and he hoped that had helped.

Not really Emma thought to herself and felt she would leave it another hour and then ring Phil Chalk.

~

Alina Usmanova had met Wil months ago. She remembered the sound of his voice and his unmistakable, soft, Welsh accent. Now, at five a.m. she was in New York, asleep, dreaming and hearing his voice in her head, once again.

237

"Alina, it's Wil, now it's your turn ...help me, Alina, can you help me."

Alina found herself responding though her lucid dream's connection, but all she could see was blackness, "Wil, how do I help? Where are you, what do I do?"

"Alex Larsson, his name is Alex Larsson, he is a Russian. If you find him, then you find me, help me," somehow, Wil knew that would be enough.

Alina's eyes suddenly opened wide she as woke up shaking in her bed, fearful for Wil. She reached for her phone and made an urgent call to London.

Christof Sorotkin was driving when he answered the call, "Alina, leave it to me I will sort this out immediately, I know who Alex Larsson is."

Christof and Larsson had not parted on good terms the last time they met. Although he was officially considered a bad boy outsider, Sorotkin still had some excellent contacts that he called on from time to time and he also had Alex Larsson's mobile phone number. Sorotkin called in a big favour and eight minutes later Larsson's phone had been tracked and Alina's rogue employee was heading towards it.

There had been no hesitation in responding to help Wil. Sorotkin berated himself for taking Larsson's dirty money and to some extent felt he was in some way to blame for Wil's predicament.

Wil had seen the large red-haired man when he'd answered the door. Despite him wearing a mask he had recognised Larsson from Phil Chalk's photograph as the man who had pestered Julia. In his semi-conscious state, Wil found himself connecting with Alina. She had been his one hope as he concentrated on her and the engraved expensive gift that she once gave him. The expensive Rolex watch which was still strapped to his wrist.

~

He is safe, I have him, was the message which pinged into Alina's mobile phone.

Sorotkin was pleasantly surprised to find the facial recognition required to open Alex Larsson's iPhone had worked so easily, considering his face was battered to a pulp. He could see Larsson's recent messages and using the same phone he took a picture of Larsson's swollen, bloody face and sent the image to Peter Brin, accompanied by a middle finger emoji.

Throwing a bowl of cold water on to Larsson's head he slowly responded. Sorotkin then asked him where Wil's car had been parked and with the threat of further punishment, he got a reasonable answer, despite the broken teeth and a fractured jaw.

Meanwhile, Wil's eyes had opened. His rescuer had sat him upright on the sofa and given him some sips of water, he was groggy but coming around.

At first sight, Wil was confused to see Christof. Sorotkin looked back at him and explained it was OK and he was getting him out of there. Sorotkin then found Wil's phone and its battery in Larsson's van, along with a red OXO Cube tin. He gave them both back to a more a coherent, but shaky Wil, along with some well-sugared strong instant coffee.

A phone rang, it was Wil's and it was Emma. A drowsy sounding Wil answered it and said he was fine, he would explain everything later, and she was not to worry. Which was the last thing she needed to hear from him, it was like a red rag to a bull. After some heated discussion, she agreed to see him later.

Christof Sorotkin had been taking his time before setting off, it was almost an hour since he had dished out the beatings. Wil had seen the aftermath after both his attackers had been placed side by side in the kitchen and he was shocked and concerned that Sorotkin might have killed one of them. He was reassured when he could see them both breathing.

Peter Brin had received the message with the image of Larsson's pumpkin effect face, 'game over' he thought to himself, wincing as he looked at it. He was furious that he had been out-thought every step of the way, but he knew then it was finished. It was time to call it a day.

CHAPTER 36
ALL FOR WHAT?

Late July 2019

It was unusual, Christof Sorotkin had felt slightly charitable. Once he had copied the entire contents of Larsson's phone across to both his own and Wil's phones, he tidied up some of the mess and then used Larsson's phone to ring 999. Claiming to be Larsson he pretended that he had just been viciously attacked by his 'boyfriend'. The contents of Larsson's phone were literally like gold dust to Christof on the black market or the dark web.

Will made a decent recovery soon after the restraints were removed and the coffee had kicked in. To begin with, he walked with tentative steps down the road with Christof towards his G wagon, before finding the life in his legs. They had about another hours drive to get to the rugby club car park and retrieve Wil's pick-up. During the drive, Christof explained that Alina had somehow got Wil's message and that's how he was able to rescue Wil.

"But I thought you worked for the fat ginger guy?" said Wil.

"We all make mistakes Wil. I think I have now stopped making mine. I'm sorry, I wasn't involved in this recent episode, I had already finished with Larsson."

Christof added, "Luckily I still had Larsson's number and could trace him otherwise it could have been bad news for you."

Gazing straight ahead, in a world of his own Wil zoned out for several minutes, wondering what the hell was he doing. Why had he decided to get caught up in all of this, and for what? Vanity, ego, curiosity, adventure, easy money from Chalk? It also crossed his mind that he knew where to lay his hands on two tonnes of gold, but he was more preoccupied with this thing, this gift, that he had been blessed with. He knew deep down he couldn't ignore his talent. For a moment, he wondered about the future for his grandchildren if the technology he was searching for were to get into the wrong hands one day. Though maybe one day he wouldn't ignore the gold either.

Christof could sense Wil had been terrified by the whole incident, he was out of his depth and offered some comfort.

"If it helps, those other guys are finished now. They won't be back, no one else will be knocking on your door, I'm sure of it. I know these things, trust me," stated Christof simply, like it had been no more than another day at the office for him.

Twenty-four hours earlier, Wil was ready to take on the world, he had been full of enthusiasm and determination. Now all he wanted to do was go home and see Emma and his family.

They had a friendly man hug at the rugby club car park. Wil said he would get round to speaking with Alina, but asked Christof to tell her that although he didn't have a private jet, she was welcome to come and stay in one of his shepherd's huts any time she wanted.

The Russian's four-litre V8 G wagon roared off. Then, before ringing Emma, Wil stayed parked up, called Phil Chalk, and explained the events of the past few hours. It was a relief to get it off his chest and speak to someone normal about it.

He also wanted to air his feelings about when this whole process might come to an end. But deep inside Wil knew he couldn't let it go. He had been roughed up, to say the least, and witnessed the aftermath of some nasty violence, yet his dogmatic desire to see it through persisted. He was like a dog with a bone.

A philosophical Phil Chalk always talked sense and was straight down the line and honest. First, of all, he wanted to put Wil's mind at rest regarding his security and said he agreed with Christof who had said Brin and Larsson were now completely exposed. Their interest in the anti-gravity aircraft was finished as they were in danger of being arrested. The last thing Larsson would want was to be imprisoned or at best kicked out of his comfortable lifestyle the USA and Peter Brin's business empire would crumble if his dodgy dealings ever came to light. The evidence on emails, bank transfers and messages from Larsson's phone was enough to throw the book at all of them.

Wil hadn't thought that through and knew Chalk was right, he instantly felt much better. For certain, he felt in a better place to have a similar conversation with Emma when he arrived home.

Never one to lose his sense of humour Wil said to Chalk, "Where was Melissa when I needed her most?"

He could hear Chalk belly laughing out loud down the phone.

Phil Chalk ended by asking if it was convenient for him to come to Wales and meet the three of them the following morning. He had already checked with Frea and she was available.

Wil agreed and they arranged to meet at his cottage near Abergavenny mid-morning.

"By the way Phil, I haven't thoroughly checked yet, but I might have a result for you with the American thing, see you tomorrow."

CHAPTER 37
WHO'S THAT MAN?

Montevideo, Uruguay - Late March 1945

Susan first met the handsome shipping magnate Jorge Rodrigues on a steamer from Brazil to Uruguay. He had helped with their luggage as she and the children transferred, having arrived from Spain to board her ship to Montevideo, for the second and final leg of her journey.

A few, occasional, brief, but mild and flirtatious conversations onboard followed. That was the last she saw of Jorge until she bumped into him at Klaus's yacht club where Jorge also happened to be a member. There at the club, the children would play for hours, as Susan read and socialised making new friends whilst she waited for Klaus to return from his sailing trips.

Jorge was a tall man, with chiselled and tanned Mediterranean features, usually sporting a white fedora hat and linen suit. He was younger than Susan and was single but came from a big family whose children were often to be found running around and mingling at the club. There was always a friendly group of women around and Klaus would return from sailing pleased that Susan was happy with a growing circle of friends, whom he had also got to know. Susan had studied languages at university in Zurich which included Spanish, so she fitted in easily, although many of her wealthy well educated new friends also spoke some English.

On one occasion Jorge invited Klaus and Susan to join him with their children, on his impressive six birth ocean-going yacht. A couple of his sisters were also going to be there with a good mixture of their children. Everything was planned, but then on the morning of the trip, Klaus twisted his ankle. Susan wanted to call it off, but the children were so upset that Klaus insisted she continued without him, she could drive so that's what she did.

Susan didn't drink much but once aboard the boat she was soon enjoying the party atmosphere and the lovely warm weather. Within an hour or so she had drunk a couple of glasses of champagne followed by some cocktails and without realising it she was beginning the get a little drunk. After two hours of sailing the boat moored in shallow water near a golden beach and all the children went ashore on a small tender. Some of the adults hung back for the second trip, including Susan who was searching below decks, looking for some towels. Jorge had been looking for his hat and was walking towards her along the narrow corridor, he offered to help her and showed her to the linen storage shelves and cupboards behind the kitchenette.

Alone, and passing close by each other in the confined space, all of a sudden, they were face to face. It was an unexpected moment, as they both made a clumsy attempt to try to squeeze by in the tight space, barely big enough for one person, not two. They both paused, momentarily looking at each other and whatever coyness had existed between them previously was forgotten. So were the towels and for several brief moments, they flung themselves in a passionate embrace until they were called as the tender was retuning. That's how it began.

They snatched moments together when Klaus went sailing and the children would be invited to go to the beach with a larger group of friends. They became lovers and were talking about planning a future together.

Susan had seen little of Klaus when he was working for the Nazis and she had spent many weeks waiting and travelling to Uruguay without him. She'd had doubts about their relationship for a long time and in the end, had acknowledged she no longer wanted to be with him, but she felt trapped.

~

Susan was aware Klaus was seeking a buyer for his knowledge, but he had been secretive about the finer details of his most recent approaches and negotiations with the Americans. Then one mid-November morning, over breakfast, with no previous hint or discussion, Klaus looked up from his coffee.

"Susan, I've met someone from the American government and explained to them what I'm capable of developing for them. And they've made me an offer."

Susan was about to take her second sip of coffee, she stopped abruptly almost spilling it before looking across at Klaus, "What do you mean, you've met someone? Where? When?"

"They came to see me privately at the yacht club, quite recently, it was all very secretive, it had to be."

Susan's saucer clattered as she put her coffee back down, "Why have you been keeping it from me? I thought we were in this together, what kind of an offer?"

"I needed to figure things out in my head, and I needed to make a decision very quickly. They were astonished at what I told and showed them and they are going to send me an advance of $1000."

Susan's normally calm voice started to rise, becoming more audible throughout the rest of the house, "Is that all? What about the rest? You said it would be worth a fortune - not $1000!"

"Susan, it will be worth a fortune, eventually - once we get to America and settle into our new home in Virginia. I will have to work with them for a while."

Clara and Tilda were attracted to the commotion and came running

245

into the kitchen squabbling, Susan stood up and uncharacteristically bellowed at them, pointing beyond them with her finger, "I'm talking with your father, go to your room. Now!"

The two children turned and scampered back upstairs.

Susan resumed glaring at her husband, "Well guess what Klaus? *You* can go on your own because *I* won't be joining you and neither will the children! That was never part of our plan was it?"

A defiant Klaus stood up to speak, "Susan, you knew we had to come to an arrangement with someone at some point, didn't you? We went through all of this, dozens of times before we left Germany."

"Yes, we did but it never involved moving to America, it just involved you selling your knowledge, that was all it was meant to be. You promised me!" Susan's eyes grew misty as she stared at Klaus.

Klaus was doing his best to reason with her, "Well things have changed, it's not that simple anymore, is it? You know that!"

"Why don't you sell it to the British? Then we can move back home to England? Why didn't we go to Switzerland in the first instance and speak to the British there?"

"You know we couldn't have risked Switzerland, it wouldn't have been safe. There were no guarantees for me."

"If you had a spine you might have found out wouldn't you, instead you've put us all through this!"

A pompous Klaus couldn't resist and reacted, "You've got a short memory, Susan. I've sacrificed everything and taken huge risks for our family. We can't live here forever, our future needs to be somewhere else."

"Well, if you weren't swanning around on your yacht and spending every penny we've saved then maybe we could! I'm sick of it all and I'm sick of you and your big ideas!"

Without thinking, Susan picked up a glass of water from the kitchen table and threw it at Klaus narrowly missing his head before it smashed into the wall. She grabbed her coat, slammed the door, and stormed up the road. Her misty eyes finally gave way to tears of anger and frustration, *"I loathe him... I loathe him."*

When she returned an hour later, Klaus could see she was still angry with him, although the walk and cool air had calmed her down a little. Her voice was more controlled, but her hands were white, clenched into fists, and her lips were pursed as she sank heavily onto the sofa.

"Klaus, I can't believe after all we've been through you couldn't be bothered to tell me what you were planning to do. You amaze me! You're unbelievable! Why...why couldn't you have told me what the hell was going on? What did you think I was going to do?"

The arrogant Klaus had never sounded more condescending, "Because Susan, I knew how you would react. I wanted to get us into a strong position first and then explain to you all the amazing possibilities for us."

Susan's head was in her hands as she spoke, "What about the children? They're happy and settled here, it's a beautiful country. There must be an alternative? There has to be?"

Klaus got up from the kitchen table, moved closer and pointed his finger near to Susan's face; he was not prepared to back down. He spoke quietly and calmly, as though issuing an instruction, "You need to listen carefully. You had better pull yourself together because we are leaving in less than a month. We will be in Virginia before Christmas. There will be no more discussion about alternatives. You will do as I say."

Klaus strode out of the room leaving Susan sobbing with a distraught look on her reddened face.

The following day Susan told Jorge what her husband was planning to do.

~

The following week, Susan was at the yacht club with some of her friends, Jorge was circulating with some of the husbands. Susan noticed he was chatting to a tall, smiling, bald man, who was wearing glasses. In conversation she casually asked Jorge's sister who the tall man speaking to Jorge was, commenting that she hadn't seen him before. The sister replied he was a business associate of Jorge's who was involved in his political activities. She said he was a German called Peter Knecht.

The sister also said she had met the man a few times before and she didn't like him. There was just something bad about him.

CHAPTER 38

PANDORA'S BOX

Wales - July 2019

By the time he arrived home after his ordeal in Oxford, Wil was shattered. It wasn't a wise move to have driven, but he'd felt well enough and had stopped a few times for leg stretches and fresh air. His head was pounding which hadn't helped matters.

Before setting off for home from the rugby club, Wil contemplated not telling Emma the whole story at all, but in the end, decided to wait until he was with her to explain. All she knew was that he had bumped into some Russians after going to Tilda's house because a foreign cleaner at the Spires had told them he was there. Christof arrived and turned out to be a good guy after all, and the Russian book that was stolen in Uruguay was beside Wil on the seat in the truck. Larsson's men had snatched Yuri Bubka's book from Emma, passed it over to Larsson, and he had been reading the book in Oxford. Wil spotted it and picked it up when he left.

Emma wasn't impressed with Wil's explanation, she knew something more serious had happened, but she wasn't going to get into an argument with him over the phone while he was driving. All that mattered was that he was fine, he was heading home, and he had a lengthy story to tell when he arrived. Wil sensed the probability of one of their rare arguments brewing.

~

It took Wil well over two hours to get home. That was almost as long as it took Emma to calm down, stop crying and shouting at him - after he had managed to explain everything that had taken place. Wil thought she was never going to stop raising her voice. When she did Emma sat and listened and appeared satisfied that whatever threat existed had now gone. The Russian's were finished. Wil was honest enough to share the doubts he'd had about the Lucidity Programme in the aftermath, but the drive home had mellowed the negatives slightly. Once again, he kept reminding himself and Emma of all he appeared to be capable of, he felt humbled and almost embarrassed by it. He couldn't get away from it even if he wanted to.

~

The next day, Wil was up early at six-thirty, he'd slept remarkably well, and it occurred it him he'd had a dream free night, which wasn't unusual for him, but it was a pleasant thought.

He sat at the breakfast bar slowly and was going through the contents of the old red OXO Cube box. It felt strange going through them, it was obvious they had been quite personal to Susan, which was why they were hidden away. Letters, notes, official papers, Wil was interested to look inside them.

He cleared the black granite island work surface and laid everything that was in the box out in front of him, fanning the items out like a deck of cards. Wil took a photo of it to ensure he knew which order, they had last been placed in the tin, he assumed by Susan. Then he placed them in sequence starting top left to right until he had formed a square with the letters and papers. Five rows across and four rows down, there were twenty different envelopes and documents and low and behold there were also a couple of old premium bonds as Tilda may have suggested. Then another photo was taken.

Wil's curiosity was first of all drawn to the three letters with the red stamps, they were from America and addressed to 'Klaus Schmitt' in

Montevideo. He remembered Lothar Muller's voice in his lucid dream when Wil was hurtling through the air and was told that Susan could stop the Americans. He was excited by what he might find inside the envelopes.

The first American letter was dated - *November 9th - 1945.*

The letter began by thanking Klaus for the telephone calls. Stating that the American defence manufacturing organisation were extremely interested in the anti-gravity device, it said they had one of their executives in the region on other business who could meet Klaus on the 12th of November at lunchtime in Montevideo. Apologising for the short notice Klaus was asked to please telephone to make firm arrangements if this date was suitable for him.

Wil knew from the information passed to him from Phil Chalk that Klaus went ahead and met the Americans on that date, because the Americans immediately followed up the meeting with an offer letter and a cheque. That was the letter which Phil Chalk was shown by his boss when the Americans had begun to challenge the ownership of the intellectual property of the anti-gravity aircraft device in recent weeks.

The second American letter was dated - *November 23rd - 1945.*

This was the letter that followed their meeting making Klaus an offer and included the cheque, which was in the OXO Cube box, for $1000 from The Bank of America and signed by the U.S, Government. But the cheque had not been paid in. It was obvious the Americans were desperately keen to get him on board as soon as possible, so hence the high-value cheque as it was at the time.

The third and final American letter was dated - *December 22nd - 1945.*

The letter had a harsher tone to it and wanted to know why they hadn't heard from Klaus and why he had not yet cashed the cheque. It stated that they intended to cancel the cheque in one week and that their letter of intent to employ him would be null and void immediately after that time.

The Americans did not know that Klaus von der Heyde had been killed when they wrote that final letter. But crucially as far as Phil Chalk and the UK government were concerned the cheque was never cashed and no money ever entered von der Heyde's account. The chances were the Americans did as they stated and made their offer null and void.

Although Susan had made the decision and divorced Jorge Rodrigues, for some reason she retained a bundle of love letters from him which were kept tied together in a red ribbon and placed in the tin. They confirmed that she had started a relationship with the Uruguayan man some months before Klaus was lost at sea and presumed dead. There were many passionate letters about the trysts that they had or were about to have. They also referred to them planning a future together and how Jorge had promised Susan the Earth if she left Klaus and remained in Uruguay. Jorge Rodrigues was determined to keep her close to him.

Then Wil found two letters to Susan parents, the first dated – *10th November – 1945.*

Posted weeks before Klaus's death, Susan had written to her parents whilst they worked in Zurich. In it, she explained the stress she was under as her husband Klaus was continually looking for a business arrangement with American companies who were interested in his scientific capabilities and expertise. She told them how unhappy she was, that she didn't love Klaus anymore and wanted to leave him. What she didn't mention in the letter to her parents was that she already had a new man in her life lined up to take Klaus's place as soon as she left him.

The second to her parents was dated – *27th November – 1948.*

The sorrowful letter sent by Susan to her father Professor Tim Blake. It transpired that her new husband Jorge had been womanising for years, which was one of the reasons she had decided to divorce him. Then she made a startling revelation, based on a conversation overheard in the kitchen of her home in Montevideo, when she was still married to Jorge. She had overheard a heated discussion between Jorge and his dubious friend, Peter Knecht.

It became apparent to Susan, that three years earlier, Jorge had hired Peter Knecht to kill Klaus when he discovered Klaus was planning to take Susan and the children to America. Susan also heard that Klaus had been a target for ex-patriot Germans and his killing was simply considered as 'two birds with one stone' when Jorge had offered some money to carry out the murder at the earliest opportunity.

There was something else said which horrified Susan. Klaus was mentioned in the conversation as being responsible 'without any doubt' for the bombing of the airbase before he fled Germany. This was the moment when Susan realised something sickening - she was the reason, on two counts, that Klaus was killed by Peter Knecht.

Susan paid a private investigator who confirmed her suspicions that Peter Knecht was a cold-blooded assassin, who was on the run and wanted by Interpol. There was no way he was nothing more than a business associate of the aspiring right-wing politician Jorge Rodrigues.

Wil wondered how these letters ended up in the tin. Susan must have found them amongst her parent's things after her father brought them back to Oxford when he and Susan's mother retired. Susan remained in Uruguay for several years after the divorce before returning to the UK, with Tilda.

~

Emma had heard Wil get up and she joined him downstairs to find him looking over his precise visual arrangement on the breakfast bar worktop. She went through some of the letters with him and found herself plucking out different ones, mostly in sequence, before she had binge read all of them. To think that so much of what they had been involved in at home and in Montevideo had such powerful connections to what was written in the letters laying before them. Emma found them so fascinating. Between them, they read every word and formed a clearer picture of what must have happened to Klaus von der Heyde and the role Susan must have inadvertently played in his death. Both he and Susan had been through so much together.

The more they read and understood the new luxurious lifestyle Susan and the children were leading with Jorge Rodrigues, the more they realised that Susan had blocked out and buried all thoughts about Klaus and his scientific know-how. The anti-gravity aircraft and the carnage it had caused her in the past was erased from her memory, other than when her daughters brought Klaus up in private conversations. Even then Susan was quiet and guarded about much of the information she chose to share with them. She had some dark secrets and deep regrets.

Wil and Emma also had gained an appreciation as to what lengths some right-wing South American politicians would have gone to just to satisfy their personal or political needs. But then wasn't that how it occurred all over the world they wondered, nothing changes. One of the other sections of papers on the square of items laid out by a focused Wil were some of the old newspaper crosswords they had found. He had also added to the mix the unrolled balls of newspaper George had retrieved from inside the cine camera case when Wil had called his son from Montevideo.

Some words were buzzing around in Wil's head and he couldn't shake them off, he had seen the words in one of Klaus's journals and again on one of the crosswords. The recurring words and phrases were: *Moulin Rouge, marriage, marriage on the films, marriage of the films.*

What was the connection? What did they mean or were they yet another red herring? Wil was shaking and scratching his head through his mop of dark curly hair, mumbling, and cursing out loud. The letters were defeating him.

~

Frea telephoned and Emma had a long telephone conversation with her about Wil's events of the previous day.

Frea was unaware until Emma told her, "Oh my God Emma, bloody hell, is he OK? Did he ring the police? Look I'm on my way over, anyway, see you soon."

She was about to set off to arrive in Abergavenny an hour before Phil Chalk's planned arrival time. That would give the three friends the chance to catch up and try to work things out. It would also give Frea time to give Wil at least some kind of a medical check over with blood pressure and some other basics including a blood sample that she would get tested the next day.

After satisfying Frea's healthcare demands and proving he was in one piece with no harm done, Wil was keen to get on with things before Phil Chalk arrived.

Wil had been correct; he did have some good news which would debunk the recent tenuous claims from the Americans concerning ownership of whatever Phil Chalk and his team were to uncover if they ever did.

Phil Chalk rang to say he was ten minutes away and Emma said she would get the kettle on. Frea had baked some vegan brownies and a banana bread cake. They were looking forward to meeting their genial associate and take him through their news face to face for a change.

As soon as he arrived, they sorted out the tea and cakes arrangements, then the first thing Chalk wanted to know about was whether Wil was suffering any after-effects from his ordeal the previous day. It wasn't a formality question either, Chalk wasn't that kind of man, he was sincere and concerned. He had been harbouring some private concerns about the team after the bag snatch and had wondered if there was worse to come. He was right and he felt responsible and guilty, he should have seen it coming but he didn't. Much to his relief, he was soon reassured by a chirpy Wil that he was fine.

Chalk wasn't finished, "I need to ask you Wil, I do have a responsibility to your welfare, believe it or not, and I think you should notify the police. How do you feel about that? Those people are mercenaries and can't be allowed to run around the UK doing stuff like that and getting away with it."

255

Wil thanked him for his concern saying, "Phil, I think it's come to an end now as far as the Russians are concerned, they took a hell of beating from our old friend Christof as well. I wouldn't be surprised if they are both still in the hospital. I'm fine, no harm done. I don't need the hassle or stress. Besides what evidence is there?"

Phil replied, "Well, they won't be coming back, I've escalated it, we've put a complete block on their future access to the UK, and we will ensure they leave the UK within days."

Wil explained to Chalk, "I've been sent everything that was on Alex Larsson's phone by Christof. You should take a look at this photo."

Wil smiled and showed Phil Chalk an image that was within a WhatsApp message. It was of a young man holding a crash helmet in one hand displaying a pair of black eyes and stitches across the bridge of a severely red swollen and broken nose.

"Maybe I'll send it to Melissa, Phil, she'd be proud of that one."

"Yes Wil, send it to her. I think she'd appreciate her handy work. Years of military and British secret service training paid off didn't it?" Chalk was glad, at least he had got something right by engaging Melissa for them.

At this point, Emma was getting tired of what was rapidly becoming a laddish conversation.

She changed the subject, "Phil we've been going through everything in our heads this morning and as you can see, we had a bit of a brainstorming session."

Phil walked across to the breakfast bar and cast his eye over the neatly laid out assortment of letters and paperwork.

"Are these items from the OXO Cube box that Wil mentioned to me yesterday? Wil you said you thought you had a result with the American issue, what did you mean?" enquired Chalk, whose gaze hadn't shifted from the breakfast bar's covering of papers.

Wil pointed out the red stamped letters and described the contents of them. Explaining with great confidence the Americans claiming the rights to the information would appear to be groundless and that they were trying it on. They didn't have a leg to stand on. Chalk scrutinised every word in the letters and picked up the uncashed Bank of America cheque.

"I think you're right Wil, looks like you've seen off the Russians and the Americans all in the space of one day. So, all we need to do now is to work out what all of this means and how the anti-gravity aircraft system operates. What is the secret technology? Any ideas anyone?"

There were blank looks all around. Everyone had reviewed all the evidence that was in front of them and everyone in the kitchen had slightly differing views and opinions. But they all agreed on one thing and that was that the anti-gravity aircraft had been for real, they were all convinced of it. The other thing they were all agreed on was somewhere within all the items and information they had was the solution to how the anti-gravity craft must have worked. The secret to its technology was all there.

"It's here somewhere Phil, we all know it, you know it, we just need to tease it out," said Frea.

As always Phil Chalk was spot on, "The one person in this room who is going to unlock it all is you Wil, you've got the answers. No pressure mate," as Chalk looked across and smiled playfully at him.

Wil shrugged his big shoulders, "Maybe you're right Phil, although maybe I have bought us some more time now that the Russians and the Americans are 'toast'. Doesn't mean the pressure is off entirely though?"

Chalk pointed out he had a team of people working through the crossword information and all of the other transcripts. That between them they should be able to throw some light on the science of it all. But then added, that no one else had uncovered the science of it for seventy-five years so it might take longer than they would hope.

As he was leaving Frea took the opportunity to mention they had one or two 'interesting' expense claims to cover off.

"There'll be no questions. Just to send them through, as long as you haven't bought any livestock." Chalk winked at Wil and Emma as he smiled and reassured Frea.

Frea left not long after Phil Chalk, after agreeing that one of her therapeutic restorative yoga sessions the next day would be a perfect tonic for them all.

CHAPTER 39
THE RIGHT THING TO DO

July 2019

Chalk had left them to recalibrate back to some form of normality. On occasions over the next few days after Wil had been thinking about the emotional and surreal connection he had made with Lothar Muller. He had been laid to rest as Lothar Haas thousands of miles from Germany, with not a soul ever knowing who he truly was or where he came from. Least of all any of his descendants at home in Germany.

Armed with everything he knew about Muller's death Wil decided he would make enquiries with the German authorities. He wanted Muller's family to learn more about the circumstances concerning what had happened to him. Muller deserved better than being another missing in action statistic. He was aware from the writings in the journals by Klaus that Lothar Muller had been single when he made his fateful flight to South America. No doubt he had parents or siblings at that time. Wil wondered if anyone had ever been interested in Muller over so many decades, or was he just history and almost irrelevant.

Following some investigation work, Wil soon discovered that an organisation existed called the German War Graves Commission. He was surprised to discover that every year they were notified of well over a thousand new graves of German servicemen.

Within a week Wil had been contacted by a young man who explained that he was Lothar's great-nephew. He was pleased to have been informed about his great uncle's final resting place and thanked Wil for letting the family know.

Wil sent on the details of the notes from the hospital and location of the grave, it made him feel good for having done it.

CHAPTER 40
MOULIN ROUGE AND THE MARRIAGE

Wales - July 2019

Wil had been home less than a week from the trip to Montevideo and was back into the swing of things, finding any excuse to help his sons out on the farm when he had finished his jobs in the campsite.

He was forever thinking and chatting with Emma about all the information they had uncovered. How the Russians had tried and failed, so had the Americans for that matter. Neither of them had succeeded in getting their hands on the films or the information, for what it was worth.

The crosswords, journals or what was left of them, were not proving to be helpful yet and may have been a red herring and a wild goose chase. The good thing was Wil and Emma were in one piece. It had been an amazing adventure, but maybe this was as far as it went. Perhaps no one would ever get to the bottom of it all.

It seemed like ages ago that Emma had said that if they ever wanted to 'stop the bus and get off' then they could do it. Maybe that's what they should have done when they met Tilda instead of getting swept along on the risky and foolish journey they had stumbled into. Their two sons would think that they were reckless fools if only they knew the full story.

That night Wil had gone to sleep listening to the rain lashing against his bedroom window in their cosy Welsh cottage, far from any more trouble and problems.

Wil had slept well all through the night until soon after dawn then he became restless and was transported in another of his lucid dreams. It was one of the strangest lucid dreams he could ever remember having. He was visualising the pair of film canisters on the coffee table in his lounge.

A familiar German voice in his head could be heard saying to him, "It's the cans Wil, the tin cans, it's all in the tin cans. In the films, they were married."

An unmistakable image of Lothar Muller, who Wil had seen in the old photograph at Edmund's home, the same man that was climbing into the anti-gravity aircraft in one of Klaus's cine films, now entered Wil's dream.

In the dream, both he and Lothar were now somehow squeezed into the tiny space of what appeared to be the anti-gravity aircraft from 1945.

Wil found himself gazing through a small round window, it looked as though he was being taken on a journey by Muller. Clouds flashed by. They were travelling at lightning-fast speeds. Wil could almost feel himself holding his breath and tightly gripping a seat.

On one occasion Wil's smiling pilot turned and spoke to him with once again in English, with a German accent, "Mach 5 Wil, superfast, eh."

They appeared to be changing altitude from time to time. Wil realised on one occasion they had zoomed high above the top of the Eiffel Tower, then headed west and passed a group of slow twin propeller-driven bombers heading home to the UK. It was exhilarating. Wil remembered the first time he went on the back of a friend's high-powered motorcycle and the adrenaline rush he got from that was remarkably similar to what he was now experiencing.

They continued to weave a rapid path over all sorts of landscapes, and Wil had the sensation of being in some kind of futuristic video game. Climbing up over what must have been the snow-capped Pyrenees, before descending following the terrain and out towards what was the Bay of Biscay. Wil thought he had glimpsed a famous old transporter bridge that he recognised from Bilbao before passing over dark volcanic sandy beaches. Maybe the Canary Islands? It was a real treat, exhilarating and exciting - this was surely a genuine rerun of one of Muller's previous trips. What a thrill Wil thought. He was still committed to the dream and let it play out. Lothar Muller was giving Wil a superfast joyride, entertaining him just for fun.

Then Wil could sense the heat from inside the aircraft as it was beginning to fail and vibrate. Lothar Muller was urging Wil on, this time he was trying to tell him where to look for something, but what.

There were numerous of his previous lucid vision flashbacks racing through Wil's mind as he dreamt. As always, he knew he was dreaming but he was compelled to stay with it and experience the sensations and emotions that often came, usually fear. This time it was the fear of crashing in the capsule or failing to parachute out before it exploded. Wil felt scared as he imagined he could smell the hot gases escaping from inside the confined space and the noise level was increasing to a deafening pitch.

Then at the end, "The cans! The cans!" Muller screamed out loud to Wil for one final time, that was the lasting message. Then one final poignant comment he said, "Oh and Wil, thank you for what you did for me." Muller was gone.

It was enough to wake Wil with a start. As a rule, it was Emma that stopped him mid-dream, but not this time. He was sweating. His body had been reacting to the imaginary heat he thought he had experienced inside the capsule with Muller together with the fear and adrenalin the whole episode had induced in him. Muller had intended to shake Wil into action, to do something, and it worked.

"He just thanked me. For what, the grave thing? Bloody hell?"

Wil left Emma in bed, went downstairs, and made himself a cup of tea. He put the mug on the coffee table and sat on the sofa gazing through their patio doors, staring at the nearby Black Mountains. He fancied a walk later to clear his head, but the rain had put paid to that for a few hours.

He now knew that somewhere or other the anti-gravity secret was in those old films. That's what he had been told by Lothar Muller and German family members. Emma and Frea had also told each other, referring to the films, 'It's in the cans' or 'it's in those tins'. Now frustratingly the previous night's dream had reaffirmed everything he already knew.

"What bloody marriage?" Wil kept wondering.

Nobody got married. It was going round and round in his head, frustrating him.

Wil decided he needed to have a much closer look at the two old films again. Phil Chalk had provided high quality digital copies, instead, Wil sent a text to his TV and film production mate. Maybe lightning could strike twice he thought, remembering his friend's creative success last year with the Scream CCTV from the art gallery. The friend replied saying that if Wil could pop around to his house in a few hours, at mid-day, he would have a look at the old films for him. Maybe his obvious technical expertise could unearth something in the films that everyone else had overlooked.

Wil retrieved the two films from the new safe they'd had installed at home. He sat on the sofa, placed the two old tins on the coffee table, ensuring he avoided his hot tea, and unscrewed their lids.

He pulled out the first spool of film and unreeled several inches, holding it up to the natural light coming in through his rainswept patio door, not knowing what he was looking for. Wil struggled to see anything, other than what looked like a dog with a small child holding its tail. Maybe that was Tilda he smiled to himself. He rolled it back up and then took a look at the second film, same procedure, again nothing jumped out at him.

Wil decided that his 'techie' mate needed to get his hands on them to see if he could find anything new.

Emma had come downstairs in her dressing gown and slippers, refilled the kettle, and flicked it on. She had stood behind a preoccupied Wil, watching him playing with the films and then asked what he was doing. Wil screwed the lids back on the tins, stood up, turned to Emma, and said that since everyone else had drawn a blank he was going to give his friend a shot at them a little later on. Reminding her about the Scream sketch success at the art gallery in Bath. She agreed it was a sensible idea and maybe there was something obvious that they weren't seeing.

As she turned towards Wil the full litre carton of milk that Emma was holding in her hand, ready to pour over her cereal, gently slid from her fingers, hit the porcelain tiled floor, split open and sprayed milk everywhere. She didn't bother to look down the mess she had made. There was an expression of utter disbelief on her face as she appeared to be frozen to the spot, gazing past Wil towards the patio door.

"Wil, oh my God, you have to look behind you," said Emma in a calm and controlled voice, she hadn't moved a muscle and looked like she had seen a ghost.

In the fraction of second it took Wil to spin around, his brain was screaming, *"Outside the patio doors? Is it one man or two men, are they armed?"*

Instead, to his astonishment, he saw both cine film tins hovering above the coffee table at chest height. They were silently spinning, not fast, at about ten or twenty RPM. He couldn't believe his eyes and he wondered for a moment if this was another of his dreams flashing through his mind. He looked and looked again, and then looked much harder. The moist sensation of a slight trickle of milk running onto the back of his foot gave him the impetus to take a couple of short, slow steps, closer to the coffee table. Wil slowly circled the two hovering objects, meticulously scrutinising them, his eyes didn't leave them. They were just 'there', at arm's length, silently spinning. What a ridiculous thing to see right there in front of him he thought.

Emma had moved slightly closer. Her hands were firmly clasped together pressing tightly into her chest and her heart was pounding, she could feel it. Wil gave her a fleeting glance before slowly reaching out his right arm towards the tins. His hand was about two inches above the nearest tin. Secretly Emma was terrified at what might happen if Wil touched the tin, but she didn't say a word. She knew her heart rate had made a dramatic increase - she was breathing hard.

With a gentle, slow approach, Wil's fingertips, at last, made contact with the centre of the first spinning disc's surface, he could feel the cool metal lid. He smiled, then gave another hint of a glance at Emma. The sensation he felt was of relief - it almost felt like sitting against the water jet inside a hot tub. It was a gentle impression of resistance. He added some pressure and the tin lowered, he took his hand away and the tin resumed its chest-high position. He touched both tins simultaneously and they both responded the same way, even when he pressed them back down to the coffee table they slowly and smoothly levitated back up to their original position.

This time, Wil carefully put his hand underneath one of the objects and slightly nudged its outer rim by the tiniest of fractions. His gentle touch had changed its spinning axis by the smallest of increments, minutes, or seconds of a degree. The effect was startling, the object darted sideways half a metre, then came to an abrupt stop. He didn't even see it; it was so fast. He realised that must have been how the speed was generated on the real aircraft. Some kind of gyroscopic principle. He remembered the Segway scooters they had rented on holidays had maybe used the same concepts, although not much of a close comparison.

"It's the lids, Emma! It's the lids!" said an excited Wil. "I've just realised, I must have screwed the lids back on to the wrong tins and that's why they are hovering."

"The secret we've all been searching for is not in the films, it's in the tins containing the film reels," Emma realised her words were coming out of her dry mouth at a super high pitch.

"I have another idea, something else has occurred to me," said Wil as using great care he captured one of the floating objects in his large cupped hands.

Wil controlled the object, unscrewed its lid, and then did the same with the other 'can' and placed the parts separately on the table.

All parts of both tins were now passive. Then Wil took out his phone and took a photograph of a blank piece of white paper. He placed his phone on the kitchen worktop and opened the photograph he had taken seconds ago - a blank white image of nothing. He then took the ends of both spools of film, matched them together and overlaid them right above his phone's bright white screen photo image. He was using his phone as an impromptu film projector to view the film strips more easily, instead of trying to hold them up to a window or a light.

"Emma, I think we have a marriage."

The first several frames of each spool, when viewed on the laptop from the USB stick, appeared to have been blank, scratchy black marks until the film of the German family or the film of the aircraft started to run as movies.

Now, as Wil manoeuvred the frames on top of each other, getting their alignment in a perfect position over his 'white' phone screen and looked closer, he paused. He then pulled out of a kitchen drawer and old magnifying glass.

"Can you see Emma, the scratches on the separate films when overlaid and aligned together form some words. Scientific gobbledygook to you and me, but meaningful formulae and instructions to someone who knows."

"Bloody brilliant," Emma was smiling as she gave her husband a hug of relief as her heart rate began to normalise.

A delighted Wil said, "I don't know how he created the initial images and filmed them but that's what he's done."

~

Eighty years earlier, the physicist Klaus von der Heyde had discovered the secret of anti-gravity technology. He had been involved in several of the Nazis covert war creations. His expert knowledge had always been focused in niche areas of chemistry and metallurgy and he had worked with a team that investigated nuclear physics. His talents then moved to try to resolve an issue concerning finding new methods of solid fuel for the V2 rockets.

Metallurgists have been aware of 'rare earth' metals for centuries. Twenty-first-century scientists are aware there is one substance called caesium which can be used as a solid fuel propellant in space rockets that is 140 times more efficient than current fuel. Hence von der Heyde's interest at that time, as he had become aware of its properties. These metals are abundant but not in one place, tiny grains of them, scattered all over the Earth and they are hugely expensive to extract.

Von der Heyde's search for new rare earth metals and combinations of them to form unique alloys led him to his accidental discovery. He had created an alloy combining the properties of several rare earth metals in a laboratory experiment whilst searching to solve durability and heat resistance problems concerning rocket engines.

For months there had been experiments using different metalworking processes and treatments. Swaging, case hardening, forging, high-temperature annealing heat treatments, immediately followed by ice bath fast quenching. These tests and experiments were all unsuccessful until they used a new process called sintering. Miniscule granules of metal and ceramic compacted together at extreme hydraulic pressures, defusing the atoms of the rare earth metals – forming a solid object. It led to him to stumbling across two uniquely created metals, when 'working together' yet 'in opposition' they caused the naturally occurring phenomena of levitation and a gyroscopic type movement. A true eureka moment.

He then had some small thin plates of the two differing metals manufactured. He had them pressed and threaded to create his pair of replica film tins and lids. This was how he kept the secret safe. There's a distinct possibility he may have shown the Americans at the Montevideo yacht club, which was why they may have become so enthusiastic as in such a short space of time. They were keen to get him to Virginia.

The tin and lid which were both stamped 'A' were made of entirely the same rare earth metal, tin 'B' and lid 'B' were manufactured from a completely different opposing metal. When the lids were switched and placed on the opposite tin, an A and B combination was created - when twisted firmly together the magic happened.

The calculated weight of the film rolls inside these rudimentary lab examples gave them the chest-high altitude. No one knew, he kept them hidden simply by keeping them in full view, he had substituted his original Kodak tins with his replica rare earth metal tin cans. He had made the odd subtle reminder in his diary noting 'Moulin Rouge' when he needed to do something secretive or go somewhere unusual relating to his amazing work. Moulin Rouge – Can Can. Over the decades, the levitational properties of the rare earth metals reacting with each other had not deteriorated, they still worked perfectly together.

The other cryptic comments regarding 'the marriage' now became clear and related to the joining of the lids from the differing tins or the overlaying of the cine films.

The anti-gravity aircraft went on to be developed by the Nazis refining and enhancing the same technology. Subtle variations, improvements of the formulas and refined rare earth metal combinations over time led to the astounding results that von der Heyde had filmed.

~

An hour later the milk and been had mopped up, the cine-film lids were on the correct tins to keep them from floating around and Wil and Emma were sat in Frea's sitting room demonstrating what they had discovered. She was jubilant as she nudged the crazy little devices as they hovered around her house.

~

They had spoken to Phil Chalk almost immediately after they made the discovery, he was over the moon. They had told him about the tins and showed him how they worked during a brief Skype call. They had never heard him laugh so much. Chalk wanted to see everything with his own eyes, so they had driven to DSTL to see him. Two hours later, having already blown Frea's mind when they showed her, the three of them were sat in the comfy DSTL meeting room with Phil Chalk.

When they arrived, Chalk thanked everyone for all the incredible work they had done to uncover this spectacular discovery. After an hour of revisiting the events endured over the last few weeks, they stood up in the meeting room to go home and he reassured them the technology would be put to good use. He emphasised it was so crucial that this knowledge had not fallen into the hands of a hostile government or even the Americans for that matter.

At the security gate, he gave them a knowing wink and said, "It definitely won't be stored away in our highly classified section, next to the aliens that were found in North Wales in the mid-seventies."

As they drove away Wil hadn't said a word for several minutes and Emma asked him what was on his mind.

Wil didn't take his eyes off the road but simply replied, "Gold Emma, 2000 kilograms of Japanese gold is on my mind."

ACKNOWLEDGEMENTS

People who were either readers of my early short stories or helped edit this book as beta-readers or proof-readers. All these people gave me motivation, helpful feedback, and the 'literary oxygen' to keep going and believe in my writing. Jan Strong, Denis Bayliss, Lauren Bayliss, Jan & Phil Thomas, Alison Pass, Caroline Schanzer, Laurance Ginsberg, Jonni Rich, Alex Iron, Jackie Huybs, Dee Bartholomew, Vicky Strong, Clare Morris at The Blue Nib, Alan Oberman, Joss Bajjada and my creative friends at the Hay Writers Circle.

Plus the numerous literary agents who politely turned me down or completely ignored me, chastening me to improve; hopefully I have.

Special thanks to:

My old friend, a former colleague and 'deadly assassin' Peter Knecht.
An old boss of mine from way back, Phil Chalk.
Some of the finest yoga, pilates and body combat teachers I know, and who provided some of my character's inspiration, Frea (Miles), (Michelle) Huckle and Melissa Benitez - namaste!
And my excellent cover designer, my son Luke.

As for 'Will Richardson' and 'Emma', they exist and were very kind people I once met, briefly, on the beautiful Pembrokeshire Coastal Path. The kindness of strangers - it's the best there is.

Finally, I couldn't have done it without the support, patience and 100s of hours of reading and common sense from my editor supremo, long-suffering and amazing wife Anne.

ABOUT THE AUTHOR

Mark Bayliss is originally from the former Welsh mining town and World Heritage Site of Blaenavon. Starting as an aerospace design engineer and then technical author, most of his career was spent as an international key account manager. He has written numerous short stories, some of his work can be found in national magazines.

To relax he's recently ridden Tour de France alpine cycling climbs, hiked the 'Camino' across Northern Spain, snowboarded Mont Blanc's Vallée Blanche and has been chased by herds of cows across his local Welsh mountains. He is a member of the Hay Writers Circle.

Mark is a dedicated yogi and occasional lucid dreamer, both are part of the inspiration for this story. He and his wife Anne live in Wales with similar views to the characters in his book. They don't own any Llama's - yet!

CONNECT WITH THE AUTHOR

Twitter: @sparkyponty

Instagram: @thelucidityprogramme @j.mark.bayliss

Images inspiring some of the amazing locations in the book will appear on my Instagram.